GO MAGIC YOURSELF

The Artemis Necklace Series Book 3

J.J. RUSSELL

Evergrowth Coach LLC

Chapter One

Why do we require the witch's presence for this menial task? Artemis huffed in my mind.

I stifled a sigh. You'd think it would be cool to own a necklace with a magical being inside, but nope. Not so much.

I glanced over at Rosalyn, the witch in question, as she set up several crystals on the carpeted floor of the small cabin. Beside me stood Alexis, a younger witch with fiery red hair and a look of pure interest as if noting the exact placement of each crystal. Neither of them had caught my internal annoyance. Which made sense since I was the only one who could hear Artemis's voice. I tried to hide the fact that I was, once again, mentally arguing with the being who was supposed to be aiding me in the whole vampire hunting thing.

Because, I silently answered, *unlike me, Rosalyn knows what she's doing and can guide me through calming down Cassandra's ghost.*

The last time I'd been in this room, I had royally pissed off the ghost of another witch in order to get information. I'd barely gotten to know Cassandra before she'd been murdered, but she had seemed like a very sweet person. I'd felt bad about causing her ghost to go all nuclear, but at the time, I'd kind of been up against a deadline to get information about who had killed her before the killer could strike again. Unfortunately, stirring up Cassandra's ghost had done a pretty good job of destroying everything in the room. Which was why it now stood completely empty save for us three and the growing number of crystals being placed on the floor.

Since I was going to live in this small cabin on the outskirts of Maine's northwestern woods, I was lucky that Rosalyn had brought in a professional cleaning service to replace the blood-stained carpet and all the broken furniture. However, it was up to me to clean up the more metaphorical mess I'd made by pissing off Cassandra's ghost.

Super.

As empty and clean as the room was, it didn't *feel* empty. I'd gotten a heavy feeling of foreboding the moment I'd stepped inside. Since then, that feeling had only grown, setting my teeth on edge. I wasn't sure if it was because I could still picture how I'd found Cassandra's body after she'd been murdered or the fact that I knew she was here somewhere as a very pissed off ghost.

We do not need the witch to disperse a ghost, Vânători. Artemis's voice dripped with contempt toward the local coven leader. *I can easily guide you through the process.*

This was not a tempting offer in the least. After successfully stopping the trio involved in the recent killings within the small Maine town of Ricketts, I'd spent the last two days mostly by myself in a motel room while Artemis tried to convince me that it was time to hunt down the uber-vampire Morvalden. Even if I could have tracked him down, there was no way I would voluntarily go after the father of all vampires when I'd only just figured out how to use the necklace to hear Artemis and access her powers. It would be like Mario skipping from level one all the way to Bowser's Castle to play the boss level. You can't jump over the levels in between! I needed to get more experience and learn how to fully use the power in the necklace before I could even think about facing Morvalden. If that meant staying here in Ricketts while I learned, so be it.

There was also the matter that this town had a somewhat friendly resident vampire and, since I needed vampire blood to make the necklace work, it only made sense to stay near such a source.

I'd already had all these arguments with Artemis. I really didn't want to rehash them while trying to focus on Rosalyn's directions for laying Cassandra's ghost to rest.

The more I use your powers, the sooner I have to get more vampire blood, I mentally explained as Alexis helped Rosalyn hobble around the room in her walking cast to place another crystal on the floor. The coven leader was chanting something under her breath that I couldn't quite hear as she worked.

If I let Rosalyn guide me through dispersing Cassandra's ghost, maybe it will limit how much power I end up using and I can go longer without vampire blood.

I heard a distinct "Harrumph" in my mind, but other than that, the necklace was quiet.

Score one point for me!

I suppressed a smile just as Rosalyn straightened from her crouch to look at me. This wasn't the environment for smiles. After all, Cassandra had been murdered only after calling me to set up a meeting. It made me feel somewhat responsible for her death.

"Is your friend safely out of the room?" Rosalyn asked with a quirked eyebrow.

For a moment I thought she meant Artemis, but then I realized she meant Ramble, my hellhound companion. Since I was the only one who could see him, Rosalyn didn't know he'd left the room earlier. She *had* heard his snort of disgust, though, when she'd started setting down crystals and chanting.

"He's outside," I reassured the head witch.

Ramble wasn't a big fan of witches since they could apparently take hellhounds as familiars. I didn't think Rosalyn was that kind of a witch and, if I was being honest, I really didn't see how she'd be able to capture the invisible, fire-breathing canine. Especially since, with a little help from me, he could pop in and out of existence.

Yep. A magical necklace only I could hear and a fire-breathing hellhound only I could see. The last few months had involved quite the learning curve. After discovering I was a vampire hunter by blood, things had been…interesting, to say the least.

Rosalyn gave me a curt, business-like nod. I wondered how she was holding up emotionally. Cassandra had been one of two witches from Rosalyn's coven who had been murdered during a coup by another witch to dethrone Rosalyn and take over the coven. I'd seen Rosalyn's powers first-hand when she'd incinerated the witch responsible for their deaths.

Rosalyn was not a witch I wanted to piss off any time soon.

"This might work better if we work as one," Rosalyn said and held out a hand.

I took it, steadying her as she shifted her weight off the broken leg. She'd been injured during the fight with the usurper witch and that witch's sidekick witch-turned-giant-monster-dog. Not for the first time, I wondered if she'd used magic to speed the healing process along. I had a hard time believing that a break that bad could heal quickly enough that a doctor would allow a walking cast so soon.

It wasn't my business though, so I kept my mouth shut.

Alexis shifted from supporting Rosalyn to merely holding

her hand, then reached out a little shyly to take my other hand. I tried to give the young witch a reassuring smile, but I've also been told I have a resting bitch-face, so hopefully my reassurance came across accurately.

We stood for a few moments, holding hands and forming a sort of misshapen ring around one of the crystals on the floor.

"Do you feel her presence yet, Vianne?" Rosalyn asked, her voice making me jump.

"Not yet," I admitted.

"Hmm." Rosalyn studied me for a moment. "Let's see if we can speed the process along with a little meditative breathing."

Oh, I'm sure that will work, Artemis said from the recesses of my mind. *Why don't we all chant together, too?*

Hush. I'm trying to concentrate, I snapped back.

"Close your eyes," Rosalyn directed. "Then take a deep breath. Hold it for a count of three, then release it slowly for a count of seven. As you breathe, think about Cassandra. Fix an image of her in your mind. Repeat her name to yourself as if you're calling her from far away, but keep your mental voice soft."

I followed her directions, breathing deeply and trying to fix an image of Cassandra in my mind. Rosalyn walked me through the breathing exercise several more times. Just as I was starting to feel a little ridiculous and wonder if Artemis was right, I felt a tiny tug at the edges of my awareness.

I opened my eyes just as a blurry, spectral being floated slowly, almost lazily, through the outer wall of the cabin and stopped. The form was so blurry and translucent that I couldn't make out any of Cassandra's features. I could only trust that the ghost was her.

I glanced over at Rosalyn who had also shut her eyes.

"She's here," I whispered. Rosalyn's eyes popped open and

immediately landed on the specter. Her hand tightened slightly on mine making me wonder what this was like for her to see Cassandra as a ghost when she'd been close to the woman in life.

"Good," Rosalyn said very softly. "See if you can draw her into the middle of the pentagram."

Say what?

I looked around, only now noticing that our little circle was formed around one of the points of what was actually a larger pentagram of crystals on the floor. It was centered exactly on the spot where Cassandra had fallen when she'd died. Though the carpet had been replaced and the cabin thoroughly cleaned by a professional cleaning company, I would forever remember the spot in that room where I'd found Cassandra, lifelessly staring up at me.

Focus, Vânători.

Artemis's voice helped me shake the mental image. I licked my lips and looked at the coven leader beside me. "How do I do that?"

"Mentally reach out to her and draw her closer."

She made it sound so easy. I took another breath and closed my eyes again. It felt more natural to stretch my hand out to Ghost-Cassandra in a sort of beckoning way, so I dropped Alexis's hand and followed those instincts. I tried to give a gentle tug at the ghostly presence I could feel in my mind. Nothing happened, so I tried again with a little more force.

I heard Rosalyn's slight intake of breath and opened my eyes to find that, not only had Ghost-Cassandra floated closer, she was also now more corporeal. I could see her features much more clearly now, even down to the clothes she'd been wearing when she'd died.

"Good," Rosalyn said. She opened her mouth to give me further instructions, but just then all hell broke loose.

Before I could blink, Cassandra's eyes fixed on mine and lit up in recognition. Her mouth dropped open and words streamed out. It was like someone turned a radio on full blast.

"Murderers! BACKSTABBERS! LIARS!" The ghost screamed.

I almost dropped Rosalyn's hand to cover my ears but forced myself to stand against the noise blasting us. An impossible wind began to whip around the room, yanking tendrils of hair loose from my braid. I was thankful the room was empty this time around. It meant she didn't have anything to throw at us.

A glance to the side showed me that Rosalyn was also steeling herself against the onslaught of noise and spectral wind. She straightened her spine and took a half-step forward.

"Cassandra. Stop." Rosalyn projected her voice like an actor in a theater. Instead of stopping though, the ghost merely jerked her head to focus solely on her previous coven leader, eyes whirling madly in recognition.

"YOU! Why didn't you STOP them?" Ghost-Cassandra demanded as she floated closer to us. The center of the pentagram was behind me. Maybe we could just walk backwards and lead her into it? But then what? Would it be like one of those ghost traps from *Ghostbusters* and suck her into it?

Rosalyn's mouth drew down at Ghost-Cassandra's accusation. "I'm sorry, Cassandra. I truly am. But this is not the afterlife you would have wanted. It is time for you to be at peace. To return to—

Ghost-Cassandra was not having it. I'd heard the phrase "flew into a rage" but this was truly an enraged ghost flying through the air. At us. Not cool. We wouldn't be able to backpedal quickly enough to lead her into the pentagram before she flew straight into us. I wasn't sure what would happen to Rosalyn and Alexis if that happened, so I jerked Rosalyn back, nearly pulling her off her good leg, then stepped in front of them with my hand raised.

"STOP." I put as much force into my voice as I could. In my last encounter with Ghost-Cassandra, I'd been able to hold her in place with my Vânători mojo. And that was before I'd had some vampire blood. Now that the necklace was actually working, I had more power than before. This should be easy, right?

The ghost halted about five inches from me, which left her screaming into my face. My hand, still outstretched, was buried in her translucent body just below her chest and felt slightly cold. I had to fight the urge to step back.

Well, this was just awesome. Now what?

This seems to be going well so far, Artemis dryly commented. *Would you like my help yet?*

I ignored her. Which sounds rude, I know, but after two days of being badgered by the necklace trying to tell me what to do, I was reluctant to accept her help. Instead, I took a deep breath and tried to think my way through the situation. I'd been able to control Ghost-Cassandra without too much trouble last time. But this was different. I didn't want to control her. We wanted to lay her to rest.

The only other time I'd interacted with a ghost, he'd wanted me to kill his vampire ex-girlfriend. Of course, Rocker Ghost had been a bit more helpful than Ghost-Cassandra was being right now. He'd just wanted to find peace, and the only way he'd been able to do that was by helping his girlfriend into the true afterlife.

I know. Kind of messed up. Listen, I don't make the rules in this weird-ass supernatural world. I'd only learned about the existence of real vampires, witches, and werewolves a few months ago, and I'd basically been flying by the seat of my pants ever since.

So, if I were a ghost and I'd been killed in my own home, what would I want?

Oh.

I looked Ghost-Cassandra in her whirling eyes and said, "Cassandra, your murderers have been killed. You have been avenged." I paused. This sounded a little too dramatic for my taste. Then again, I was standing in front of the ghost of a witch who had been killed by another witch just so she could become leader of the local coven. It didn't get more dramatic than that. I guess I could deal with some drama if it meant helping Cassandra find a little peace.

My attempt made no difference.

I still had an angry ghost screaming five inches from my face. I glanced at Rosalyn to see if she had any ideas. I'd have simply asked her, but she probably wouldn't have heard me over the screaming.

Luckily, Rosalyn understood the desperate expression on my face. She turned to Alexis, and they must have shared some unspoken thought, because the younger witch closed her eyes, and a moment later, I sensed something sweep from Alexis then through Rosalyn to reach me. I gasped as a tingling, pins-and-needles kind of feeling spread from my hand, up my arm, and into my chest. My core felt immediately warmed. If you've ever taken a swig of a hot coffee on a really cold day, it was like that. The energy Alexis had sent into me made me feel warm all over.

Rosalyn gave me a little smile and a nod of encouragement.

Um. Okay then. I guess she wanted me to try again?

I turned back to the screaming ghost and closed my eyes since I seemed to do better at this stuff with them closed. I focused on the warm energy resting at my core. The sensation was an odd juxtaposition to how cold my other hand was where I had it raised in Ghost-Cassandra's chest.

Maybe I should use the energy Alexis had given me to warm up Ghost-Cassandra? Seemed worth a shot. I focused my attention on the warmth radiating from my chest and mentally nudged it toward my upraised arm...and damned if it didn't respond to my request! I almost opened my eyes in surprise but managed to remember that I was supposed to be focusing here.

I nudged the energy from my upper arm, into my forearm, then into my hand, and finally into the tips of my fingers. I held it there for a few seconds and said, "Cassandra, your time here is over. Your enemies have been vanquished. Be at peace." Then I pushed the energy out of my fingers and into the ghost.

The screaming cut off like I'd flipped a switch.

My eyes snapped open at the sudden silence. Cassandra now stood fully formed before us, no longer transparent. If I hadn't still had my hand in her chest, I wouldn't have thought she was a ghost.

She no longer looked angry and instead wore a peaceful smile. This was more like how I'd initially seen her ghost form the first time I'd come to her home after she'd been murdered. She'd been a little more transparent then, but the serene expression was the same.

"Listen to Rosalyn," I said and shifted slightly so that Cassandra could see her coven leader more clearly. I kept my hand where it was and added, "She's here to help you rest."

Cassandra shifted her gaze to the witch.

"I'm sorry, Rosalyn."

Rosalyn moved so that she was standing beside me once more. She still gripped my hand, but it was more for balance as she maneuvered her cast around.

"There's nothing to be sorry for, Cassandra. You were always a bright light in an ever-dimming world. It's time to return to the light now." Her voice didn't waver, but as she spoke, a tear slipped down her face. "Merry meet again, sister."

Cassandra smiled. "Merry meet again." As she spoke, both her body and voice faded until she was nothing more than a glimmer of light. Then, even that winked out of existence.

The atmosphere in the house had completely changed. Now it just felt...neutral. Like nothing supernatural or bad had ever happened here.

What a complete waste of energy, Vânători.

Ignoring the necklace, I let out a long breath and slowly lowered my hand. Rosalyn dropped my other hand to brush away tears, and Alexis stood in quiet comfort to her coven leader. We stayed like that in the dark for a few moments, none of us wanting to break the sense of tranquility that had filled the room.

A snort of annoyance broke the spell.

The witches and I turned as one to find Ramble staring at us from the doorway. Well, I could see him, but the witches couldn't, though they'd clearly heard him.

"Someone sounds a little impatient," Rosalyn coolly observed.

"I'm pretty sure he's just reminding me that it's time for supper."

Another snort.

"I see." Rosalyn's demeanor suddenly shifted, and she became a little more like the no-nonsense woman I'd grown accustomed to. Dropping Alexis's hand, she limped over to retrieve the crutch she'd left propped against a wall near the door. With a quick glance at where she thought Ramble was, she turned her attention back to me.

"So, do you want to move in here tonight?"

Chapter Two

"**T**onight?" My automatic response would have been hell no but that didn't seem appropriate given that Rosalyn was doing me a favor by letting me stay in the cabin. I mean, we had just exorcised a ghost in here! There was no way I was going to stay in this creepy place tonight.

"Um, I hadn't planned on it, so all my stuff's back at the motel."

As excuses went, it was pretty thin. It wasn't like I had much stuff. More like a sad backpack filled with a few odds and ends. After doing some time in jail for a string of DUI's, I'd struggled to build up any kind of personal belongings. Add to that the discovery that I was the descendent of a famous vampire hunter—famous in the supernatural community anyways—and that I was on the run from freakin' vampires, and you have the perfect recipe for living a life with no belongings. I'm pretty sure I could give hardcore minimalists a run for their money.

"I see," Rosalyn said. "Well, when you're ready to move in, here are the keys." She fished in her jacket pocket to jingle keys attached to a black cat figurine keychain. "I have an extra set, so if you accidentally get locked out, let me know."

I took the keys with a nod, careful not to make any statements about the keychain.

The coven leader turned to Alexis who had begun picking up the crystals and placing them in a black velvet bag. "You're okay to finish up here?"

Alexis nodded with a neutral expression, but her tone suggested annoyance at the question. "I'll be *fine*."

I realized I had no idea how old the younger witch was and was suddenly curious at the teenager-like tone.

Rosalyn gave the witch a small smile and when Alexis turned away, shot me a look and a shrug as if to say, "Youngsters. What can you do?"

We left the living room together and paused in the small foyer at the front door. Though most of the furniture still remained, with the exception of the living room set, Cassandra's more personal belongings had been removed. I was grateful for that. If I'd had to see her pink mud boots waiting for her by the door again, I'm not sure I could have lived in the cabin. I was still a little weirded out as it was, but I was also tired of living in a motel room. Plus, this place had a washer and dryer. You don't turn your nose up at a place that comes with that amenity.

"Are you really sure this is okay? I feel like I'm overstepping here. Especially since you won't let me pay for the first month's rent."

The witch waved away my concern with her free hand as she turned to face me, leaning on her crutch.

"The coven owes you a debt for helping us stand against Gabriella and the monster she created. If you decide to stay past the first month, you can start paying rent." She stopped with her head cocked, as if listening to a far-off voice only she could hear. I knew what that was like. "But something tells me you might be staying a little longer..." Then she shrugged one shoulder and smiled. "Then again, precognition isn't my gift so what do I know?

With one last glance at the doorway to the living room, she said, "Let me know if you need anything!" It was loud enough to be directed at both me and Alexis. Then she hobbled out the front door and carefully maneuvered the steps down the front porch and over to her car. Ramble and I watched as she gave us a little wave before turning out of the driveway.

On top of being the local coven leader, Rosalyn's gift as a witch was knowing what people wanted. I guess it must have told her that I didn't want to stay at a motel owned by the only vampire in town who had almost killed me before Ramble helped me incapacitate him so that I could drink his blood and regain the powers of the necklace.

Have I mentioned yet that my life is a weird, complicated mess?

Of course, the jolt from the vampire blood had worked, but it wouldn't last forever. I'd already lost most of my super-strength. If I didn't drink more blood soon, I'd lose my ability to hear Artemis. After that, the really scary stuff would start as she lost the ability to shield me from Morvalden entering my dreams like a much scarier Freddy Krueger.

I still do not understand why you wish to stay in the witch's cabin, Artemis complained. *We should be where the vampire is. If you're not going to drink the vampire's blood and you refuse to use the energy from the ghost, then how will you maintain your Vânători powers?*

"We're moving out here so we can have some privacy," I said out loud. Normally I only answered Artemis mentally, but I didn't think Alexis would be able to hear us out here. And honestly, who cared if she did?

I turned and walked back inside the cabin. I'd decided to

do a quick inventory of what I'd need to buy from town before moving in tomorrow. I still had a little money left from when I'd hit up some ATMs with a fake credit card before coming to Ricketts. That seemed like a lifetime ago, but in reality, it had only been about a week.

The only reason I had any cash left was because Louis hadn't charged me for any of my stay at the motel. I'd tried to pay the young girl at the counter this morning, but she'd said everything had already been taken care of.

Maybe Louis felt bad for almost killing me? I guess I still felt a little bad about almost draining him, too, but mostly I was just glad neither of us had died. I figured we were even.

Then he went and didn't let me pay for the motel, which made me feel like I owed him again.

Gah. Vampires.

I thought about what Artemis had said as I browsed the kitchen cabinets, making a mental list of what I needed to buy tomorrow. I paused when my brain caught up to her last sentence. *And what do you mean 'use the energy from the ghost?'*

It is possible you could have used the ghost's energy to prolong your powers without imbibing vampire blood, she explained. Over the past few days, Artemis had slowly lost the sound of absolute contempt when she spoke those two words: vampire blood. I think it was because she'd actually begun to annoy herself with how much she railed at me for not securing a promise of more blood from Louis.

That gave me pause. Having to drink vampire blood was kind of a sticking point for me. For starters, it was gross. I mean, come on. Secondly, it bothered me that since I wasn't a direct female descendent of the first Vânători, I didn't have enough Vânători blood running through my veins to make the necklace work on my own. It irked me that I needed vampire blood to make it work. And quite frankly, I didn't know why it had to be vampire blood and not, say hellhound blood or the blood of some other supernatural creature. Not that I'd tried those yet...

Lastly, though I didn't want to admit it to myself, I had really liked drinking vampire blood. It sounded ridiculous, I know, but that moment of latching onto Louis and drawing his blood into my mouth...

I suppressed a shiver.

How could I possibly be grossed out by something yet simultaneously crave it? It didn't make sense, but it also wasn't an entirely new feeling for me. Without the necklace and vampire blood, I struggled with alcoholism. Somehow, vampire blood insulated me from my need for a drink. But powering up the necklace had introduced me to a new high that alcohol would never be able to touch. Lately I'd been dreaming about drinking from Louis. Sometimes the dreams involved reliving those moments on the floor of the jail cell where I'd almost died before drinking Louis's blood.

Other times, my dreams of Louis were, well... a little embarrassing.

I had to stifle another shiver though this time for an altogether different reason.

No, I told Artemis when I managed to pull myself back from thinking about Louis. *You said it's possible we could prolong your power, but you're not sure. I wouldn't put Cassandra's ghost through something like that. I mean, what would that do to her? Would she get to have an afterlife? I mean,* I paused, *if there is an afterlife?*

She's a ghost, Vânători. Your job is to protect humans. She doesn't fit that category.

I shook my head, though I was pretty sure Artemis couldn't actually see me, and closed the last cupboard before leaving the kitchen with my mental list.

"Last time I checked, I've been conscripted into being some sort of lawman—lawwoman—for the supernatural community. I think that means more than just protecting humans." I stalked to the bedroom, not caring now that Alexis might hear my one-sided conversation. Was she even still here? Surely she'd finished cleaning up our little cleansing ritual by now.

I flicked on the light. A naked mattress on a plain wooden bedframe sat against the far wall with a window to one side of the headboard. A dresser on the other side of the bed matched the headboard.

Though it meant I'd have to buy a sheet set and blankets, I appreciated that someone had removed most of Cassandra's linens. I was already moving into her home and using her furniture and kitchen stuff. It would have felt weird to also sleep on her sheets. I was thankful someone had taken them since, if they'd still been here, I would have struggled to spend the money on something I already had. They'd left the curtains, but I could handle using those.

I added a few more things to my mental list then jumped about a mile when I found Alexis standing in the bedroom doorway

"Sorry," she said with a grimace. "I didn't want to interrupt your...conversation."

Uh huh. Sounded like a polite way of saying she didn't want to offend the lady who was clearly talking to herself.

When my heart had recovered from its trip to my throat, I asked, "Is there anything else you need help taking out of here?"

She held up a plastic caddy of cleaning supplies that magazines always suggested a good homeowner should keep on hand. "Nope. All done." She looked around the room then back to me. "If you're going to buy sheets and stuff, you might check out Mardens. They usually have some pretty good deals on stuff like that."

"Thanks."

"No problem. Good luck!" She flashed me a smile and left.

The moment she was gone, the cabin felt a lot colder. Ramble chose that moment to pop his head around the bedroom doorway.

"Am I forgetting anything?" I asked him.

He snorted and jerked his head in a "follow me" gesture. We'd gotten fairly good at the nonverbal communication. I obliged him, and he led me back to the living room. For a scary second, I thought maybe he was going to tell me that Cassandra's ghost wasn't gone. Instead, he stopped in front of the woodstove and stared at it.

"Do you want me to light it or something?"

I'd never lived in a house that was heated with a wood-stove. And seeing as how I'd ended up stuck in Maine over the winter, I was definitely going to have to figure out how to use the dang stove.

He gave me the negative huff that also suggested I was a dumbass.

Okay. What else then?

After another moment of staring at me, Ramble turned his attention to an empty metal rack not far from the wood-stove. Finally, it clicked.

"Oh. We need firewood."

Yup. That's me. Super-genius with vampire-fighting super-powers. Just watch me solve mysteries and vanquish the bad guys with my faithful hellhound.

"Let's double-check to make sure there isn't any wood outside. If not, maybe I can ask Rosalyn where Cassandra got her firewood from."

How much would firewood cost? How much would I even need? I had no idea. I made sure all the lights were turned off before stepping onto the front porch and locking up. When I turned around, I noticed a small pile of wood stacked up on the porch against the side of the house. It wasn't much. Maybe, ten or so pieces of split wood.

Using my cell phone as a flashlight, we traipsed around the cabin but didn't see any other piles of wood. Maybe Cassandra just hadn't had any wood delivered before she'd been murdered?

I added figuring out how to get firewood to my list of things to do tomorrow and resolved myself to a trip into a bigger town to use the fake credit card. I hated to do it, but if I was going to stay here for a little while longer, I'd need more cash soon.

Before getting in the car, I looked up to find that the sky was filled with more stars than I'd ever seen before. Being away from downtown Ricketts and at least an hour from the next biggest town meant no light pollution. For a moment, I just stared at the sky. It was faint, but I could just make out the path of the milky way.

Maybe it wouldn't be so bad staying out here after all.

Are we staying here or going back to the Inn, Vânători? Artemis's voice cut through my thoughts.

"Yes. We're going back to the *motel*," I purposefully corrected her as I got in the car. If she was going to exist in this century, then she needed to get used to the lingo.

It was a clear night which meant no snow on the road. I didn't look forward to driving these roads when winter really set in here. So far, staying at the motel in town had meant I hadn't had to drive too much on roads made treacherous by snow or sleet.

Before the whole running-from-vampires thing, I'd lived in Indianapolis. They got plenty of snow, but the city had a fleet of snowplows that kept roadways pretty clear. Plus, it was pretty flat out there. Here, it seemed like every hill ended in a tight turn I'd have to carefully maneuver if I didn't want to end up down a snowy embankment.

We hit up the drive thru of a fast-food joint then ate in the car because I didn't want to deal with any other people tonight. The necklace was oddly silent for the drive back to the motel. Rather than worry about what Artemis had up her sleeve, I rolled down the passenger window so I could watch Ramble stick his head out. It made for a freezing ride, but at least it got the hamburger smell out of the car. Plus, the sight of a hellhound with his spiky hair whipping in the wind and a giant doggy smile on his face was always fun.

The moment we got to the motel and I shut the door behind me, the necklace couldn't seem to keep her feelings to herself anymore. Assuming she still had feelings.

Vânători, you must stop playing this childish game of keep-away from the vampire. You need his blood. Moving into the woods will not change that fact.

"I know moving won't change anything, Artemis." I rolled my eyes at Ramble when he lifted an eyebrow at me. He'd heard this argument before. He let out a snuff and headed for the front door. I opened it before he had to ask to be let out. Bear in mind that Ramble didn't ask to be let out like a normal dog would by scratching at the door. Oh no. Mr. Fire-breather preferred to stare at me as if I was his personal assistant and was letting him down by not taking care of his unspoken needs.

At this point, we'd grown kind of used to each other. I knew Ramble's general routine now and figured it was just easier to let him out without him having to ask. If I didn't, I'd end up on the receiving end of one of his withering stares.

That and I thought it would royally suck to be a super-intelligent being in a dog's body trying to navigate a world built for humans. I also knew that Ramble was the real deal. He was an actual hellhound. I mean, I guess I knew that since he met all the other descriptors of a hellhound. Breathes fire?

Check. Invisible to everyone else? Check. Could pop in and out of existence? Check.

However, I'd kind of always wondered if he might fall into a different category. Like maybe a cousin to hellhounds or something. Everything I'd read said hellhounds were supposed to have three heads. I'd only ever seen Ramble with one head... until I'd called him into one of my dreams to defend me against Morvalden.

In the dream, he'd still had only one head but only because the other two had been lopped off at some point.

I had no idea what had actually happened or even how he'd been captured by the vampires who'd stuck him in their basement—which is where I'd found him and accidentally made a deal with him. All I knew was that he'd stuck by my side since then and had fought numerous monsters for me so far. I hoped now that I had the Artemis necklace working, I could be a little better at fighting by his side instead of having to hide behind him all the time.

I am talking to you, Vânâtori.

"I'm sorry." I sighed and closed the door before returning to my seat at the end of the bed. "I didn't hear you."

I'm in your head. How could you not hear me? Her voice ratcheted up a notch. Clearly this was going to be a big blowout if I didn't stop to hear her out.

It was times like this I was tempted to just take the damn necklace off.

I stifled another sigh. "I'm listening now, Artemis. What do you want to say?"

You cannot keep pretending that you don't need the blood, Vânâtori. If you continue on as you are, you will end up as Morvalden's plaything when he drags you from your dreams.

That was... not a fun thing to think about. It had come close to happening. Too close. It was actually the reason I'd needed Ramble to pop into my dreams and save me from the uber-vampire.

"Artemis. Come on. I'm not pretending anything. I know I need more vampire blood. I get it. But I'm not going to guzzle down blood everyday just to keep you powered up. There are going to be times when you're going to have to, I dunno, power down a little I guess." I wasn't sure what the right words were for this situation.

Power down? Her voice was right on the edge now. My attempt to calm her down was backfiring. Badly. Her voice grew in volume with each word now and I could feel her anger starting to boil to the surface. It made me kind of glad that I was the only one who could hear her.

I am not one of your machines that you can just turn on and off. I am a goddess *trapped in a* necklace *and I am at the mercy of a half-Vânători who does not seem to take the world seriously!*

"Whoa, whoa, there. Let's just cut the name calling. I might not be a full Vânători, but I've almost died several times just to get you. Not to mention I came pretty close to dying just a few days ago just so I could find out how to make you work." I realized that my voice had risen a bit to match hers. Apparently now it was my turn to get worked up.

I took a deep, calming breath and used my best I'm-being-patient-with-you customer service voice that didn't quite drop into condescension as I said, "I am not pretending anything. And I don't think you're a machine. I know that I need vampire blood to continue receiving your assistance." I could feel a tiny tug of appreciation emanating from her presence in my mind at that. "You know I'm not looking forward to asking for more blood, but we need to know how long I can actually go without blood before my ability to communicate with you wears off."

That bought me a few seconds of thoughtful silence. *I see,* she finally said.

"We know that with a little blood, like what Constancia made me drink, that I can only hear you for a limited time before you fade away again. But with the amount I got from Louis, the super strength lasted a little longer and I've been able to hear you for far longer."

So, she said hesitantly as if feeling her way forward, *you are gauging the amount of blood needed to stay connected to your Vână-tori abilities.*

"Yes. And also determining if there is an optimum amount of blood for keeping me connected to you. The less I need to drink, the better."

It disgusted me how all this talk about drinking blood was making me want it.

Right now.

Bad.

Somehow it was worse than my alcohol dependence had been. Or was. I wasn't magically completely cured of alcoholism. The moment I stopped drinking blood and the necklace's abilities wore off, I would revert back to craving alcohol. It had happened before.

Then again, now that I thought about it, I didn't think alcohol would ever scratch that same itch again. Thinking about a cold beer or a nip of vodka just didn't send that feeling of need through me. But when I pictured Louis and thought about the coppery, cold taste of his blood and his personal scent of vanilla...

I dragged in a gulp of air. My body definitely wanted Louis for more than just his blood.

Was this what Louis felt like when he thought of drinking human blood? Maybe we needed to start a blood-addicts anonymous group.

Clearing my throat, I tried to change the subject. "Actually, I've been wanting to ask you about something else. After our fight with the beast and Gabriella, you told me that the

Vânători had acted as lawmen for the supernatural community."

That was the wolf's word and not quite accurate. It is not a mere job that you can quit at will. It is who you are. A better term might be an enforcer. The Vânători are tasked with maintaining an order among those who are other.

"Other?" I asked.

Those who are not human. For many centuries, I worked with your ancestors to protect those within what you are calling the "supernatural community." We kept peace among them. We weighed arguments and handed down decisions that were respected in their finality.

I thought about how to carefully word my next question. "But something must have changed. You haven't seemed too interested in the well-being of the werewolves and witches we've met here. Let alone vampires."

Over time, those we determined to be at fault or who lost an argument didn't want to accept our ruling. They fought back or, in some instances, stopped calling upon us at all during such disagreements, choosing instead to settle the matter among themselves. Mostly through combat or cloak and dagger tactics. The Vânători and I changed with the times and began only to seek out those who preyed on humans. Over time, our purpose as an enforcer was at best ignored and at worst, seen as overstepping.

I paused to think about this. "So, you're no longer interested in the well-being of the supernatural community because they didn't want to play with you anymore?"

Maybe that was a harsh way to put it, but that's about how it sounded.

No, Vânători. I am not a child to act out of selfish revenge. I am protecting the supernatural community by keeping humans ignorant of its existence. Look at the weapons humans wield today. Do you think they would peacefully open their arms and embrace vampires and werewolves were they to discover the existence of other creatures different from them?

Actually, judging by the popularity of some vampire romance fiction, I had a feeling there were quite a few folks out there who would do just that. Or who would want to become a vampire.

But Artemis was right. There were far, far more people who would immediately run for their pitchforks. Or AR-15s. Different weapons for different times, I guess.

A light grumble outside interrupted my thoughts, and I hopped up to let Ramble back inside. Maybe I should invest in a dog-door for the cabin so he could go out when he wanted. Then again. I didn't plan to stay there forever. That and I wasn't sure they made dog doors big enough for the hellhound to fit through.

"Ready for bed?" I asked him. He snuffed neutrally in response then lay on the floor to clean his feet. It was the start of his pre-bedtime ritual and usually something he did while I brushed my teeth.

I sighed, wanting to go get ready for bed myself, but I had one more thing I needed to do tonight.

"I'm going to see if I can catch Louis in the office before we go to bed."

Good, Artemis said in the back of my mind.

Ramble's eyes flicked to mine to acknowledge he'd heard me but continued cleaning his feet. I guess he was no longer concerned about me being alone with the vampire. I wasn't so sure he had the right feeling about that. Louis had said there were no hard feelings for me almost draining him, but I hadn't spoken to the vampire since that night. For some reason, it felt like I was trying to corner the vampire after a one-night stand: Awkward, embarrassing, and you just wanted it to be over.

I slipped outside and headed toward the office. The

window was dark, and the open sign had been flipped around to the "Closed" side. Just in case, I tried the door handle and wasn't surprised to find it locked.

Blowing out a breath of annoyance that Louis was dodging me, I also gave a mental sigh of relief at not having to talk to him tonight. I had wanted to tell him that I was moving out of the motel tomorrow, but I knew we also needed to have the awkward conversation around me needing more of his blood in the future.

I didn't plan to ask about the blood tonight, though. Not yet. I mean, yes, I really wanted it, but I didn't really *need* it right now. And though I'd had a valid excuse for Artemis, the truth was that I was scared at the thought of being alone with the vampire again. Not because I thought he'd harm me, but because I thought I might really drain him completely this time without someone to stop me.

That and the thought of drinking from him again had become a lot more sexually charged. Was I afraid I'd rip his pants off and have my way with him?

Maybe.

With my plans to chat with Louis thwarted, I headed back to the motel room. As I neared the door, I stopped.

Was that lawn gnome there earlier when we came out? I silently asked Artemis.

Someone had left a three-foot tall garden gnome in front of our door. It had the requisite pointed red hat with a blue robe and brown pants. A grey beard covered the lower part of his face and hung down almost to his little knees. His feet were bare, showing off long, gnarly toenails that looked chapped and blistered. What a weird detail to add to a garden ornament. The other thing that struck me as odd was the small knife in his hand.

No. It was not. On your guard, Vânători.

I felt a surge of adrenaline followed by an underlying thrill as Artemis readied for a fight.

Moving more cautiously, I approached the door. Was this some sort of distraction? I tried to keep my head on a swivel as my previous hunter-mentor, Jax, would have suggested. If the gnome was a distraction, then it was likely someone would try to sneak up on me from behind.

And then the gnome moved.

He turned and craned his head up at me to demand, "Where the fuck have you been?"

Chapter Three

❧

My mouth dropped open in surprise. Just when I thought I knew what to expect out of this weird-ass world of the supernatural, something new popped up. How many times had I lamented the need for a manual on this stuff?

I heard Ramble on the other side of the door give a low rumble.

Sure, now he warns me.

The gnome stared at me, clearly waiting for an answer.

"Um, I...can I help you?"

"Can you help me?" He looked up at the sky as if praying for strength. "I chase after the Vânători all day and when I finally catch up to her, she asks me, 'Um, c-c-c-can I help you?'" His voice rose to a falsetto as he made fun of me.

I would have been more annoyed by his response, but I was still stuck being taken aback. Not only because I was talking to a freakin' lawn gnome, but because he was so angry at me.

"Um. Well...if you've chased me around all day, and now

you've caught up to me, why don't you tell me what you want instead of being a dick about it?"

Okay, maybe I was a little annoyed.

Ignore the little man, Artemis haughtily suggested. *He is of no consequence.*

What? I mentally responded. *Less than ten minutes ago, you said it's my job as a Vânători to protect those in the supernatural community. If this guy doesn't count as part of that community, I don't know who does.*

He is a lesser being in the hierarchy of things. What can a gnome do for you in return? Watch your garden? Tend your lawn? Water your flowers? His problem is not worth your time, Vânători.

It was news to me that there was some kind of hierarchy in the supernatural community. See? I needed a manual! But what pissed me off and made me decide to help the gnome was that I was not a fan of a social caste system. Who was I to say that this gnome was less important than, say, Louis or Rosalyn? Plus, I wasn't aware that we were expecting some sort of kickback for Vânători protection.

Since when do we help others in return for favors? I asked.

Don't be a child, Vânători. We aren't here for charity. We are here to build up alliances with creatures who will be able to stand with us against the vampires when they inevitably come for you.

News to me.

Throughout my internal conversation with Artemis, the gnome stood glaring at me. It was as if he knew I was otherwise mentally occupied. Weird.

"If you would invite me in, I'll tell you why I'm here," he said when I'd finished speaking with Artemis.

I quirked an eyebrow at him and crossed my arms over my chest. He might not look like that much of a threat because of his size, but if I'd learned anything about the supernatural community, it was that looks could be deceiving.

The gnome suddenly looked a little embarrassed. He

tucked his knife into a leather sheath at the small of his back and, without looking at me said in a quiet voice, "I'd rather not tell you out here in the open. It's a...sensitive matter."

Hmm. I wasn't sure I believed him, and I was hesitant to let him into our room. What if he had a magic talisman that allowed him to just *look* like a harmless gnome but was actually a giant monster who would swallow me whole as soon as we were behind closed doors. Then again, it wouldn't just be me in the room with him. I'd have Ramble at my back and the powers of the necklace. I guess we could handle him. And if we couldn't, what would keep him from just hulking out right now? Might as well see what he wanted.

"Fine." I leaned over him and pushed open the door.

Ramble stood to the side of the doorway. As the gnome entered the room, he gave the invisible hellhound a wide berth as if he could see him or sense he was there.

Interesting.

I closed the door behind us, and the gnome settled into a cross-legged position on the floor with his back against the end of the bed. He'd pulled off his pointy red hat, revealing long, wiry grey hair that matched his beard. I started to pull a chair away from the table before I realized that it would leave me towering over him. So I left the chair and sat on the floor across from him, mimicking his cross-legged sitting position. Ramble padded to my side, making us a united front as I studied the gnome.

Now that I knew he wasn't just a statue, his poor abused feet that had been exposed to the cold seemed even more pitiful. His nose was also red from the cold. Did he stay outside all winter?

"Okay. We're inside now. Away from listening ears—"

At that, the gnome looked straight at Ramble and ticked up an eyebrow.

So he *could* see Ramble. Huh. I tucked that knowledge

away and continued "—with the exception of Ramble here, of course. But he's part of the team, so he stays."

Now both the gnome's brows shot to his forehead. "You named the hellhound?"

I stifled a groan. Seriously. I was never gonna live this down.

"Yes. I named a hellhound and now we work together. Can we move this along?" I tried not to look longingly at the bed as a wave of exhaustion hit me. I hadn't realized I'd used so much energy to lay Cassandra's ghost to rest.

The gnome crossed his arms over his chest and glowered at me. Great. I ignored his glower and decided to try a different tactic.

"I'm Vianne, by the way. And you've met Ramble now. What's your name?"

He continued to glower at me. I didn't have time for this shit. I was ready to drop into bed. Just as I started to hop up and kick him out, he finally spoke.

"I'm Hyssop—Yes, before you ask, like the flower."

Since I'd been about to ask just that, I quickly changed what I'd been about to say. "Nice to meet you, Hyssop. Now, what's got you waiting outside my room in your bare feet in the middle of winter?"

"I've been kicked out of my garden and I need your help taking it back."

"Okay..." I said, drawing it out so I could figure out what to ask next. Ramble snorted and hopped up onto the bed, clearly done with this conversation since it didn't involve killing vampires and breathing fire on anyone.

"Who kicked you out of your garden?" I asked to distract the gnome from Ramble's apathy.

"The human who lived at the house died of old age two years ago and her prick son turned around and sold the house to some nitwit who wouldn't know a hoe handle if it smacked him in the head." Here Hyssop had to pause as his voice hitched with emotion on his next words. "He *ripped out* the whole garden last spring. *Everything* I'd kept alive for years in that garden just, poof, gone! Even my *namesake,* the beautiful hyssop bush! Gone in an afternoon when the oaf decided he wanted a gravel backyard filled with raised garden beds. Gravel! Who does that? I mean, straw, sure. Or I've even seen cardboard like what Goldie's house does to keep the weeds down in their veg patch, but—

"Goldie?" I cut him off.

"Goldenrod. Good chap. He's the guardian of the garden a few houses down from mine. Small plot but he does a real nice job—but that's not the point, Vânători." Hyssop's brows drew down in consternation. "The point is that my garden is *gone*."

I had no idea what to say to that, so I went with, "I'm very sorry for your loss." And then realized that his story wasn't quite making sense. "But hold on now. You said you'd been kicked out of your garden, but it sounds more like the garden was removed."

"It was *destroyed,*" he corrected with angry glare, "but then I was kicked out."

"What happened? I mean, why were you kicked out?"

He'd wrapped the end of his beard around the index finger of one hand as he spoke and now was winding and unwinding it in a nervous gesture.

"Well, as you can imagine, I was very upset with that addle-brained human, so I...I..." suddenly his voice dropped to an almost whisper, "I stopped his veggies from growing." Hyssop threw his hands up in an exasperated gesture, but one hand, still wound up in his beard, jerked his chin up with it. He untangled his hand and smoothed his beard back down before continuing. "I know, I know. Purposely ruining the growth of any living plant is against the way of the gnome, but you've got to understand, he was—is—ruining my garden! He may as well have salted and burned that backyard!"

Tears filled his eyes and dripped down his cheeks to disappear in his beard.

I'd been planning to ask him if we could just find him a new garden to care for, but I had a feeling he was attached to that plot of land. Instead, I settled on asking, "How has the new homeowner been taking it when his raised garden keeps failing to produce anything?"

Hyssop sucked in a breath and whispered, "He adds *chemicals* to the soil."

"Oh." I tried to sound appropriately offended for Hyssop's sake. I was still missing something though. "So when did he kick you out of the garden? And how did he know it was you keeping things from growing? I'm assuming he doesn't know about gnomes and other creatures of the supernatural community.

"Supernatural community?"

I sighed and flapped my hand at the gnome. "You know what I mean. Does he know you're not just a garden statue? Or do you even let him see you?"

"Of course he sees me. What, do you think I just magically twiddle my thumbs and vanish like your useless hellhound there?"

This elicited a grumble from Ramble, but he didn't bother to even raise his head. Even Artemis was silent. Which was more than odd and made me a little wary. Apparently, this was my ballgame.

"Okay, so he *sees* you, but does he know you're real?"

"He only sees a statue."

"So why would he kick a statue out of his garden?"

"Because he keeps throwing me away," Hyssop huffed, "and I keep climbing out of the trash can and back into his garden."

"I see. So what's stopping you from just going back to the garden again?"

"Let's just say he thinks I'm more than a statue now."

I twirled my finger in a circle to suggest that the gnome should elaborate. He sighed but explained, "He caught me trying to put those garden chemicals in his morning coffee and freaked out. Instead of trying to throw me away, this time he got a hammer...so I jumped out of his hands and ran away. That was two weeks ago. I've been garden-hopping ever since."

I had to suppress a laugh. I could just picture some guy walking into his kitchen and catching Hyssop mid-act as he was pouring plant fertilizer into the guy's coffee cup. I wish I could have seen the look of surprise on the guy's face when Hyssop leapt out of his hands to avoid getting thwacked by a hammer.

There were worse ways to discover the world of the supernatural, I guess.

"I see," I said, and when Hyssop just looked at me like he was expecting more, I added, "What would you like me to do about it? I'm not sure it's the best idea for you to try and go back there."

"But, Vânători, that's my *garden*. It's my plot of land in this life and I'm sworn to it. Look," he held up a callused foot, blistered by the cold. "I'm already losing my magic against the elements. If I don't go back soon, I'll likely fade away altogether. Maybe if you could just talk to him, help him understand why he has to change the garden back, then everything could go back to normal?"

He was pleading now. How do you say no to someone begging you for their help? It would have been different if he'd continued being a jerk, but as soon as he'd started crying, I knew I'd have to help him.

You're too soft-hearted, Vânători, Artemis said, and I could almost hear her rolling her nonexistent eyes. *We cannot help every gnome, fairy, or nymph who shows up on your doorstep.*

Why? I silently asked. *Why shouldn't we help him? We don't have anything else going on right now and it might be a good opportunity for me to get more comfortable using your powers.*

Not that I thought I'd need to use the necklace to talk a human into letting Hyssop return to his garden, but I thought it was a better argument than saying I wanted to help because I felt bad for the guy.

I felt Artemis mulling it over before she finally relented. *Fine, but if a more important case comes up, it takes precedence over the gardenless gnome.*

"Fine," I said and realized too late that I'd said it out loud rather than silently. Hyssop perked right up.

"You'll help me?"

"Yes, but not tonight. I need to get some sleep, but first thing in the morning, we'll head over to your garden and I'll see if I can talk to the guy who bought the house.

Gratitude transformed Hyssop's face, making him suddenly appear much younger. "Thank you so much, Vânători!"

How old was this guy? I would have guessed mid-forties if he'd been human, but now I wondered if he might actually be far younger than that. I waved away his thanks and focused on the next issue at hand.

"Since you can't go back to your garden tonight, do you need a place to stay?"

Hyssop shook his head, "I have a friend nearby who guards the town center garden. He'll let me stay there tonight."

I got the details of where Hyssop's garden was located, which took some time since he didn't know the street address. After showing him a map of the town on my phone, he was able to point it out. He left shortly after that and I breathed a sigh of relief as soon as I was able to shut the door. Turning, I found Ramble giving me the stink eye.

"What?"

He didn't bother to lift his head and chose instead to roll his eyes at me. Then he whined like a normal dog would when begging for something. He was definitely making fun of me for giving in to help Hyssop.

"Whatever. You probably wanted to help him, too, but you're just pretending to be a hard-ass with a cold heart."

He snorted at me.

Whatever.

"Alright," I said around a jaw-cracking yawn. "Time for bed for me. I'll figure out what to say to the home-owner tomorrow. We'll do that first thing, then go to a bigger town for house stuff after that.

And knock off an ATM while we're there, I thought to myself with a sigh. I hated using the fake credit card, but unless I got a real job here in Ricketts, I wouldn't have any money coming in anytime soon.

One would think that the life of a vampire hunter from a legendary family would involve having a lot more cash flow. Instead, here I was, once again wondering how to stretch out my current savings to buy household goods, food, and gas. Not to mention paying rent next month if I was here that long.

Story of my life.

Chapter Four

Though Ramble was not much of a morning hellhound, I thought we'd had a pretty pleasant morning. I'd gotten on his good side by coaxing him out of bed with some free breakfast from the motel office "buffet" (which mostly consisted of yogurt, prepackaged muffins, and terrible coffee).

Ramble ate everything I brought him then slipped outside to do his business while I showered and got dressed. It didn't take me long. It wasn't like I had a closet of clothes to pick from and I didn't exactly wear a ton of makeup. My beauty routine consisted of blow-drying my hair before braiding it, then hydrating my face with the hotel lotion. It wasn't meant to be used on your face but screw it. The cold Maine winter was doing a number on my skin and I'd rather be slightly greasy than deal with flaking, painful skin on my face.

Since I planned to stay in Cassandra's cabin tonight rather than returning here, I grabbed my backpack, did a once over of the room to make sure we hadn't missed anything, and headed outside with Ramble on my heels. There was still no sign of Louis, so I left the key with the front office clerk.

When I turned to meet Ramble at the car, I practically tripped over the hellhound when I found he was right outside the office door.

"What?" I quietly asked him. "Afraid I might get into trouble with the kid at the front desk?"

Ramble huffed at me, then turned to stare pointedly at the parking lot. I followed his gaze. It took me a few minutes to realize the problem.

"Where the hell is our car?"

I'd parked it right across from the motel room door last night. I must have been so preoccupied in figuring out how to start my conversation with the guy who'd kicked Hyssop out of his garden that I hadn't noticed it was gone until now.

"Holy shit, Ramble," I said, looking at the hellhound. "Someone stole our stolen car!"

"More like moved it."

I turned at the familiar voice to find Donavon parked in an unfamiliar, puke green car near the front office. I mentally kicked myself for not noticing him as he extracted his muscular self from the small car. It would have been funny had I not been fuming about my missing car and slightly embarrassed at my lack of attention to my surroundings.

Slipups like this could be your death, Vânători. You cannot let the enemy sneak up on you like that.

"He's not exactly the enemy," I said under my breath as Donavon approached.

Once free of the car, Donavon stretched his arms behind him until his back audibly popped. I did my best not to ogle the muscles under his tight sweater and briefly wondered how all that stretching didn't burst the piece of fabric at the seams.

As he stretched, he gave me a look and said, "Of course I'm not the enemy."

Argh. I really needed to get used to the whole supernatural-hearing thing when working with nonhumans.

He may not be the enemy today. But tomorrow? Tomorrow could be another story.

That's my trusty magical necklace, trying to make enemies out of allies.

Donavon was a werewolf and the leader of the local Pack. We'd worked together to figure out who was behind the murders in town, so it was hard to see him as an enemy. Though, now that I thought about it, he *had* known that the car I was driving around was stolen.

Shit.

"What did you do?" I crossed my arms over my chest. "And why would you move my car?"

He stopped a few feet away at the hostility in my voice. Good. I liked Donavon, but if he thought he could take my car without my permission, then he was overstepping. We were friends, but not that good of friends.

Okay, I might have almost jumped his bones a few days ago, but in my defense, I was slightly hypothermic and was going through alcohol withdrawal. It's not my fault I tend to replace the need for alcohol with a more carnal desire.

Sometimes I wasn't sure if it was a good thing or a bad thing that we'd been interrupted before anything had happened. Probably a good thing since the person I was currently having very intimate dreams about was Louis. And since Donavon and Louis considered each other brothers, it seemed like the best bet was to just steer clear of both of them when it came to sex.

I could still admire the view though. Even if I was pissed at him.

Donavon put up his hand in a placating gesture. "You can't keep driving a stolen car around town, Vianne. You don't exactly keep a low profile, and Bart can't keep pretending he doesn't know it's stolen."

It took me a minute to remember that Bart meant Sheriff Allen.

"What did you do with my car, *Donavon?*"

He put his hand down with a sigh. "I had one of my guys drive it a few towns over and drop it in the middle of nowhere. Then they called the local law enforcement to say they'd seen an abandoned car."

"What!?" I threw my hands up. "What the hell, Donavon! How am I supposed to get around now? It's not like I have oodles of money and can just buy a new car!"

"You can't keep driving a stolen car around town!" He insisted.

"Says who?" I suddenly felt like a teenager arguing with her parents.

We were getting loud, but I didn't care. Though the motel was on the main road, the parking lot we stood in was on the back side of the building. The only person to witness our argument would be the front desk clerk, and she'd probably gone back to listening to her earbuds already.

Donavon took a deep breath, closed his eyes, and blew the air out through his mouth before opening his eyes again. I was relieved to see they were still a regular human color and hadn't shifted as they did when he started to wolf-out.

"Vianne," his tone was that of an adult clearly being patient with an unruly child. "This is a tiny town. *Everyone* knows you stole that car. Bart has been dropping hints at me for the last two days that if you didn't leave town, then your car needed to. Get it? So I did you a favor and had the car moved somewhere that it could be found and returned to its rightful owner without implicating you."

I did not care for his tone.

Do you think that if we punched him in the face that he'd stop talking to us like that? I mentally asked Artemis.

I think that if you punched him in the face, Vânători, he would stop speaking completely because we would break his jaw. But I believe that we would only have the power to wield such damage against the werewolf for the rest of today. After that, we will need more power to injure him.

By power, she meant blood. Well, I sure as hell wasn't drinking vampire blood today. Which meant I needed to play nice with the damn werewolf. I took a cleansing breath of my own before responding.

"If I don't have a car, Donavon, how do you recommend that I get around town? It's not like you have public transportation here.

A grin spread over his face and I knew the answer to my question even before he pointed at the puke green car behind him. "I have an extra car. You can use it while you're here, but you're responsible for the maintenance and upkeep. If you decide you want to keep it, we can talk about payments."

I was glad he hadn't said I'd be responsible for the insurance. As someone who'd skipped out on parole, trying to get insurance in my real name would be a bad idea. And if the cops could find me, then so could Morvalden and his crony vampires.

"So, you just have an extra car sitting around?" I asked.

I know, I know. I should have just said, "Thank you," but I wasn't used to people trying to help me. I'd just been operating on my own for so long, even before the vampire hunter thing, that it was kind of hard to suddenly switch gears and accept help.

"Well..." he said, giving me a look that said I'd hit on something that he didn't really want to talk about, "it's my car now, but only because Samuel left it to me."

Samuel had been one of Donavon's werewolves before

he'd been murdered by the giant monster-dog. And, I remembered, he'd been murdered right outside his car. *This* car.

Great. Just what I needed. But what the hell, I was already going to be staying in the house where Cassandra had been murdered. Why not add a murder-car to the mix?

It wasn't really like I had a choice at this point. My only other option for transportation was to steal another car, and that wasn't going to happen in a town where everyone knew each other and would immediately spot the theft.

I felt Artemis stir in the back of my mind. *I don't like this, Vânători. First you take favors from the witch and her coven and now you're accepting a gift from the werewolf. If you're not careful, you'll be beholden to them and won't be able to act as a neutral party when called upon to make a judgement as a Vânători.*

First, I mentally responded, *this isn't a gift. Donavon already said I'd have to pay him if I drove it for more than a month. Second, I'm not here to make any kind of judgments.*

The fact didn't escape me that both Rosalyn and Donavon had both given me the spiel about paying if I stayed for more than a month. It was obviously more than a coincidence. They'd clearly collaborated on this for some reason. It made me wonder why exactly a month? Hopefully it wasn't because there was some crazy ritual that they wanted me to take part in as the ritual sacrifice.

Maybe I should start dropping hints that I wasn't a virgin or something.

Or maybe I should just put on my big girl pants and ask them outright what was up.

"I appreciate the gesture," I told Donavon, trying and failing to sound sincere when I didn't know what his motives were, "but why are both you and Rosalyn being so nice to me? She's letting me stay in Cassandra's house for a month, and now you're loaning me a car for a month. I can't help but wonder why."

He opened his mouth, thought better about what he'd been planning to say, then shut it again. Hmm. Suspicious much?

Finally, he came to a decision and stepped closer to quietly say, "Rosalyn and I both think it's good for the town—for, you know, *our* people—to have you stay longer. In the past few years, we've had more folks like us moving here to make Ricketts their home. And while that's great, it also means more *incidents* among the...supernatural community."

He suppressed a wince as he used my phrase. Why did everyone think it was weird or funny? If someone had a better idea for what to call a collective gathering of witches, werewolves, vampires, gnomes, trolls, and who knew what else, I was happy to use their suggestion. But until then, I needed a term which described folks who weren't exactly human. "Nonhuman" sounded a little too hateful for my ears, so "supernatural community" it was.

"What kind of people?" I asked, genuinely curious as I dropped my angry stance. I was still pretty sure that Donavon wasn't wise to the fact that the owners of the Flying Pie restaurant were trolls. They had a deal with Rosalyn to act as the coven's muscle in return for a bit of magic that made them appear and smell human.

If Donavon didn't know about them, he might not know that gnomes like Hyssop were living here either. Huh. Who else had moved into Ricketts recently that didn't fall into the witch, vampire, or werewolf categories? Interesting that he hadn't mentioned any other supernatural beings when we'd been investigating the monster-dog murders together.

Donavon shrugged one giant shoulder. "Other shifters, a goblin family, and a clan of faeries.

We should find out where the goblins live. They eat human babies, Vânători. We must strike them before they make their first kill.

I would have ignored Artemis, but it would be difficult to look the other way if someone in town was eating babies.

"Goblins? Aren't they known for having a particular kind of appetite?"

"These ones swear they're vegans."

"Okay," I said, trying to get this conversation back on track, "so you and Rosalyn want me to, what? Help keep the peace among the supernatural community and stay here longer than a month?"

"Exactly." He smiled, clearly glad I understood and wasn't mad.

How little he knew me. I hadn't planned on staying even this long, yet here he and Rosalyn were, making plans for me without my knowing. Without asking me. While I wanted to enjoy the fact that they wanted me to stay, I couldn't forget that it wasn't because they liked me and thought I was a great person.

It was because I was supposed to be some all-powerful vampire hunter who could keep the peace in their town.

"You know that Morvalden is going to come after me, right?" I asked quietly.

Donavon flinched.

Good. At least I didn't have to try and convince him how scared he should be of the vampire.

"If I stay here too long, Donavon, he'll eventually come to your town. I don't think you want that."

What game are you playing, Vânători?

No game, I mentally responded. *I just don't like people assuming they know me when they don't know the first thing about me.*

You're acting like a spoiled child. I don't like accepting favors from the wolf either, but you will need the vehicle.

Fine.

Donavon had opened his mouth to say something, but I

44

started moving toward the car and cut him off before he could respond. "Thank you for loaning me the car. I'll need it for the next week or so while I'm here." Sensing my mood, Ramble shouldered his way past the werewolf and followed me to the car. Being shoulder-checked by an invisible hellhound would throw anybody off, and Donavon was no exception.

He stumbled to the left a few steps, and when he recovered, his eyes were the silvery-white of being on the edge of angry. Good. I didn't want to be the only one pissed off here.

"What is your deal, Vianne? I did you a favor by getting rid of the stolen car, and now I'm loaning you this one."

"Ah. Gotcha. So two favors then. Look how lucky I am." I set my backpack down next to the car. It would have been more dramatic to drop it, but I didn't want to damage the laptop inside. Or the gun.

I straightened up and turned to face Donavon again. "My *deal* is that you took my vehicle without asking me, then decided to make me beholden to you by loaning me a car." I could feel Artemis preening at my use of her word. Whatever. "If you thought you were doing me a favor, why didn't you just talk to me beforehand about the stolen car instead of taking it in the middle of the night?"

"I... I didn't think you'd be on board with it."

"Uh huh. And why didn't you think I'd be on board with it?"

He sighed. "Because then you'd feel that you owed me one, but," he perked up as if he'd just remembered something, "you don't owe me anything. This is me returning your favor since you helped us take down the deputy and the witch he was working with."

Though the deputy had been part-witch, he could only turn into the giant dog-monster-beast thing with the help of a magical device the witch Gabriella had given him. Donavon made it sound like the deputy had been the brains behind the killings when he'd mostly been following Gabriella's orders.

"Did Rosalyn tell you to say that?"

"Uh."

How had this guy become the alpha of the local werewolf pack? I shook my head and held out my hand for the keys. "Fine. I'll take it. But only because I don't have anything else to drive, and I have a job to get to this morning."

"You got a job in town?" He asked as he dropped the keys in his hands.

"Sort of." I mean, it didn't *pay,* but it was still a job, right?

Perhaps you should *charge the gnome,* Artemis added. *It wasn't unusual for Vânători to be paid for their services.*

Hmm. That was something to think about. Then again...

What is Hyssop gonna pay me in? Flowers?

Do not underestimate the lesser non-humans, Vânători.

Seriously? You just told me last night that he wasn't worth it, and you literally just called him "lesser." He's either worth our time or he isn't.

I felt her give a mental shrug rather than answer.

Donavon was staring at me. Shit. This whole business of carrying on two conversations wasn't as easy as I thought it would be. What had we been talking about again? Oh right. The job.

"It's not a paying job," I admitted, picking up my bag again and heading for the trunk.

"Someone in town has already asked for your help?"

"Yup." I popped the trunk open and deposited my bag inside. Next, I opened the passenger door for Ramble while Donavon followed me around the car.

Before Ramble could get in, Donavon stepped in his path. "Actually, before you head to your job, I need a ride back to my place since I drove this car over here."

I stared at him for a minute before looking at Ramble to

see what he thought. He huffed and rolled his eyes but pushed past Donavon again to hop through the passenger side door and into the back.

"Fine." I said again. Apparently, this was going to be my word of the day.

He hesitated to get in. "Um…is he…?" He jerked his head toward the passenger seat, and I remembered that he couldn't see Ramble.

"Afraid of pissing off the hellhound?" I asked, suddenly grinning. Ramble grinned back…which was a little scary if I'm being honest. My quip earned me a look from the werewolf.

I relented and told Donavon, "He's in the back. It's safe for you to get in."

It took me a few seconds to get the seat and the mirrors where I wanted them. I cranked the car and, though it was an ugly thing, it started just fine.

"Shit. Is that the right time?" I asked.

"Yeah. Why? What time's your job?"

"Like, right now. I don't think I'm gonna have time to drop you off." I yanked the seatbelt on and waited expectantly for Donavon to get out.

Instead, because my morning wasn't going badly enough already, he smiled and said, "Alright. I'll just come with you."

How had this werewolf learned to grind my gears so quickly?

Whatever. My options were limited at this point. It looked like helping Hyssop was going to be a group effort.

"Fine."

Yup. Word of the day.

Chapter Five

"I don't think this is a good idea," I said a few minutes later as I halted the car at a four-way stop.

"It's fine. I know all the supernatural creatures in town. Maybe I can help. Turn left here."

Since I hadn't been able to convince Donavon to get out of the car, I'd decided to make him useful, so now he was navigating us to Hyssop's garden. Not that he really needed the phone's directions in such a small town once he saw where our destination was.

"Great. Except that this job also involves humans," I explained.

"So?"

I glanced over at him. Was he hunching over so his head wouldn't hit the roof? He looked like a giant in this tiny vehicle. I wondered how Samuel had managed to get in and out of it.

"So...I dunno. It's my first job, and I don't want to feel like I have a babysitter."

"Do you need a babysitter?" He flashed his perfect white teeth at me in a grin that sent a little shiver down my spine.

Shit. I thought my attraction for him had been a one-off type thing. A substitute for needing a drink. I didn't have time to go lusting after a werewolf for his body and a vampire for his blood. Besides, I wasn't that kind of girl to go after two guys at once. Especially two guys who considered each other brothers.

"Whatever," I said and looked away, hoping he hadn't caught the scent of my body's interest in him. After turning through the stop sign, I started fiddling with the heater controls. Not that it really mattered right now since Ramble had his head out the open window in the back. Though it meant I was freezing my butt off up front, it seemed like the least I could do for making him ride in the back.

"Um," Donavon's expression changed as he watched me fail to get the heat going. "The heat doesn't work in this car."

"Seriously?" I put my hand back on the wheel. "It's winter. In Maine. You couldn't lend me a car with a heater that works?"

"If you're just driving around town, it's not like you'll be in it for long."

"Says the guy with heated leather seats in his car."

He pointedly ignored my comment. "The house is up here on the right."

A little adrenaline shot through me as we approached the house and parked at the curb. It was a decent-size place with a fancy Victorian style that I didn't think I'd ever be able to afford. The outside was an interesting shade of lavender with white trim. The front lawn was immaculately maintained, as were the rose bushes out front.

Hmm. It looked like the new owner hadn't gotten rid of all the flowers after all. It made me wonder if Hyssop had been exaggerating what the new owner had done to his garden out back. I couldn't tell from here, though, since a tall wooden privacy fence blocked any view of the backyard. The fence looked pretty new. Maybe the owner had added it to keep Hyssop out?

I put the car in park and thought about my plan of approach. Everything I'd come up with the night before had sounded great in theory, but now that I was here, I wasn't so sure my arguments for letting Hyssop back in and changing the garden back would stand up in the light of the day. Not to mention, I now had a werewolf tagging along.

"Is there any chance I could convince you to stay in the car?"

"Nope," Donavon's smile was...mischievous. Argh. It made me want to punch him in the face. Or hop in the sack with him. It was a toss-up.

We do not fraternize with non-humans, Vânători.

Thanks for the ground rules, Mom, I shot back.

I sighed and got out of the car. I had not had enough coffee yet to deal with this kind of ridiculousness. And I was just getting started.

I looked at Ramble with his head still hanging out the rear driver's side window. "You coming with or staying here?"

He huffed and rested his head on the window. I took that to mean he'd stay here.

Super. Just me and the nosy, pushy, hot werewolf.

There was no sign of Hyssop yet, but maybe that was a good thing. I wasn't sure what the new owner would think of me if I was running around with a gnome who wasn't supposed to exist. At least the guy wouldn't be able to immediately tell that Donavon was a werewolf.

Donavon and I walked to the front door together, but he motioned me to take the lead as we approached.

"Your show," he said with that damn grin again.

Seriously. I needed to wipe that grin off his face.

I wrapped my knuckles on the door when I didn't see a doorbell, and it was only a matter of seconds before it was answered. When the door opened, it revealed a man who dressed as immaculately as he kept his front lawn. His suit was more expensive than every piece of clothing I owned put together—which I guess wasn't saying much since my jacket and boots were from a second-hand clothing store and most of my other items were from big box stores.

"Can I help you?" The man asked with just the right level of curiosity mixed with annoyance for showing up on his front porch without invitation.

Lawyer or doctor? I mentally wondered. There were only so many vocations that taught someone that mixed level of greeting.

"Hi, I'm Violet Mason," I said with what I hoped looked like an endearing smile. Yep, still going with my fake identity. No reason to have humans asking after me with my real name and tipping off the authorities or the vampires to my location. I started to launch into one of my prepared spiels before realizing I needed to introduce the giant beside me.

"This is Donavon." I gestured at the giant werewolf beside me who had maintained his welcoming grin. "I'm renovating a house a few streets over and heard from some of your neighbors that you have quite the garden set up in your backyard! I'm just in the process of figuring out what to do with my backyard and thought I'd come check out the garden everyone's been talking about. Would you mind if we just took a peek at it?"

Okay, it might seem like I was chickening out of confronting the guy for Hyssop, but the thing was, what would I even be confronting him about? Looking at his front yard and the roses had made me realize that this guy had a side to the argument that I hadn't heard. Maybe I was letting my respect for human laws—okay, *most* human laws—get the better of me, but if this guy had bought the house, then didn't he have a right to change the backyard however he wanted?

The man's expression turned sour. "Did Karen next door put you up to this?" He shook his head in disgust. "I swear, that woman is nosier than a damn toucan. Always peering down from her upstairs windows into my backyard."

"Uh..." I'm not sure what kind of response I'd expected, but it wasn't this.

The man went on. "From the minute I moved in, I felt like I've been under a microscope. It's like the neighbors are always watching me. Do you know what's that like? And then weird stuff started happening."

"Weird stuff?" I helpfully supplied. Maybe he'd talk about seeing a gnome come to life and make my job easier.

It was as if he'd been drowning in a flood of complaints, and I'd just blown up the dam holding them back.

"Gardening tools going missing. Hoses suddenly springing leaks. Do you know how many hoses I had to buy this summer? I might as well become a partner in the local hardware store. Do you know," he stepped closer, "they *laugh* at me when I go into that store now? Me! I was the top defense lawyer in Portland, and the locals here *laugh* at me. But oh no, 'take a less stressful job,' my doctors said. 'Find a slower pace of life.'" He pointed a finger at my chest and suddenly I felt like I was on a witness stand being cross-examined. "If a less stressful life involves getting made fun of by backwoods locals and constantly feeling like I'm under surveillance by my NOSY NEIGHBORS," he turned and shouted that last part at the house next door before turning back to us, "then I want nothing to do with it."

With that, he retreated inside and slammed the door in our faces.

"Well, that went well." Donavon said.

"Shut up." I turned and retreated to the car.

"What was that all about anyways?" He asked after he'd shoved his giant body back in the tiny car.

I jumped when Hyssop responded from the back seat. "That was a Vânători losing her nerve and backing out of a deal."

The gnome was perched on the edge of the backseat, far away from Ramble, his blistered feet dangling in the air. His cheeks were red, but I didn't think it was from the cold.

"We had a deal, Vânători. You make the human let me back into the garden and tell him to put it back the way it was."

"No." I corrected. "I agreed to talk to him. By human law, he owns the house. I can't *make* him do anything, so I have to do this a different way."

"Uh," Donavon said, clearly at a loss for words at the appearance of a gnome in the backseat.

I guess it wasn't just the trolls that the werewolves didn't know about.

"Donavon, this is Hyssop. He's a gnome who says he lost his garden to the man we just spoke to. Hyssop, meet Donavon. He's the alpha of the local werewolf Pack."

"If you brought muscles here," the gnome jerked his head at Donavon, "why didn't you use him? He coulda grabbed that scallywag and thrown him into the street where he belongs!"

"We're not throwing anyone into the street." I stopped, remembering what the lawyer had said. "Hyssop, did you steal garden tools from him? And ruin his watering hoses?"

"So what if I did? He *destroyed* my entire garden, Vânători! What's a few hoses compared to that? And it's not like he knew how to use them. His whole system was wrong. Even if I didn't sabotage his plants, they'd have died anyways. That guy wouldn't know a green thumb if someone stuck one up his ass."

"Thanks for the lovely mental picture." I said and glanced over at Ramble. He'd made space for Hyssop and didn't seem to mind the gnome's presence. I quirked an eyebrow at my four-legged partner. "Thanks for the warning that Hyssop was waiting for us in the car."

The hellhound glanced at the gnome and licked his chops pointedly.

"No. Don't eat him yet." I sighed. "I said I'd help him, and I will, but I need to see both sides of the story."

I twisted back around to face forward again while Donavon continued to stare into the backseat.

"He's a gnome?" The big, bad, alpha werewolf almost squeaked.

"Yep. He's a gnome."

Ha! Artemis laughed in my head, *Wait until he learns about the trolls.*

"I know, right?" I answered.

Donavon tore his eyes away from Hyssop and drilled them into me. "How long have you known there was a gnome in town?"

I started the car and drove a little way down the road before answering. "Since yesterday evening when he showed up outside my motel room asking for help." I turned left at the next intersection, drove a few houses down to find an empty spot and then parked the car again.

"It looked like he was heading into work, right?" I asked.

"What? Who?"

"The lawyer." I looked over at Donavon who had twisted around to stare at Hyssop again. "Will you quit staring at him? You act like you've never met a gnome before."

"I haven't. We don't have gnomes in this town."

"Uh," Hyssop piped up from the backseat, "who do you think keeps all those roses outside your house alive, wolf? Because it sure isn't you with your terrible watering habits. Did you think your roses just put out amazing blooms with zero work? No, it's Blush who feeds your roses banana peels and painstakingly prunes them back to life. You just throw a plant in a hole and expect it to grow. If humans weren't around, you'd probably lift your leg and—

"Whoa, hey now." I whirled around and stared at the gnome. "If you haven't noticed, he's kind of on our side."

"'Kind of' being the key words here," Hyssop grumbled.

I decided to step into the conversation before they *really* stopped being civil. "You really didn't think there were other creatures in town that you didn't know about?" I asked Donavon. "It sounds to me like Hyssop and the other gnomes have been here for a while."

"One-hundred and twenty-three years I've lived in this place," Hyssop spat out, "and seventy-five of those years were spent right there, in that garden. Until that *monster* ripped my beautiful plants from the ground and walled me out." The gnome was on the brink of crying. "And now look at me." He smacked his feet. "I'm losing more of my magic every day. Pretty soon there'll be nothing left of me."

"I'm working on it, Hyssop. I'm just waiting for him to leave so we can check out the backyard." I glanced at the time on the car's dashboard. I'd give it another ten minutes, then we could head over. I was guessing Mr. Lawyer drove the brand new Mercedes parked in front of his house. Once that car was gone, I'd feel more comfortable snooping around.

I thought about what Hyssop had said. Not the part about being over a hundred years old. Boy had I guessed wrong on his age. But the part about the wall. "Wait, did that guy put up a fence after he tried to hit you with a hammer?"

That must have stirred something protective in the wolf because Donavon suddenly perked up. "He tried to hit you with a hammer?"

"Yes. He tried to hit Hyssop with a hammer because he caught him trying to poison his coffee."

Hyssop waved away my comment. "It wouldn't have killed him, Vânători. And my garden has *never* been walled in like that. Well, except for the cute fieldstone rock wall, but that fell long ago when they bulldozed most of the site to make way for the house."

I closed my eyes in thought. "Wait, hold on a second." I turned around and popped my eyes open to watch the gnome. "If they bulldozed the site, then they must have destroyed the garden. So you've lost your plants before. What makes this time different?"

"Aye, they destroyed *most* of my plants, but I was able to save some of them and restart the garden with that."

"So..." I really didn't know how I was going to get that lawyer to agree to let Hyssop back into the garden, so I was reaching for straws now. "Couldn't you just take some seeds from this garden and start over somewhere else?"

"No! Are you listening, Vânători, or are you just daft? It's not the seeds that are special, it's the *ground* where they're planted."

"I see." Did I? No, not really. *Do you want to explain this to me, Artemis?*

Oh, I see you need my help now. Not going to go to the witches for assistance this time?

What I wouldn't give for just a tiny bit of vampire blood right now. I bet it would take the edge off.

"You know what? Everybody just shut up."

Only after I said it did I realize I was really the only one talking. Whatever.

"Here's what's gonna happen. You two," I pointed at Hyssop and Donavon, "Are gonna stay in the car. And Ramble and I are gonna go and check out this guy's garden once he's gone."

I didn't really have the authority to boss the hellhound around, so I added, "Right, Ramble?" Which kind of killed the whole take charge thing, but I tried not to care.

Ramble stood in the backseat and shook himself. I

popped the door open and got out, leaving it open for Ramble. When he hopped into the front seat, he smacked Donavon with the tip of his tail.

"Watch it, dog," The werewolf partially growled.

Ramble ignored him and jumped down to the blacktop beside me. I could have sworn I saw him grinning.

Yet another reason why we got along so well.

I shut the door before the other two could protest and headed back down the street and around the corner with Ramble padding along beside me. One of the perks of having an invisible hellhound sidekick was that he could go anywhere at any time without being seen.

Well, with the apparent exception of gnomes, I amended.

"How do you feel about sneaking around the house and checking through the windows just to make sure he's gone?" I murmured to Ramble as we walked.

He gave a nonchalant grunt that sounded like a yes.

We neared the house. "I think that was his car parked out front earlier, but it looks like it's gone. I'm gonna hang out here while you check the place out."

I guess Ramble agreed because he sauntered off toward the house. I looked at my phone and pretended to be texting someone while I watched Ramble.

The hellhound walked right up onto the front porch, then silently padded over to each window before retreating back down the steps and over to the side of the house. These windows were further off the ground and he had to go up on his back legs with his front paws braced against the house to look inside.

It didn't take him long to return to my side and give a negative huff.

All right. That meant the coast was clear. I tucked my phone into the back pocket of my jeans and headed for the garden gate on the right side of the house. I had the weird feeling that I was being watched. I looked around but didn't see anyone.

It took a few seconds to figure out how to open the gate. Once Ramble and I were inside, I shut it behind us. No reason to arouse suspicion with the neighbors, right?

When I turned around, I sucked in a gasp.

The backyard was like a mini oasis.

A deck had been installed across half of the backyard and took up its entire width. Where the deck ended, white gravel began. A raised walkway made of the same wood as the deck and wide enough for two people carved a meandering path through the white gravel from the deck to the back section of the yard. There, a small garden pond had been dug out but had not yet been filled in with water yet. Or maybe he planned to fill it with water in the spring. For now, a mound of dirt he'd dug from the hole sat next to it, marring the pristine landscaping.

Here and there among the gravel were raised garden beds with a few frozen plants still visible. Those must have been the plants that Hyssop had sabotaged. With it being winter, it seemed like the plants would have died and frozen even without the gnome's meddling.

Though I thought this place was amazing, I could see why Hyssop would be upset.

I do not think the gnome will gain much by returning to this garden, Artemis said.

There wasn't really anywhere for him to grow a full garden here anymore. Not straight out of the ground anyways.

"Any chance you think he could survive just growing things in those planter boxes?" I asked her.

Ramble snorted in the negative at the same time as Artemis said.

He could try, but I do not think it would be a long life. Nor a happy life. Gnomes thrive on and gain their magic from the relation-

ship between the ground and the growth of seeds. Those sad little boxes will not be enough to keep the gnome alive. And the dirt in those boxes is not from this ground. I do not sense any magic in it.

"Wait, can you sense magic in the ground?"

Yes. But it is faint. The man has smothered it in painted rock and tainted wood. It is but a flicker of what it once might have been with the gnome's cultivation.

As I spoke with Artemis, Ramble wandered over to one of the planter boxes and sniffed it. I hoped he didn't get it in his head to pee on it. I wasn't his mom though, so I wasn't about to chastise him. Plus, I liked to keep my eyebrows unsinged.

I started to tell him we should leave when I got that feeling right between my shoulder blades of being watched again. I looked around and then up at the houses on either side of the garden. In one of the windows on the third floor of the house next door, an older woman peered down at me. Seeing someone watching me made me jerk a little and my movement caught Ramble's attention.

"There's a woman watching us up there." I said with a glance at the hellhound before looking back up at the woman.

Was this the Karen next door that the lawyer had complained had been watching him?

Seemed like it.

I caught my breath when I realized that the woman was no longer looking at me but was looking at Ramble. Wait, maybe it was just because I'd looked over at him then back up at her? So she'd just looked in the direction I had?

"Ramble," I murmured trying not to move my lips, "I think that woman can see you. Will you walk toward the dry pond back there and see if she follows your movement?"

I do not think the woman can see your hellhound, Vânători. You are, as they say, jumping to conclusions.

Except that as Ramble followed my request, the woman's eyes *did* track him across the yard.

Shit. What did that mean?

You were saying? I dryly asked Artemis. *Wait, you can feel magic in the ground, can you tell if that lady is magic? Or if she's something other than human?*

Perhaps... Artemis was silent for a few seconds and suddenly I started to feel a little drained. Like I'd just finished a long walk and was ready for a cold drink. Or a hot one. Like vampire blood.

Dammit. What are you doing? Are you pulling energy from me or something?

You asked me to assess the woman. That is what I am doing. Stop complaining, Vânători. Almost under her breath she added, *Your predecessors were never this whiny.*

I rolled my eyes. "Ramble, let's get out of here. This lady is giving me the creeps." I'd give Artemis the few seconds it would take for Ramble to get back to us before I stopped whatever the goddess was doing.

The fact did not escape me that I lived a very weird life now.

This is...strange. I cannot seem to feel anything from the woman.

"Is she too far away to get a reading on or something?"

No. It's more that she's a blank slate. Which is not normal, Vânători. Every being has an aura but, oddly, I cannot see hers.

Hmm. I didn't like the sound of that. First the creepy lady next door could see Ramble, and now Artemis was saying that she was not exactly the normal, run-of-the mill, nosy neighbor.

"Okay. Let's go." We backtracked through the gate, down the street, and back to the car where Donavon and Hyssop waited for us.

As soon as I opened the door to let Ramble in, I knew something was up. The tension was so thick in the air I could have karate chopped it. If I knew how to do that, I guess.

"It seems you two have been getting along."

They both spoke at the same time.

"We need to have a meeting of the heads of the nonhumans, Vianne," Donavon demanded.

"I will not be ordered around by some fur-faced, muscle-brained, idiot who couldn't grow a thistle in a field full of daisies!"

Um, was that a thing? I shook my head.

"Whoa, guys! Chill out. Jeeze. I leave you alone for five minutes, and you guys can't keep it together?" I held up a hand when they both began to speak simultaneously again. "Nope!" I said over both of them. "I have other things I need to get done today, and I'm not sitting here listening to you two argue. Hyssop? That's a pretty elaborate set up that the lawyer-guy has in that backyard. I'm not gonna be able to convince him to change it back. By law, it's his property."

"By *human law* you mean. By gnome law, that piece of property is mine until the day I die...which will be sooner rather than later if I don't get my garden back, Vânätori."

"Granted," I said, trying to take the edge out of my voice, "you could keep trying to sneak in, but you'd have to content yourself with cultivating whatever he puts in those planter boxes. However, it's my understanding that those wouldn't actually give you the magic you need to live. That the magic or whatever comes from the ground itself, right?"

The gnome squinted his eyes at me in mistrust. "That is correct, Vânätori."

"I cannot give you your garden back, but...what if I could get you the dirt from the garden and then relocate your garden to somewhere else by moving the dirt?"

This earned me a shocked look of disgust. "That's *blasphemous*, Vânätori. We can't do that! And besides, it's the ground that's got the magic, not the dirt, *girl*."

I squinted back at him, ignoring that he'd just referred to

me as "girl," like it was derogatory. "Do you know, 100%, that it won't work?"

He ignored my question. "Why can't you just send muscles here," he hooked his thumb at Donavon, "to get rid of the human?"

"We can't do that, Hyssop. I might be here to keep the peace among the supernatural community, but in my mind, that includes not tipping off the local authorities as to the existence of that community. We can't go around murdering every human who gets in your way or doesn't know the laws of your kind."

His eyebrows shot to his forehead at the same time that Donavon's did. Uh oh. What had I said this time?

"My *kind,* eh, Vânători? Perhaps you haven't noticed, miss, but you're not exactly human yourself."

"That's not what I meant. Look, I want to help you. I do. But I can't help you by killing the lawyer. That's not what I'm here for. What I *can* help you do is take your ground back by stealing a shitload of dirt from him and moving it elsewhere. So, what do you say? Are you in, or do you want to keep skulking around your old garden, being reminded of all your old flowers, and staying at your friends' gardens until you just lose your magic altogether?"

I felt like a bully, but I couldn't see any other option to help Hyssop reclaim his garden. I had zero confidence that I could convince the lawyer to change the yard back into its former state. This seemed like the best bet for keeping Hyssop alive.

"Fine." He crossed his arms over his chest. "But I don't like it."

I nodded then changed the subject. "By the way, what's up with the nosy-neighbor next door? She doesn't have an aura, and she could see Ramble when we were out back."

"Oh," He shrugged. "I'm not entirely sure what she is.

Definitely not human though. Me and the lads have bets that she's either a banshee or a lamprey."

I shuddered. I'd met a lamprey once. It had almost sucked the life force out of me. If that lady was a lamprey, then I had a feeling I'd be dealing with her sooner rather than later. I hadn't worked out my exact role here, but it definitely didn't involve looking the other way while those in the supernatural community picked off the human population.

Not a lamprey, Vânători. Lamprey's have an aura. And I do not believe that she is a banshee, either. I am not sure what that woman was. It may be worth looking into....

I'd rather not go looking for trouble, thank you very much, I told the necklace. *I have enough of it at my door as it is.*

"A lamprey! In my town? Not on my watch." Donavon was already opening the door when I grabbed his arm to keep him in the car. Though I didn't have the uber-strength that I'd had after first drinking Louis's blood, I did still have some super-natural strength.

He stopped and gave me a look that suggested I should let him go or get dragged along.

"She's not a lamprey. She doesn't have an aura, and lamprey's do. And I don't think she's a banshee, either." He didn't look convinced. "Look, as far as we know, she's just a lady next door who hasn't done anything wrong."

This finally convinced him not to go after a potentially innocent woman. He shifted his weight back to the middle of the seat and pulled the door closed again.

Now for a plan...which I was making up as I went along. "Hyssop, you'll need to find a suitable place for us to put your new garden. Do you know somewhere that might work?"

"I'm not sure, Vânători. One doesn't usually contemplate uprooting his whole garden—his whole life—among *my kind*."

I guess I deserved that. "Look, I'm sorry I implied that

we're different. I didn't mean it that way, but I know it sounded bad. I apologize."

Apparently, Hyssop knew that I meant it because he looked away for a moment then back to me as if having made some decision. "I need to ask around about a new place. Make sure some of the ones I'm thinking of haven't been claimed."

"Okay. Come find me when you figure out where you want your new home to be. By the way, I'm not going back to the motel tonight." I rattled off the address of the cabin, then showed him on my phone how to get there.

We ended up dropping him off at the center of town. When he was gone, I looked at Donavon. "Where do you want me to drop you off?"

"Here's fine, but listen, about the car—"

I waved him off. "It's fine. I appreciate that you're letting me borrow it. I don't know how long I'll stay, but if I decide to stay longer than a month, then I'll start making payments like you asked."

Honestly, I was still a little pissed about how he and Rosalyn had made decisions on what they wanted my future to look like in their town, but my need for him to get out of the car and leave Ramble and me to ourselves was much greater than my anger right then.

And if we continued to chat, I didn't think it would be long before he brought up Louis and me needing more of his blood. Donavon was not a fan of me drinking his brother's blood. I couldn't say that I was a fan of the idea itself...but I was definitely a fan of how it made me feel afterwards.

I really didn't want to have that conversation with him right now.

"Um, okay," he responded, though his expression suggested he didn't trust my sudden change in opinion about the car.

"Great. I'll see you around then."

He finally got out of the car and watched me drive away. I breathed a sigh of relief when he disappeared from the rearview mirror.

"Just you and me again, Ramble. Ready to go shopping?"

The hellhound whuffed, then stuck his head out the window to catch the chill November air in his face as we drove out of town.

Chapter Six

I *have never met a Vânători who cared so much about her material things,* Artemis complained for the fifth or maybe hundredth time.

"It's not so much that I care about things," I murmured as I pushed the cart through Mardens, "it's that I care about not spending a lot of money. That means you can't just grab the first thing off the shelf. You have to pay attention to how much things cost, and that means sometimes going to several stores to find the cheapest price."

This was the third store we'd visited. I wasn't familiar with this retailer, but I figured I'd give Alexis's recommendation a whirl since everywhere I'd been had been a little too pricey for my wallet. So far, she hadn't been wrong. Though the store didn't carry everything on my list, the stuff they did have was way cheaper than anywhere else we'd been so far.

I'd even found a giant water bowl for Ramble for less than a buck. He'd rolled his eyes at me when I told him what it was for, but I think (hoped?) he was secretly pleased that I was thinking of him. I almost splurged on the giant dog bed, but I think that might have crossed the line of being too dog-like. I fully expected him to sleep on the same bed as me since that's what he'd been doing since I'd rescued him from the vampire's basement. He took up a lot of space, but his presence made me feel a heck of a lot safer at night.

That and when I sometimes had nightmares about the vampires, he'd wake me up. Not to mention that when I'd had dreams in which Morvalden showed up and had been able to actually harm me, Ramble had come to my rescue. Who knows if he would have heard me call for him if he hadn't been in the same bed as me that night?

I pulled my brain away from such negative thoughts and grabbed a big box of heavy-duty garbage bags from the shelf. Hopefully they were durable enough to carry dirt without bursting.

Do you think that moving the dirt from Hyssop's garden to another location will really work? I asked Artemis.

I felt her give a mental shrug. *I do not know another option unless you think you can convince the human to allow him back into the garden to change it back to the way it was.*

It didn't seem like there was a chance in hell that the lawyer would allow that to happen. I also couldn't imagine convincing him that Hyssop actually existed, let alone that the gnome had rights to the lawyer's backyard. Bypassing that conversation altogether and trying a different strategy seemed like the best option.

I wheeled over to the check-out registers while Ramble waited for me by the door.

"Getting ready for college, huh?" The woman at the register asked.

"Actually, I just got a new place." I tried and failed to drum up some fake enthusiasm. It had already been a long day, and I still had to actually set up the cabin.

"How exciting!" Her enthusiasm was more than enough for both of us. "I remember when I moved into my first place! It was so exciting to pick everything out! It's smart of you to just get the basics first. I went a little crazy with my first place and got everything before even moving in, then ended up having to take back half of the furniture because it didn't fit the apartment!"

"Yeah, I'll definitely make sure to measure before I buy any furniture," I softened my lack of excitement with a smile but was thinking that new furniture was not in my future. I'd already written off using the living room since it didn't have anything in it, and I couldn't afford to buy any. I was just happy to have a real kitchen. It meant I could save a lot of money by not eating out all the time.

After Mardens, we hit up a big grocery store where I basically spent most of the rest of my money. I saved a little for gas, but that was it.

I'd have to make a decision soon: Do I use the fake credit card one more time here? Or do I find another way to make money while in Ricketts?

Using the credit card in a town so close to Ricketts seemed like a bad plan. Especially now that I would be driving the same car for a while. If the card was flagged already, then it would be too easy for someone to witness me getting money out and then report the memorable car to cops who started asking around.

Damn it. I sighed. I guess that meant having to find another way to make money. Maybe there was a pawn shop in Ricketts where they could pay me under the table. I couldn't officially apply anywhere since Violet Mason didn't have a social security number, and I didn't dare use my real name for fear of drawing any vampire attention.

On the drive home, I decided to make one last stop before heading out to the cabin. A little while later, I walked into the secondhand clothing store alone. Ramble had decided to wait in the car. Actually, I'm pretty sure if I had tried to get him to go into one more store, he might lose it and just start burning everything in sight with his fire breath.

Apparently, the hellhound had limits when it came to shopping.

Rosalyn looked up at the sound of the bell on the front door and smiled when she saw it was me. I hoped that was a real smile and not a fake, customer service one. I was pretty familiar with those.

"Hi, Vianne. What can I do for you today?"

"Hey Rosalyn, I was about to head out to the cabin, but thought I'd better stop in and see if you have any gloves and a winter hat?" I glanced around the store for them. "Donavon is loaning me a car, but it doesn't have a heater."

"Ah, winter accessories are over on that table." She pointed to a low display table that held several bins and added, "I'd heard Donavon was going to do that." I couldn't ignore the mischievous gleam in her eyes.

I'm sure you did, I thought with twinge of annoyance.

I've told you a thousand times, Vânători, witches are sneaky. Artemis's tone held more heat than necessary. Apparently, she was still pissed that I'd asked for Rosalyn's help with laying Cassandra to rest.

Um, you've never said that to me, I mentally responded. *You know that I'm not the same Vânători that you've talked to in the past, right?*

Clearly.

I considered calling Rosalyn out for being in cohorts with Donavon and trying to get me to stay, but what would I say? How dare you try to make me feel more welcome here? That sounded pretty lame. Instead, I quickly shifted my focus and decided to stick to what I'd come here to ask about. "Did you also hear that I'm helping a gnome find a new garden?"

The witch's eyebrows climbed her forehead. "Oh? A gnome? I've never seen any of them, but I knew they were around. They rarely let others see them. It must be an honor to have one request your help."

I wasn't sure I'd call it an honor. More like a pain in my ass. I picked up a pair of purple gloves and tried them on to hide any expression I might make at thinking of Hyssop.

"Actually, I was wondering how familiar you are with gnomes. There's a possibility he may have to move the location of his garden. I guess gnomes usually stay in one spot their whole lives. He says his magic is tied to the ground. I was thinking that if I move the dirt from his garden, that maybe it would allow him to relocate. What do you think?"

The witch shook her head. "That's not really my territory, Vianne. Gnomes are a fairly secretive people. It's news to me that their magic comes from the ground."

Shit. Maybe I shouldn't have told Rosalyn about Hyssop's magic. It was tricky not to give other creature's secrets away when I didn't know who knew what. I already had to keep the local trolls' existence a secret from the werewolves. Now I'd need to keep my mouth shut about the gnomes' magic, too, I guess.

"Oh. Okay." I found a pair of boring green gloves that fit perfect and were within my sad budget. The winter beanie was a little easier since there were only two available: black and orange. I picked the black one in case I needed to retrieve the dirt from Hyssop's garden at night. I'd rather not stick out in the dark because I was wearing hunter orange.

Rosalyn stilled as I neared the register to pay. "Was there something else you needed?"

I started to say no, then reconsidered. Rosalyn's gift as a witch, besides blasting evil witches to smithereens, was that she was able to tell when people needed something. She had been instrumental to helping me accept that I needed vampire blood to make the Artemis necklace work. So, while I was still miffed at her about speaking with Donavon behind my back, I couldn't overlook the fact that she'd helped me in the past. Maybe she could give me some insight now.

"Actually...I was thinking about looking for a job? Just a temporary one." I quickly added when I saw a small smile tug at the corners of her mouth. "I just need some spending money, really."

She hid her smile behind a mask of serious thought. "A job that, I'm assuming, won't require your real name?"

Relief washed over me that she understood without me having to explain the delicate nature of me applying for a position. "Something like that."

"Hmm. We aren't a large town with a lot of extra opportunities available, but there are always the odd jobs here and there to pick up under the table. Though, mind you, those are usually labor intensive and typically given to men. Anything particular you had in mind?

"I have some experience working in retail at a pawn shop and some fast-food places."

"I would bring you on here, but I honestly don't have the financial ability to hire right now. The shop doesn't exactly rake in the dough, as they say." She smiled at me to soften the blow, but I was a little disappointed. It would have been easier to work for Rosalyn since she knew my real story and wouldn't be running any background checks on me.

"That's okay, but if you hear of anything that might be a good fit, would you let me know?"

"Of course. Oh," she paused, hand on her chin in thought, "you know, Cheri's job at the diner is open if that's something that might interest you. I could talk to Dave, the owner, and see if he'd bring you on without too many questions."

"Uhh..."

I know, I know. Beggars can't be choosers, but it seemed a little weird to take the job of someone I'd had a hand in killing. I mean, I hadn't killed Cheri on purpose when I'd yanked some magic off me and flung it at the waitress, but since it had ended up squeezing the life from her, I definitely felt responsible. Not that she was innocent or anything. She'd taken pride in working with the deputy to murder Cassandra, but I'd never set out to end her or anybody else's life.

Okay, except maybe for the asshat deputy who had stabbed me in the stomach. He'd definitely had it coming.

Luckily, Rosalyn easily read my facial expression. "You're right. It might be a little weird to work there. Maybe leave it as a last resort."

"Thanks, though," I squeaked out. I paid for the gloves and hat then made my goodbyes and returned to the car.

It is getting dark out, Vânători. It would be wise to visit the vampire now.

Somehow, Ramble and I had managed to spend the whole afternoon shopping. It would definitely be full dark by the time we got back to the cabin. Yippee for returning to a dark, recently haunted cabin in the middle of the scary Maine woods.

"Not tonight, Artemis. I still have to put all the groceries away, not to mention setting up the house so we can sleep in it tonight."

Okay, there really wasn't that much to do tonight other than get the sheets out and make the bed. I would have preferred to wash them first before sleeping on them, but that would just have to wait until tomorrow. And, I thought to myself with a weird sense of glee, I could wash and dry all my clothes right there at the cabin without having to haul everything to the laundromat!

If you've ever had to use a laundromat for an extended period of time, you understand the luxury of doing your laundry at home.

It's the little things, people.

You are going to let me fade away again, aren't you, Vânători?

I rolled my eyes at Ramble where he sat next to me in the passenger seat. He'd finally pulled his head inside and let me roll the window up since it was getting pretty cold with the sun gone from the sky.

"Artemis, I'm not gonna let you fade away. I'm just tired. It was a long day and I just want to get the cabin set up and get some sleep." Ramble huffed in solidarity with me about how annoying the necklace was getting with her harping about talking to Louis. "Look, how about this. We'll go and talk to Louis tomorrow night, I promise."

Fine.

"Great. Now let's focus on—"

I stopped talking as police cruiser lights lit up behind me.

"Shit."

What did you do, Vânători?

"What? I didn't do anything!" I glanced down at the speedometer. I was going *under* the speed limit by like one mile an hour. What could he possibly be pulling me over for? "Maybe he's just trying to get around me?"

I slowly pulled the car onto the small shoulder which still left us with half the car on the road.

The cruiser pulled in behind us and stopped.

"Shit," I said again.

Now what? Not only did I not need to have my driver's license run since it was fake, I also didn't have a registration or insurance for this car. And, I remembered, I had a gun sitting in my backpack in the trunk.

This was...not good.

Should I drive off and try to make a run for it? It wasn't so much the potential to go to jail for having skipped out on my parole, but more that the vampires were likely to find me if the police hauled me in. I'd be trapped in a jail. The vampires could just stroll in, hypnotize the police on duty, then drag me out to Morvalden.

Did I mention this was not a good situation?

We can get rid of the human lawman, Vânători.

"We are not getting rid of the lawman," I said aloud, making Ramble raise an eyebrow at me. "Even if we did, we'd have to hide his car."

Ramble let a little smoke ring float from his mouth.

"You think you could incinerate the cop *and* his car?" I asked.

The hellhound shrugged.

It says a lot about my state of mind right then that I considered his offer. But hey, it was only for a second. By then, the officer was almost to the driver's side door.

"No," I said quietly but firmly. "No incinerating anyone, got it?"

Ramble huffed and hunkered down on the seat, clearly disappointed that his services weren't needed.

I rolled down my window, letting the chilly night air in— not that it was much warmer inside the car without the heater working—and found myself looking at Sheriff Allen.

"What seems to be the problem, Sheriff?" I said, cringing at the line I'd heard a million times on TV.

"Miss Mason. I didn't recognize the car. You had a different one before, right?"

"I did, but it was acting up," I quickly lied, "and Donavon was kind enough to lend me this one." I was suddenly thankful that I'd had the chance to explain that I was borrowing this car since it would explain why the registration wouldn't be in my name. Let's just hope he didn't ask for proof of insurance or try to run a search on my driver's license.

"Hmm. You know this was his friend Samuel Vance's car, right?"

"He mentioned that, yes." I wasn't sure how I should react to that, so I just kept my voice neutral.

"You two seem to be getting awfully close if he's letting you borrow Samuel's car, eh?"

I couldn't keep my eyebrow from quirking up on its own. How was that any of the sheriff's business? I almost said as much but decided that getting snippy was not the best way to get out of this situation.

Instead, I forced my facial expressions to behave and said, "We're just friends, Sheriff." Then, to move things along, I asked, "Was there a reason that you stopped me?"

He straightened up and looked at the back of the car. "One of your taillights is out."

"Oh." Seriously? He'd pulled me over for that? A gut feeling told me that he'd known exactly who was driving this car and had welcomed the opportunity to pull me over.

The sheriff's deputy, Ken Smith, was the murdering asshole who, upon learning that there were more than just humans running around town, had decided to slowly take out anything not human. I had hoped that the sheriff wouldn't be as closed-minded as his deputy had been. After all, he'd been willing to accept Donavon's help with the murder investigation even though he knew that Donavon was something more than human.

Was I about to find out if the sheriff was anti-nonhuman? I hoped not. If so, I might have to take Ramble up on his offer.

"Yeah," the sheriff went on, "you'll definitely want to get that fixed if you're gonna be running these roads at night. I, uh, hear that you'll be staying out this way for a time?"

Boy, word sure did travel fast around here.

"Just for a short time," I reassured him. "I have some business to attend to, then I plan to be on my way."

"Huh. That's a pity. I'd thought you might want to stay on a bit longer. It could be useful having someone like you around to help the department with, uh, interspecies relations. As a consultant, of course."

What now? Ignoring the interspecies relations bit, I had a bad feeling where this was going.

"Um," I said, mentally flailing around for a valid excuse for why I couldn't take that kind of gig. Something like that would need a background check, right? "I'm not sure that would be such a great idea." At the sheriff's questioning look, I quickly added, "I'm not really cut out for law enforcement work and it might not go over well with the, uh, supernatural community, if they thought I was siding more with humans than them."

He gave me a searching look that made me wonder if I'd said too much before he finally grunted in ascent. "I understand," he said, and I tried not to let my breath out in a whoosh of relief.

He smacked the hood of the car twice with his open hand, "Alright, get that taillight fixed so I don't have to stop you again."

"Will do," I said with a forced grin.

I started rolling up my window as he walked away but paused when I heard the alarming sound of snapping branches in the woods beside the car. Ramble jerked to a stand, ears pricked at the sound. A small warning growl escaped his throat.

Brace yourself. Something is coming!

Chapter Seven

Whatever was in the woods was fast and, judging by the sounds, it was heading straight for us.

A blurry shape darted out from the woods and went straight for the sheriff. It was so fast that I only caught a glimpse of antlers before it tackled the sheriff and sent them both flying down the embankment on the other side of the road.

"Holy shit!" I said out loud. I scrambled to open the door and Ramble pushed past me to get to the sheriff first.

Weapons, Vânătorĭ! I felt Artemis trying to reign in her excitement at the idea of a fight.

"No time!" I shouted back. It would only slow me down to stop and open the trunk and fumble in my backpack for the gun or my knife. I had no idea how I'd help the sheriff without weapons, but maybe just acting as a distraction to his attacker would be enough.

The bottom of the embankment was surrounded by pine trees and so shrouded in darkness that, from the top of the hill, I couldn't even see where the sheriff and his attacker had rolled to. Ramble scrambled down the hill ahead of me and let out a vicious growl from deep in his belly that made the hair on the back of my neck stand up.

"Sheriff Allen!" I shouted, starting down the embankment and trying not to fall on my face while stumbling over rocks and sticks. There was a muffled response to my shout, but I couldn't actually make out any words. Then the sheriff's voice cut off in a yelp of pain.

Maybe I should have grabbed a weapon after all, I thought.

Too late now, Artemis helpfully responded.

"Sheriff!" I called again. I was just above the bottom of the embankment, and my eyes were starting to adjust to the dark. I could make out the dark shape of the sheriff against the ground where he lay under a canopy of pine trees. He was pinned down by his attacker and was barely holding it off.

From here, his attacker looked humanoid. I briefly wondered why I'd thought the attacker had antlers, then Ramble and I hit level ground and were sprinting to help the sheriff.

Suddenly, Ramble came to a halt in front me so quickly that my legs smacked his shoulders. I flipped right over him and landed hard on the rocky ground. Pain shot through my shoulder when it connected with a partially uncovered rock and I let out a yelp.

Get up, Vânători!

I forced myself to sit up and found Ramble standing between me and whatever had attacked the sheriff. It had abandoned the sheriff—who still looked like he was moving— and decided I was better prey.

I couldn't exactly blame it. After all, I'd just tripped over my own sidekick like one of the Three Stooges.

Why had Ramble suddenly stopped in front of me like that? Ramble's hackles were all the way up. He growled and spit at the thing that strode toward us on two legs like a human. It was still weirdly blurry, but I could definitely see that it had something like antlers on its head.

It completely ignored Ramble's threats and was closing the ground between us. I quickly weighed my options and, realizing it was too late to run, I shakily stood behind my hellhound who immediately pressed his back against my legs.

Ramble shot me a quick glance that felt like a push for me to run.

Wait. Was Ramble *scared* of this thing? Fear suddenly dropped into my belly. What would a hellhound be afraid of?

Vânători, I know you do not trust me, but you must let me take over your body. Right now. Or this being is going to end us before we've even gotten started.

What? No way!

You will die if you do not let me take control, *Vânători!*

Not only did I not trust Artemis, but as a recovering alcoholic, control was a big deal. There was no way I was just going to hand over my freewill to a being I barely knew.

Then again, what good was control if I Ramble and I were dead?

The antler-guy was almost to us now. I was on the edge of turning all control over to Artemis when gunshots split the night and made me jump.

The sheriff had managed to get up on one knee and was carefully firing at our attacker.

Antler-guy jerked to a stop and whipped around. Ramble took the opportunity to spew a gout of fire at him. The thing let out a weird bugle as the smell of singed hair filled the woods. It turned toward me one more time, but another gunshot by the sheriff changed its mind. It took off and disappeared into the woods.

I stood rooted to the spot for a second before I remembered the sound of pain the sheriff had made earlier. I briefly touched Ramble on the shoulder in thanks, then stepped past the hellhound to help the sheriff up.

He was able to stand without too much assistance, but he kept his right shoulder cradled close to his body.

"Did it bite you in the arm?" I asked, wondering how injured he was and also whether a bite from such a creature would turn the sheriff into something other than human.

"I pulled something rolling down that damn hill." He jerked his head at the steep embankment that we were about to have to climb back up.

"Were you able to get a good look at it?" I asked. "I couldn't see much of it in the dark."

"Me neither. It was on me so fast I didn't know what hit me. And then when it had me pinned, it just held me down and I started to feel weak. Like I couldn't move or speak anymore." We started toward the hill, but he paused and turned toward me.

"Did you...did you just throw fire at that thing?" His voice held a little bit of awe mixed with disbelief.

"Not exactly." I glanced down at Ramble beside me and started walking forward again. The less the sheriff knew about me and my four-legged companion, the better. Then again, I didn't want to take credit for scaring the thing off, and it might actually be good if the sheriff knew that Ramble existed even if he didn't know what he was.

"Let's just say that I rarely travel alone. My friend was the one who made the flames."

The sheriff grunted but started up the hill beside me. I only had to help steady him once or twice during the climb. When we were back on the road, he stopped and turned to me. "I have to file a report about why I fired my weapon. I don't suppose you'd want to come down to the department and make a statement to corroborate that we were attacked by a bear after I stopped you, and I fired warning shots to scare it off?"

I was impressed with his quick story. "Weren't her two little cubs just the cutest?" I asked then smiled. "Actually, it would be better if my name wasn't involved."

He stared at me for a second, assessing me. Maybe weighing my character and what he thought he knew about me.

Well, I got news for you buddy, I thought. *I don't even know the measure of me anymore.*

He finally gave a sharp nod. "Get that taillight fixed, Miss Mason!" With that, he walked over and got in his car, then waited for me to do the same thing before he drove off.

When we were back on the road, I threw a look at Ramble and asked him and the Artemis, "Anybody care to tell me just who or what exactly antler-guy was? You clearly knew something, Ramble, or you wouldn't have stopped like that."

I do not know what the hellhound knows about the attacker, Vânători, but I can tell you that it is a Power.

"What do you mean it's a power? What the hell does that mean?"

As Artemis spoke, I relayed her words to Ramble. Information was its own type of weapon, and I wanted to make sure we were all on the same page and amply armed.

Beings like witches, nymphs, and the other creatures like them have power or magic as you call it. But there are also beings who, simply put, are made *of power and are the very spirit and embodiment of a piece of nature. They do not merely wield magic—they* are *magic, through and through. We call them Powers, and we avoid them at all costs.*

She paused in consideration before adding, *We must leave, Vânători. We should take the vampire with us and go through the Between. We cannot fight a Power and win. Our only option is to flee. Especially now that it has seen you.*

Escaping into the Between was a tricky thing. First there was the issue of even finding a door that would take us Between, and then there was the fun part that when you stepped into that weird dimension, you tended to lose a lot of time. I wasn't ready to run away just yet without more information.

"We're not just going to leave. I promised Hyssop we'd help him figure out his garden issue. Plus, I'm pretty sure Louis might protest being forcibly kidnapped."

This is much bigger than a gnome, Vânători!

I jerked at the urgency in her voice.

No Vânători has ever gone up against a Power and won. Gawyn, the first Vânători, almost lost her life against the Etna Power, and she was the most powerful Vânători to ever live. I only managed to keep her breathing because I convinced her to flee. Vânători have avoided tangling with Powers ever since.

I finally pulled into the cabin's driveway but didn't kill the car's engine just yet.

"Wait, Etna, as in *Mount* Etna? The volcano in Sicily?"

The very same. You should avoid visiting anywhere near there. Powers have a long memory. She paused in thought. *I do not know what spirit of nature this Power embodies, but we should not wait around to find out.*

Good to know. Hopefully no trips Between would ever spit us out near the angry volcano.

I sat in the running car for a few more seconds, thinking through the events of the attack. If the thing that had attacked us was one of these Power beings, then it might be smart to heed the necklace's warning. Then again, I couldn't just kidnap Louis, nor did I think I'd be able to convince him to come with us. He had a life here as the owner of the only motel in town. I didn't think he'd agree to run away from the big Power spirit thing in order to be my personal milkshake that I could grab a drink from anytime I wanted.

"Let's not be hasty," I said, earning a look from Ramble and a note of surprise from the necklace. "This is the first time we've run into that thing, and if it was so powerful, why would it run from mere bullets? Besides, if it's against us, why show up now and not when we were out in the middle of the night investigating all those murders? And why hasn't it attacked any of the other people in the supernatural community?"

I let those questions hang in the air as I got out of the car, went around to the trunk, and put on my backpack before gathering the bags from our shopping spree earlier in the day. Artemis spluttered at me the whole time about how I was the dumbest *Vânători* she'd ever worked with and how I was going to get killed and she'd wind up back in the hands of Morvalden.

Blah, blah, blah.

Hands full and necklace nagging me, I finally cut her off.

"Listen, you can either suck it up and help me figure out how to avoid that thing or be quiet. I appreciate your suggestion to run away, but in case you didn't notice, that Power or whatever didn't attack us until we tried to help the sheriff. So maybe it's not hell bent on coming after us like you seem to think."

Perhaps it didn't sense you until you approached it, but now it knows you're here Vânători, it will be drawn to you.

"Well, I guess we'll just have to wait and see what it does because we're not running away. Not yet."

That said, I started up the dark porch steps and paused.

"What is that, Ramble?"

Something had been dropped at the top of the stairs. I made a mental note to start leaving the porch light on. Or to get one of those motion sensor things. Listen to me. Like I was suddenly made out of money or something.

Carefully, Ramble slipped gracefully up the stairs to investigate, sniffing the air as he went. When he reached the top step, he let out a snort of amusement. My heart went back to beating like normal. Whatever it was, it wasn't dangerous.

As I hauled my cargo up the stairs to join Ramble, something that wasn't snow crunched under my feet on the last two stairs. "Broken glass?"

Ramble huffed and sauntered over to the front door, went up on his back paws, and flipped on the outdoor lights.

Someone had left a welcome basket on the front porch. Which was nice, except that they'd clearly dropped the thing on the porch and left. Or maybe they'd just tossed it there. The broken glass came from a shattered bottle of red wine that stained the top stairs. Whoever had left it for me clearly didn't know me terribly well, or they'd know that alcohol as a gift for me, a recovering alcoholic, was not terribly thoughtful.

"Huh." Who would know to leave me a welcome basket on my first night at the cabin? The list wasn't exactly extensive. My guess was it was either Rosalyn or Donavon.

I shrugged and walked around the basket, struggling to shift the plastic bags that were now cutting in my wrists so that I could fish the key out of my pocket and unlock the door.

With a sigh of relief, I finally got the door open and hauled the bags the last few feet into the kitchen to leave them on the floor. Ramble went over to the woodstove while I went back outside to retrieve the basket. I didn't want the wine, but I wasn't about to turn down the free snacks I'd seen in there.

Back inside with the door closed and locked behind me, I put the basket on the kitchen counter and removed the snacks that were covered in wine, washing off their packaging in one sink and leaving them to drain in the other sink compartment.

I found a handwritten card underneath the snacks, soaked in wine.

"'Welcome to your new home! I hope you enjoy your stay, Rosalyn.' Well, that explains that, I guess," I said before realizing I was pretty much talking to myself. Artemis had gone quiet on me since I'd told her to chill out, and Ramble was somewhere else in the house doing his own thing.

I started putting groceries into random cupboards. I didn't exactly have a system for where things would go yet and figuring it out helped me release some of the jitters from the attack earlier. It also gave me space to think while my hands were busy. After a bit, Ramble came and laid down just outside the kitchen doorway.

I turned to him. "What do you think, Ramble? Should we run off like the necklace wants us to?"

He looked at me for a moment and cocked his head to the side a little, indicating he was considering it. Then he snorted in the negative.

Okay. So he either didn't think we should run because we didn't know enough about the antler-guy, or he didn't want to admit he was scared of it.

Oh yes. Good plan. Take advice from a hound of hell who is so great at protection that he is missing his other two heads. Yes. I'm sure that will work out well for you.

I was glad that Ramble couldn't hear Artemis. I'd tried on several occasions to find out what had happened to Ramble's other heads and quickly learned that he didn't want to talk about it. I couldn't see the severed necks in the normal world, but when he'd popped into my dream to save me from Morvalden, I'd been able to see them. Just because I couldn't see them now didn't mean they weren't there.

Listen here, Artemis. You're just a being trapped in a magical necklace who doesn't always want to share information with me. Sure, you've saved my butt a couple of times, but Ramble has saved my ass more times than I can count. So, yeah, I'm gonna listen to his opinion on the matter.

This got me blessed silence once again.

When I finished putting away groceries, I realized I'd need to tackle something I hadn't been looking forward to: starting the fire.

And I'd forgotten to ask Rosalyn about where Cassandra had gotten her firewood. Shit. Not that I had any money left anyways. The little pile of wood was still outside on the porch, so I brought it all inside and set it in the rack that was a few feet away from the woodstove.

"Okay. This can't be that hard, right?" I asked Ramble where he watched me from a safe distance. He didn't offer any comment, so after a little searching, I found some old telephone books and ripped out a few pages to crumple up and throw in the woodstove. Next, I loaded a few pieces of wood on top of the crumpled papers, then started looking around for a lighter or matches. It took a few more minutes, but I finally located a box of long matches.

I struck one of the matches, then held my breath as I touched it to the newspaper. It caught quickly and soon the other papers were burning away.

"That wasn't so hard," I murmured mostly to myself, then shut the door to the woodstove.

The fire immediately died.

After several more tries and some trial and error once I discovered the little lever for opening and closing the flue to let air in, I was able to close the door and keep the papers lit, but I just couldn't get the logs to stay lit. I was close to looking up videos on how to start and maintain a fire in a woodstove when Ramble huffed impatiently behind me.

His expression plainly said that I was terrible at this and to let him try.

"Fine. By all means, go ahead." I gestured at the open woodstove door.

He nudged the door closed until it was only open a crack, then took a deep breath, and with his mouth right up to the crack in the door, he blew out a small spray of fire but maintained it for longer than I'd ever seen before. When he finally ran out of air, he stepped away to show me that the wood had caught and the fire was truly going now.

I heard my phone ring in the kitchen and moved to shut the woodstove door the rest of the way, but Ramble huffed at me. "Okay, fine. But it's your party. Don't let it burn the house down, please."

I heard him grumbling to himself as I hurried into the kitchen and snatched up my phone from the counter after a quick glance at the screen.

"Hi Rosalyn," I said. Should I mention the whole no-no on the wine or just be grateful? "I just got home. Thanks for the gift basket." Grateful it was. Besides, why risk offending her when she might be able to connect me to a job?

"Oh," She paused briefly, sounding distracted, which wasn't like her. "I'm glad you liked it, Vianne. Actually, I was calling to ask if you'd seen or heard from Alexis? She was supposed to drop the basket off at the cabin and come home after that."

"Drop" being the key word here. I kept the comment to myself.

"No. I just found the basket on the front porch."

"Oh, I see. Okay. Thank you, Vianne."

I knew I'd regret it, but Rosalyn sounded so worried about the young witch that I couldn't help but ask, "Everything okay? Maybe she just went into town or something?"

"Maybe. She was supposed to drop the basket off at the cabin and come back here for our afternoon lesson. She never showed up or called though. It's not like her."

I suddenly saw the state of the basket in a different light. "Not to make you more worried, but when I got home, I found the basket on its side like it had been dropped. It hit the porch hard enough to break the wine bottle."

"Was there anything else wrong? Is Alexis's car still there?"

"No, her car's not here."

"Oh," Rosalyn's voice was tight with worry. "I guess she must have left there and gone somewhere else..." She trailed off, clearly lost in thought.

"Do you want some help looking for her? I can come over—"

"No, no," The quick response told me something else was going on that she wasn't telling me. I immediately thought of the antler-guy that Artemis and Ramble were so afraid of. Should I mention my encounter with him to Rosalyn? It seemed unlikely that the two events—me running into antler-guy and Alexis disappearing—would be related.

I started to tell Rosalyn about the incident just in case, but she cut me off before I could.

"Thanks, Vianne. I'm sorry about the wine. I'll send you over another bottle tomorrow."

"Oh no. That's okay. I don't drink."

"Please give me a call if you hear from Alexis, would you?"

"Of course," I said, though honestly, it seemed unlikely that Alexis would contact me before Rosalyn. "Let me know if I can help."

We hung up, and I looked at Ramble who'd rejoined me in the kitchen. "That was weird." I told him about Alexis, and he asked to go back outside. I let him out and watched as he sniffed around the porch, the stairs, and the path leading up to the porch. Finally, he came back inside and gave me a huff that suggested he hadn't found anything

"Well, at least you checked." I made a mental note to

check in with Rosalyn tomorrow and then grabbed more shopping bags and my backpack before retreating to the bedroom to continue unpacking and make the bed with the new sheets and blankets. By the time I finished, Ramble had joined me. He climbed onto the bed as soon as I'd made it and claimed his two-thirds of the mattress.

I was just pulling my clothes from the backpack and putting them away in the empty dresser when it hit me: I had a real place to live again. I could unpack my backpack. I could make my own meals. I had a place to call home, even if it would only be for a short time.

I blinked back tears and tried to hide them from Ramble. Thankfully, the necklace didn't comment.

When everything was in its place, I brushed my teeth and checked the fire. Ramble had managed to shut the door to the woodstove which now radiated a steady heat. It might take a little bit for its warmth to reach the bedroom, but the house was already feeling a lot cozier. I looked around the living room to make sure there were no remnants of Ghost-Cassandra, then double-checked that the front door was locked.

After a bit of internal debate about whether I should keep the bedroom door open so the warmth from the fire could reach the bedroom or if I should shut it as an added layer of protection, I finally decided to shut it. I could always open it later if it got too cold.

I climbed into bed beside Ramble. He sighed and moved a little closer to me, letting me have some of his body heat.

This wasn't such a bad life, right?

I drifted off to sleep making plans for how to help Hyssop move his dirt and where else I might ask around for a job the next day.

Chapter Eight

I wore a red, silky dress that hugged every curve of my body and left no impression of undergarments. I lay on a deliciously soft, four poster bed with black velvet curtains drawn closed around it. For one panic-filled moment, I thought Morvalden had found his way into my dreams again and that he would come tearing through the curtains at any moment...

...and then the scent of vanilla filled my senses.

The smell was safe and spoke of soft sheets and smooth, salty skin. It made me lust for vampire blood...and more.

The curtains parted to reveal Louis in tight black leather pants and no shirt, showing off his marble-hard abs and a tasteful bit of happy trail that disappeared beneath the leather.

The moment he saw me laying languidly on the bed, his entire body came to attention. His dark eyes became difficult to look away from, and his fangs slipped over his bottom lip. I remembered the prick of pain those fangs had sent through me followed by the almost ecstatic pleasure of tasting Louis's coppery blood.

The memory sent a jolt of need radiating from my groin. Breathlessly I said, "Louis," and held out a beckoning hand.

Slowly—almost painfully so—Louis languidly crawled onto the

bed, his eyes never leaving mine. I felt paralyzed. He could do anything to me in this moment and I wouldn't mind. In fact, I'd welcome it.

Slowly, ever so slowly, Louis reached out and ran a hand from my naked thigh, over my silky dress, up my stomach, lightly over my breast, and to my neck where he stopped with a finger on my pulse point. His touch left waves of electricity in its wake.

I reached up and grasped his hand, pulling him on top of me, then moved my hand to caress the back of his neck, pulling him down for a long kiss.

Things seemed to move quickly from there as he lost the will to resist me. To resist the call of my blood.

His hands moved to hike up my dress, and I fumbled to unzip his leather pants. He moved his hand to my breast, squeezing. I pulled his hips toward me and—

—I was jerked out of the pleasantly sensual dream by a loud thud outside the cabin. It took me a moment to orient myself in the unfamiliar bed. Ramble stood at attention on the end of the bed, staring at the closed bedroom door. I was suddenly glad I'd decided to shut it.

We waited, holding our breath and keeping as still as possible, straining to hear if the sound would come again or for some other sound to indicate that someone—or something—was outside.

Arm yourself, Vânători.

I almost jumped out of my skin at Artemis's voice. I know I was the only one who could hear her, but my nerves had been so wound up that she startled me and made me jump, earning me a dirty look from Ramble.

Rather than ignore her, I decided to follow her directions this time. I didn't want to end up weaponless again if it was the blurry, antler-man outside. I slipped out from underneath the covers as quietly as I could and opened the nightstand drawer to retrieve the Glock. I was glad I'd put it there just in case. After a moment's thought, I pulled the slide back to chamber a round. It wouldn't do me any good if I got attacked before I could ready the gun to shoot.

I was as ready as I was going to get, though what I really wanted to do was crawl back into bed and hide under the covers until whatever was outside went away. Apparently, when you're the descendent of a semi-famous vampire hunter, that's not an option.

Slowly, Vânători, check out the window.

There were two windows in the bedroom. One looked out on the side of the cabin and the other afforded a view out front. Since I thought the noise had come from the front of the cabin, I left the light off and crept over to that window. Slowly, I peeked around the curtain.

With the porch light off, it was pitch black out. I waited in case my eyes would adjust to the dark, but even after a few seconds of staring out the window, I could only make out the darker shapes of the porch and the car parked in the driveway. I waited another few seconds, but nothing moved and everything stayed silent.

Stepping away from the window, I whispered to Ramble, "Do you see anything moving out there?"

He gave a barely audible negative huff.

"Me neither," I agreed. I took a deep breath to try and calm my jangling nerves. Something about creeping around a dark house in just my boxers and a t-shirt while holding a gun put my teeth on edge. "Should we check the porch? It sounded like the noise came from there, right?"

Remembering the thud, I thought it had sounded suspiciously like a body thudding to the floor. I had a lot more experience at identifying that sound now than I cared to admit.

Ramble thought for a second, then gave a jerky nod of his head before leading the way to the door. I opened it for us, and we crept down the short hall and into the foyer with Ramble still in the lead. We paused at the front door. Unfortunately, there wasn't a peephole to look through, so we'd have to take our chances on what or who we might find on the other side.

I slowly unlocked the front door, afraid something would burst through it at any second. When that was done, I put my left hand on the doorknob and glanced at Ramble. He nodded. In a flash, I turned the knob and yanked the door open.

Ramble cleared the door first which was why he stumbled into and over the body that lay on the porch in front of the door. I was thankfully able to come to a halt before following him ass over teakettle. The smell of blood and death assaulted my senses. Gun shaking slightly, I kept an eye on the body at my feet while scanning the rest of the porch and yard beyond that for any signs of movement or danger.

There were way too many shadows on this porch, I realized. Anything could be lurking in those small pockets of darkness. If I stayed here for long, I made a mental note to splurge on a motion sensor light. Not that it would probably do much against any magical creatures in the supernatural community.

When nothing immediately jumped out to grab me, I reached back and snapped on the porch light... and immediately regretted that decision. At my feet was a deer with huge antlers. A buck, I vaguely remembered. Blood splatters marked the porch and the front door. A pool of blood was growing larger underneath the body, and I had to step back to avoid stepping in any more of it.

I breathed a sigh of relief that it was an animal and not a human body on my porch. I mean, don't get me wrong, I felt bad for the buck, especially when I spotted the giant bite that had been taken from its neck. Was that how it had died?

Ramble was sniffing around the body while daintily stepping around the blood. Finally, satisfied with whatever evidence he'd collected, he trotted down the porch steps, nose to the ground, and out to a spot about ten feet from the porch. When he finished his inspection, he trotted back up to me and bared his teeth while pinning his ears back.

Uh oh. That couldn't be good.

"You know what dropped this on our porch?"

Look at the porch, Vânători. There are no tracks in the blood. The buck was not dropped on the porch. It was thrown at your door.

I looked again at the large, bloody mark on the door just below the doorhandle. Shit. She was right. I looked back at Ramble. "The spot you stopped at in the driveway, was that where they threw the deer from?"

Rambled whuffed an affirmative.

What do you think could have thrown a 200-pound buck across that distance, Vânători? I will give you a hint: You recently met it and it is more than three feet high.

"You think the antler-man—

The Power, Vânători, Artemis corrected.

"You think this Power guy threw a deer at our door in the middle of the night? Why? What purpose would that serve?" I removed the round from the Glock's chamber. It was obvious that the thing that had done this was already long gone or had no intention of attacking us.

Perhaps to warn you off? Artemis suggested.

"Maybe, but why not just show up and threaten us in person? Or attack us. It doesn't seem like a very clear message if it wants to scare us off." I paused and thought for a minute. "It honestly feels more like a cat leaving us a dead mouse, you know?"

I have never had a cat.

That's my magical necklace. Super helpful.

"Well, regardless of why someone left it, what the hell am I supposed to do with it?"

What do you mean? Leave the body, pack your bags, attain the vampire, and go Between.

"We've already had this conversation," I groaned. "I'm not leaving yet. We don't even know what the deer's body means."

If you're not going to leave town, then you'll need to move the body somewhere else, so it won't attract predators.

I sighed. She was right. I was going to have to move that big ass deer somewhere. There was a shed on the other side of the cabin. If it was unlocked, maybe that would do for now? I wasn't up to hauling the carcass to the car and burying it. Honestly, I was a little too creeped out to go running around in the woods at night just to bury a deer.

I stomped inside and back to the bedroom. If I was going to clean up a body, I really didn't want to do it in my pajamas. I left the gun on the nightstand and made a mental plan as I changed clothes, shucking off the boxers and pulling on my worst pair of jeans. (I only owned two pairs, so it was easy to tell the difference between the ripped, bloodstained pair and the somewhat newer pair from Rosalyn's shop.) I donned a black, long sleeved shirt. It was one of my only good shirts, but the color wouldn't show bloodstains as much as something lighter would.

While lacing up my boots, I decided to just freeze my butt off rather than sully my only jacket. At the last second, I remembered the beanie I'd gotten from Rosalyn's shop and pulled it on. I also grabbed the house keys from the kitchen in case there was a lock on the shed. When I was finally ready, I stepped back onto the porch where Ramble was waiting for me.

"Okay, here's the plan," I said. "Let's see if we can drag the thing to the shed out back. I'll check to make sure it's unlocked." I jogged over the shed and found it padlocked.

Luckily, one of the keys Rosalyn had left me fit the lock, so the plan was still a go.

Back on the porch, I grabbed the buck's antlers, Ramble grabbed one of its back feet in his mouth, and we dragged it across the porch. It wasn't the cleanest way to move a body. Nor, it turned out, the smartest. After only a few steps, the buck's head suddenly ripped clean off its neck. I stumbled backward and landed hard on my butt, staring at the deer's head now in my lap.

Super.

My stomach roiled at the sight of the headless deer. It was a close thing to keep my dinner down. Rather than make more of a mess with the head, I left it on the porch and ran inside for a garbage bag to put it in. Good thing I'd bought the contractor size! The bag minimized the extra gore from the head, but we still had to drag the rest of its damn body across the porch and down the steps, leaving a bloody trail in our wake.

I was doubly lucky that I still had some extra strength left over from Louis's blood, otherwise there's no way I would have been able to budge the buck's heavy carcass.

After a lot of huffing and puffing broken up by several breaks, we managed to get the deer into the shed. I put the bag with the head in there too, then locked the shed. That was as good as we were going to get for body storage tonight.

"Now for the task of cleaning up," I said to Ramble. He snorted and retreated to the porch, clearly letting me know that he felt he'd done his duty for the night. "Fine," I called after him, "but see if I make you breakfast in the morning!"

He looked pointedly at the shed.

My mouth fell open. "You'd eat raw deer for breakfast?"

Ramble shrugged then picked his way carefully around the blood-stained porch to disappear inside.

You used a lot strength to move the deer, Vânători. We will need to seek out the vampire sooner than your plan anticipated.

"I know," I said out loud. I could feel it too. I was definitely weaker now, and I could tell the necklace wasn't quite as loud in my mind. "It's kind of late to be calling him now, though."

Vânători...vampires are nocturnal.

Oh yeah. "Good point." I followed Ramble's example of avoiding the blood on the porch and was about to go inside when I slammed to a stop.

"Ramble..." The hellhound peaked his head out of the kitchen where he must have been getting water from his new bowl. I was too spooked by what I'd seen on the porch to find the water dripping from his lips funny right now. "Is it just me or is there more firewood on the porch now than when we went to bed?"

Ramble slipped back to the doorway to peek out and stopped. He looked at the pile of wood, then back to me in obvious surprise.

When we'd gone to bed, I'd left maybe three pieces of firewood on the porch. Now the pile was back to ten or twelve neatly stacked pieces. Someone had replenished it during the night.

"Do you think it was the same person who left the deer?"

After sniffing the woodpile, Ramble snorted in the negative. He didn't get the same smell from the pile that he'd gotten from the deer. That meant it was probably a different person.

Our night was just getting way too full of mysteries. I needed to ask for some help.

I retreated inside with Ramble and shut the door.

It was time to call Louis. Maybe I could use the excuse of the deer to ask for his help and then ease into the whole asking for more blood thing.

It was worth a shot, right?

I blew out a sigh and called the number for the motel, waiting with bated breath at every ring. Was I relieved when he didn't pick up and the call switched over to voicemail? Maybe a little.

"Hey Louis," I said to the machine, wondering what I could say that wouldn't sound like I was an addict calling my dealer for her next fix. The thought made me flash on that feeling of ecstasy I'd had from Louis's blood coursing through me.

The image did not help. I realized I'd paused for too long in my voicemail. "Um, hey, it's Vianne. I wasn't able to get in touch with you before I left the motel, but I've moved into Cassandra's place. Um, so, weird story. I just found a dead deer on the front porch, and I just wondered if you might have any ideas as to who might have left it? I'll touch base with Rosalyn tomorrow to see if she has any clue, but I figured I'd call you first since, you know, you'd be awake."

I decided not to mention the mysteriously appearing woodpile. I already sounded like enough of an idiot as it was.

"Anyways, I put the deer in the woodshed for now. I guess I'll figure out what to do with it tomorrow..." Okay now I was just rambling. Even Ramble looked up at me with a raised eyebrow.

"Okay. Uh, any information would be helpful. Talk to you later." I hung up, then tapped the phone against my forehead. What was wrong with me? I mean, sure, I really, *really* wanted a fix of vampire blood, but that ridiculously babbled message had sounded more like a teenager calling her crush.

Surely I didn't *like* Louis, right? Like, you know, like-like him?

Ugh. Now I was sounding like a teenager in my own head. Not good.

Instead of standing around lusting after vampire blood, I

decided to clean up the deer blood all over the front door and porch. Luckily, Alexis had left the caddy of household cleaners under the sink along with a partially used roll of paper towels. Armed with these, I tackled cleaning the door, which was the easier job, and then worked on the front porch.

Unfortunately, it turned out that wood soaks in blood. So, while I could get rid of the blood itself, there were still stains left over no matter how hard I scrubbed. Also, it turns out that paper towels are the absolute worst at trying to clean blood off wood. I wasn't about to ruin my new bath towels though.

When I'd done what I could for the porch, I went inside, locked the door, and took a hot shower. Though scrubbing the porch had taken my mind off vampire blood, the hot shower only brought that and other needs crashing back into my mind. I inhaled sharply at the thought of Louis's teeth sinking into my neck. The mental image elicited an almost electric spark of need.

Cold shower it is, I thought and cranked the cold handle up.

By the time I got out of the shower, I was shivering so hard my teeth were rattling in my head. I wrapped myself in the big bath towel and went to sit in front of the fire to get warm. Ramble was already there, cleaning his front paws. Through some pantomiming gymnastics, he indicated that I needed to add wood to the fire. Once that was done, I sat near the woodstove and stared into the flames.

You should get some sleep, Vânători. If you're going to anger a Power, you need to be in top shape when he responds.

"I'm not angering anyone that I know of," I leaned my chin on my hand. "We don't know what the dead deer even means yet. Let's ask around before we jump to conclusions. I'm not convinced we're dealing with that kind of being. And if this guy *is* so powerful, then why not just kill me when we were down that embankment? Instead, he ran away from the sheriff shooting at him. To me, that means he's not invincible."

I shook my head. It would be nice if there were instructions for how to handle this kind of thing. Until then, I would just have to play it by ear and get as much advice as I could from a magic necklace and an invisible hellhound.

Yup. Totally normal life.

Chapter Nine

I stared at the empty coffee pot in the kitchen. Morning light streamed in through the kitchen window, making the room cozy and warm in conjunction with the roaring fireplace. I had my own kitchen to make breakfast in, but somehow, I had forgotten to buy coffee. Did I buy coffee filters? Yup. Had I bought the actual coffee? Nope.

"Next time, I'll make a real list. None of this mental list bullshit where I forget the most important item." I said to Ramble as I pulled a pan of eggs and bacon off the stove and pushed more than half of it onto a plate that I placed on the floor for him. He ignored my bitching and immediately chowed down. I tried to overlook the pools of drool he'd left on the kitchen tile from watching me cook.

Rosalyn had left me the kitchen table and two chairs. I plopped down in the chair that faced the big kitchen window and looked out at the woods out back. I tried not to think about what creatures might be shuffling around those woods at night. How many of them would have the strength to toss a deer carcass on my porch or worse?

A layer of frost coated the short section of grass between

the cabin and the trees. It had definitely gotten cold last night if the ground was getting frosty. I'd already made it through one early snowstorm on Halloween night in Ricketts, but I wasn't sure I wanted to spend a whole winter up here.

I was having a lot of trouble shaking the fog of sleep from my brain without coffee. I'd finally gotten some sleep about an hour after cleaning up the deer gore from the porch, but it had been fitful and full of carnal dreams about Louis. I was definitely not going to be running on all four cylinders today unless I got some damn coffee.

After forcing myself to finish breakfast, I took another shower to try and wake up. It helped dissipate some of the brain fog, and I was able to start planning my day a little better. Obviously, the first thing on the agenda would be getting coffee. However, I also needed to call Rosalyn since I hadn't heard back from Louis.

You'd think the guy could at least call a girl back...

I stifled my annoyance and was about to sit down and create an actual to-do list on my phone when a car door slammed outside. Both Ramble and I whirled to face the front door.

Gun or no gun? I decided against it since whoever was out there hadn't been trying to hide their presence if they were slamming car doors.

A moment later, someone knocked on the front door. I once again lamented the lack of a peephole and instead took the extra few seconds to slip into the living room and look out the window.

A sheriff's cruiser sat in the driveway behind my car. Great. That's all I needed this morning. A visit from the cops. I tried to keep my heartbeat from speeding up. Just the idea of law enforcement made me panic. What if the sheriff had come back because he'd discovered who I really was? What if he was here to arrest me and sent me back to Indiana for skipping parole?

Ramble moseyed back to the living room doorway and plopped down facing the front door. I guess he was gonna watch the show from there.

Seeing Ramble's nonchalant reaction to the sheriff helped me shove the panic away. I forced myself to walk to the front door and open it.

"Morning, Sheriff. What can I do for you?"

He'd moved back from the door to kneel down and look at the blood-stained porch. Yep. That was gonna be fun to explain.

"Something happen here that you care to tell me about?"

I opened my mouth to lie but decided against it at the last second. If the sheriff was going to truly do his job and provide protection and enforce laws for everyone in the community, including those not considered human, then maybe he might start by helping me get a better understanding of the Power that had thrown the damn deer at my door. I hadn't considered the sheriff as an avenue for help, but what hell? He knew a little about the supernatural community and he was already here. Might as well try.

"I'll show you. Just one sec," I said and retreated to the kitchen to grab the house keys and my jacket. On my way back through the foyer, I pulled on my boots and quickly laced them up. Ramble was still lying in the doorway to the living room, enjoying the heat radiating from the woodstove. I raised an eyebrow at him in question and he laid his head down between his paws. I guess he was staying inside where it was warm.

I returned to the porch and walked past the sheriff who had straightened from his crouching inspection.

"Someone left me a little present in the middle of the night," I said and motioned for him to follow me around the side of the cabin. When I opened the shed and stepped back to reveal the deer, his mouth dropped open.

"They left a decapitated deer on your front porch?" He asked, entering the shed to get a better look.

"Well," I admitted, "the head was mostly attached and just came off when I was moving it from the porch to here."

He glanced back at me. "And you moved it all the way over here by yourself?"

I shrugged. "I had a little help." He looked at me for another second, waiting for more of an explanation. When he realized that was all the info he was going to get, he returned his attention back to the buck.

"I'm guessing you haven't had a spate of dead deer left on porches in the middle of the night, huh?" I asked dryly.

"Not to my knowledge." He pointed at the torn flesh around the deer's neck. "Was there a bite taken out of it?"

"That's what it looked like." I crossed my arms over my chest to keep warm. Though I wasn't a big fan of the cold, I was grateful it kept the body from decomposing. Once it warmed up later in the day though, it would probably start to smell and attract critters and who knew what else from the woods.

"Huh." His tone was perfectly neutral. "What about the scorch marks?"

"What scorch marks?"

He waved me to follow him, and we retraced our steps to the porch stairs. He was moving pretty well today so the tumble down the embankment must have left him more bruised than broken. At least that was something.

He stopped in front of the stairs and pointed at a black burn mark on the bottom step, then knelt down and pointed at the grass around it. "Whatever it was burned the grass and the stairs."

Somehow, I'd completely missed it. Ramble must have

been listening from inside because he emerged from the cabin and ghosted down the stairs to give them a quiet sniff. His ears flicked forward and back as he gathered information. I was dying to ask him if he'd smelled the scorched areas yesterday or not.

"Huh." I said, echoing the sheriff.

When he stared at me, I decided to give him a little more information. After all, if I wanted his actual help here, then I needed to extend a little trust here.

"I'm not sure about the scorch marks, but I think the deer was left here by the thing that attacked us yesterday. The person who helped me move the body has a keen sense of smell, and he said it had the same scent as our attacker."

"Is that so?" He straightened up and turned to face me.

"I trust his judgement. I'm just not sure if the deer was left as a warning or more as—

—a gift." We finished in unison.

I raised my eyebrows in question.

"Seems like if it was a warning, the body would have been a lot more, I dunno, grisly. But if there were no other marks on it other than the killing stroke—or bite in this case—then it looks to me like it was more of a gift than a warning."

I had to hand it to the sheriff, I was impressed that he had an open mind about this. I'm not sure I could have done the same if the antler-guy had tackled me yesterday and rolled me down a huge embankment. My thought process must have shown on my face because the sheriff suddenly gave me a warm smile.

"I've lived here in Ricketts all my life. I've seen a few odd things here and there that I couldn't really explain. The last sheriff generally turned a blind eye to anything that was strange and let the locals in those little pockets of the community take care of their own business. Personally, I'd rather know a little more about what's going on in my town than that. Hard to help folks if I don't know what's happening, Miss Mason." He paused to look me dead in the eye, "Or should I say, Vianne Vanator?"

I flinched at his use of my real name. Shit.

I'd initially told him it was Violet Mason while helping Donavon investigate the monster-dog murders. How had he found out who I was? And a much better question: Could I escape from him if he decided to haul me in?

Kill him, Vânători, Artemis demanded. *Do it quick before he brings Morvalden's attention down on you.*

Before I could make a decision of whether to flee or fight, the sheriff put out a placating hand.

"There's no reason to run. I don't intend to arrest you for violating parole unless you cause problems in my town." He shrugged. "After everything at the mausoleum, Donavon called you Vânători. It stuck with me and after yesterday's incident, I decided to look you up. It didn't take long to find someone with a close enough name. Plus, you've got several social media profiles with your real name and face."

If I wasn't still standing stock still, I would have facepalmed. How could I not think to delete my social media profiles?

I do not understand, Artemis said, clearly clueless.

I'll explain later when we don't have a cop on our lawn. I guess I hadn't explained the internet to her, let alone what social media was. That was going to be interesting.

When Sheriff Allen didn't say anything more, I asked, "So...you know who I am but you're not gonna arrest me?"

"Not unless you give me a reason to."

Hmm. I didn't really have much choice but to take him at his word. I mean, I could wait until he left and make a run for it, but I didn't really have anywhere else to go. And the only option I had for getting vampire blood was here in this town.

The sheriff was still staring at me, waiting for what my response would be.

"Okay. I don't intend to cause trouble in your town."

"Trouble seems to follow you around though, huh?" He jerked his head at the dead deer.

"Sometimes," I admitted, "but I'll remind you that your deputy was murdering people long before I arrived. So that definitely wasn't me."

He sighed, and all the tension slipped from the conversation. "True." Suddenly he shifted gears. "What do you plan to do with the deer? I don't recommend keeping it out here much longer, otherwise you'll have all kinds of unwelcome guests."

I hoped he just meant foxes and bears and not some monster from the woods.

"I guess I was going to bury it out here somewhere." I'd noticed a shovel in a pile of tools at the back of the shed earlier. At least I wouldn't have to waste money buying one. That was something.

The sheriff frowned and rubbed his chin in thought. "Not sure that's the best idea. You'd want to bury it pretty far away. Helluva thing hauling that big of a deer around the Maine backwoods without an ATV. Plus," He looked over at me, "if the deer was intended as a gift, the thing that attacked us might be watching to see what you do with it. I'm not sure what message it would send to basically throw away its gift by burying it in the woods."

Crap. I hadn't considered that.

What do you think? I asked Artemis.

You know my opinion, Vânători.

She still wanted me to pack up and make a run for it. Not super helpful.

"Do you have a recommendation for what I should do with the body?" I asked the sheriff.

He shrugged. "You could have it butchered and keep the meat. Venison makes a mean winter stew." Seeing my expression, he smiled. "I know a guy who might be willing to pick up the body from you." The sheriff looked back at the deer head. "That buck had a pretty good rack of antlers. My buddy might be willing to butcher the deer at a steep discount if you give him the head. I can give him a call if you like."

He could take the whole damn deer if it meant getting rid of the thing. I sure as hell didn't have the strength to haul it around again. Not without more vampire blood, anyways.

"That would be great, thanks."

I'd just have to scrape up some more money to pay the guy. It looked like the day was gonna consist of a job search.

Super.

When the sheriff didn't make any move to leave, I remembered that he must have come here for something else. We'd just been sidetracked by the deer.

"Was there something else I could help you with?"

Clearly the sheriff had been waiting for my cue because he smiled in appreciation for me broaching the subject. "Actually, I wanted to follow up on my consultant role offer. I thought maybe your hesitation might stem from thinking I'd find out about your criminal background if you worked for the department." He shrugged. "I wanted to make sure you knew that your history wouldn't be a problem. Not if you're a consultant anyway."

I started to tell him I wasn't interested, then stopped myself. I needed the money, and I didn't have any other ideas for where to start looking for employment under the table. I *really* didn't want to take Cheri's job at the diner, either. That would just be too weird.

This is a bad idea, Vânători.

You're the one who said that the Vânători were historically seen as enforcers and lawmen. Well, what better work than consulting with actual human law enforcement?

The sheriff's smile slowly started to slide from his face as we waited for a response. Perhaps he could sense the internal conversation that was occurring and was rethinking his offer.

"Okay," I quickly said before he could change his mind.

He regarded me for a moment before he stuck out a hand. "Good. Welcome to the team."

I grasped his hand to seal the deal.

"I'm glad to have you on board," he continued, "because I have a case that requires your services." He grimaced as he asked, "Got any experience with an invisible body?"

Chapter Ten

I stood at the edge of a small parking area and looked out at the lake's surface as it rippled in the light morning breeze. Though it had been cold last night, the day promised to be one of the warmest I'd experienced yet in Maine—at least, according to the weather app on my phone.

Ramble had immediately darted over to the lake and begun sniffing around its semi-sandy perimeter, sometimes hopping onto the large, smooth flat boulders that lay here and there, partially hidden beneath the dirt. They were big enough to lay down on, and, if it were a bit warmer, I might have been tempted to do just that since I still hadn't gotten my morning cup of coffee.

I idly wondered if Ramble ever got sand or other stuff up his nose while sniffing the ground like that. As I looked around, I realized I'd been to this lake once before with Rosalyn, but we had parked at a different area where there had been a couple of picnic tables. That had been more of a public park while this section of the lake was a privately run campsite.

I'd opted to follow Sheriff Allen in my own car rather than

ride with him, that way I could hit up a grocery store after-wards for coffee. Also, I didn't want to have to figure out how to let Ramble into his cruiser without the sheriff realizing the hellhound was there. My life was already complicated enough without the added headache of explaining the existence of my hellhound sidekick to the sheriff.

The sheriff stood with a young couple near their tent which was about one-hundred feet away from the water line. He glanced my way, and I remembered that I was supposed to be working here. I quickly continued scanning the campsite, looking for some sign of an invisible body.

Yeah. The sheriff hadn't been joking about that.

"Vi!" The sheriff called. When I looked up, he waved me over. Ramble continued sniffing around the waterline while I trudged up the small incline to the campsite.

"This is Violet Mason, a consultant in these kinds of things," the sheriff explained to the couple. He started to say more but the woman cut him off.

"She specializes in freaking fairies?"

It was a close thing, but I was able to keep the surprise off my face, though just barely. I knew we were looking for an invisible body, but a fairy? That was new.

"Fairies and a few other things that aren't always visible to the naked eye," I said. I would have paired it with my rendi-tion of a warm smile, but my lack of coffee paired with the woman's tone kind of pissed me off. That and the way she had looked me up and down, assessing my cheap outfit and second-hand jacket, made me think that I was not going to like her. Before she could say anything to worsen my mood, I asked, "Can you tell me what happened?"

"We *just* told the sheriff," the woman icily replied, flicking her perfectly styled hair behind her shoulder.

I didn't think she and I were gonna be BFF's.

She wore L.L. Bean flannel pajamas that I was a little

envious of. I wondered how she could manage such a perfect hairstyle while camping, but then I caught a glimpse inside their family-sized tent.

Rather than sleeping bags, they had a full-size bed that had been perfectly made with crisp, white bedding and decorative pillows. Next to the bed was a white nightstand complete with a table lamp. White Christmas tree lights hung from the ceiling of the tent inside. It looked like something straight from a magazine.

This couple wasn't camping. They were *glamping*.

The sheriff saw my gaze and gave a tiny shrug as if to say, *We get all kinds here.*

"Derek and Lisa here are newlyweds who are on their honeymoon. They were woken up in the middle of the night by music—"

"I didn't say music," Lisa interrupted. "I said it sounded like *musical voices*." She gave a put-upon sigh and turned to me as if the sheriff couldn't be trusted to finish the story. "I heard musical voices outside the tent and woke Derek up. He said he couldn't hear anything and didn't believe me, which, like, *really*? So I crept over to the tent door and unzipped it fast enough to see two things fly toward the lake." She pointed to where I'd been standing only moments before. "It was dark so I couldn't tell what they were. I followed them to the edge of the water and started videoing them on my phone. Derek followed me down to the water—"

"—I couldn't see anything though," Derek forcefully interjected. He looked like he'd lost a fight against a thorny rosebush. He had long scratches and cuts all over his face and hands. His dark flannel pajamas were completely soaked, and I wondered how he could stand there without freezing to death. Derek's build and the way he carried himself made me think he might be military, but his shaggy yet trendy hairstyle suggested otherwise.

One thing was for sure, Derek did *not* want us to think he believed in fairies.

"I was just following Lisa," he added for clarification.

Lisa glared at him. Clearly, he was going to get an earful later. She shifted her focus back to me and picked up the story thread again. *"Anyways*, they let me get close to them and when I did, I could see that they were tiny men with wings."* She put a hand on her heart. "I know that sounds crazy, but I swear, that's what I saw."

"Okay. Sounds like fairies," I said, then mentally asked Artemis, *Right?*

Fairies or pixies. Fairies are a bit more serious while pixies are the pranksters of what you've been calling the supernatural community. Without seeing the body, I am unable to tell which the woman saw.

Perhaps Ramble would be able to tell me whether it was a pixy or a fairy by smell—if it was even either one of those creatures. So far, the only thing I was sure of with the supernatural community was that I only knew enough to get myself in trouble.

It was interesting that Lisa had been able to see the fairy, yet her husband Derek couldn't.

"So, what happened next? I was told there was an invisible body here somewhere?"

Derek clenched his jaw a little like he dreaded what was about to come next while Lisa glanced at him and then back to me to continue her story.

"I told Derek to get his fishing net so we could try to capture one of them. We weren't going to hurt it. We were just going to see if we could take a picture of it. Do you know what kind of publicity a picture of a real-life fairy could get? I mean, I have over a hundred thousand followers. That could put me in the millions!"

That explained the glamping, perfect hair, and expertly done makeup. They were having the picture-perfect honeymoon so she could share it on social media with her followers. Except they'd chosen the wrong place to camp and found themselves face-to-face with things that didn't fit their version of reality.

Welcome to the club, I thought.

"Okay, so you get the net, and Derek tries to capture whatever you saw. Then what?" I asked Lisa

"I had to tell him where to swing the net—"

"Because I couldn't see anything," Derek explained though I thought he would have preferred to say because he didn't think there was actually anything there. I kind of felt for Lisa. Her new husband probably thought she'd had a break with reality. Then again, he was still standing here beside her, so maybe that meant something. Then again, who was I to say. I hadn't had a real relationship in, like, ever.

"But with me giving directions," Lisa said, "and Derek's speed—he's an MMA fighter, you know—we were able to capture one!"

Surprising twist. I looked around for the net but didn't see it anywhere nearby.

"But then," she continued, "the other fairy whistled and, like, a ton of them suddenly came flying out of everywhere with tiny swords and knives to attack Derek."

Derek seemed unsure of himself now, but explained, "It felt like...like I'd kicked up a swarm of bees, and they were stinging me. So I dove into the water to get away from them."

Taking a closer look at his pajamas, I noticed now that there were gashes here and there in the soaked material. I'd never seen a bee that could rip through cloth like that. I wondered how someone could write off that kind of damage to both his clothing and his skin as the result of a swarm bees.

"But he brought the net with him, and it went underwater..." Lisa said.

It wasn't hard to figure out what happened from there.

"And the fairy drowned in the net," I said, careful to keep my tone neutral.

Lisa nodded sadly but Derek seemed unphased. Perhaps it was easier for him to believe that the fairies had really just been a swarm of bees he couldn't see than the fact that he had killed another living being. Of course, his disbelief was only reinforced by the fact that he couldn't see the fairy's body.

These two are a lost cause, Artemis said. *You will not be able to save them from the fairies. Or the pixies if that was what they murdered. Both creatures will follow them and cause mischief and mayhem until they end their own lives.*

Well, shit. I couldn't let that happen. *Is there nothing that can be done?*

Artemis was silent for a moment as she considered the situation. *If it was a pixy, their forgiveness might be bought. It's possible you could negotiate with them, Vânâtori. But if they murdered a fairy, they are already marked for a life of suffering and eventually death.*

Great. I tried to suppress a sigh. Maybe this job would have seemed more doable if I'd had a cup of coffee first.

"I see." I finally said when I realized both the couple and the sheriff were staring at me, waiting for a response. "Where's the body? I'll need to see it to figure out what to do next."

"We left it in the water, but it looks like your dog already found it," Lisa said.

What?

"What dog?" The sheriff asked.

I ignored him and turned to find Ramble emerging from the lake with a wooden fishing net in his mouth. He put the net down for a second to shake the water from his fur, then retrieved it before trotting up to us.

The two men were startled into silence as they watched the net slowly make its way through the air toward us, carried by an invisible dog. Derek looked a little pale, but the sheriff had his mouth screwed down. Clearly, he wasn't very happy that I hadn't told him I'd brought my partner with us.

Lisa, however, seemed perfectly okay as she watched Ramble carry the net over.

She can see your hellhound, Vânători, Artemis helpfully said.

No shit. It was the only response I could muster right then. This was the second person in two days who had been able to see Ramble. Wait, I couldn't leave out Hyssop. Make that three people who could see Ramble.

At this rate, he wouldn't be much of a secret weapon.

I looked at Lisa. *Is she a witch?* I asked Artemis.

Oh! Surprise and then a note of embarrassment lit up the back of my mind as Artemis assessed the woman. *Yes. I see now that she is a witch. Her powers are not developed though. Which is why I did not sense them before.*

Hmm. Judging by her embarrassment, it was more likely that Artemis just hadn't bothered to check to see if the woman was more than human. It was something that could easily cost me my life in the future, but I let it slide. For now, anyways. I'd made my share of mistakes and was likely to make a lot more as I figured out the whole Vânători thing. I'd rather store Artemis's mistake away for later use when she would inevitably berate me for doing something stupid in the future.

Instead I mentally said, *But Rosalyn is a witch and can only sense Ramble's presence. She can't see him.*

Perhaps this witch has the gift of Sight? It would explain her ability to see the fairies as well.

It made me wonder about the lady living next door to Hyssop's old house. Artemis had said she didn't sense an aura around the woman, but maybe she was also a witch who could hide her aura or something? I didn't have time to think about it right then, so I tucked the thought away for later inspection.

Ramble finally reached us, and my mind was forced back to the present as the hellhound very gently placed the net on the ground. Tangled within was the limp body of a tiny man wearing brightly colored clothing. One translucent wing half covered his body while the other one had gotten tangled in one of the threads of the net.

Well? I asked the necklace, holding my breath for her answer.

These foolish children may be in luck. It's a pixy, Vânători. There may be hope yet for negotiation.

Good. What should we use to negotiate? What would they want?

Artemis was quiet as she considered the question. *I am not sure, but it does not matter at this juncture. Pixies tend to emerge during in-between times such as dusk and dawn. I do not think they could come out during full daylight.*

Well, damn. That meant I'd have to deal with this couple a second time today and come back to their camp at dusk.

The sheriff looked down at the net which he clearly saw as empty, then around the space where Ramble was before turning his gaze to me with a raised eyebrow. I ignored his pointed question regarding my four-legged companion and focused my attention on the couple.

"You've killed a pixy," I told Derek and Lisa. Though Derek might have been the one responsible for the actual drowning, it was Lisa who had suggested he try to capture the pixy just so she could get a picture and a few more followers. I viewed them as being equally responsible for the pixy's death.

"You can see it?" Derek said. His voice was an odd mix of disbelief and guilt.

"I can see *him*," I corrected. I looked at him and his wife for a moment before coming to a decision on how to handle this. Finally, I bent down and gingerly began to extract the little pixy from the netting. I spoke as I worked and made sure to occasionally look up to meet both Lisa and Derek's eyes.

"There are other beings who live in this world beside humans. For the most part, they keep to themselves and don't want to be bothered." That was mostly true. "Some live seemingly normal lives in plain sight." I thought about Mitchell and Deloris, the trolls who ran a local restaurant known for its many pies. "While others can't pass as human and so must live at the outskirts of our cities and towns, getting by on a smaller and smaller amount of land as humans turn wild spaces into shopping malls," I looked around, "or campsites."

I finally freed the pixy from the net and placed him gently on my left palm. He was just tall enough that my middle finger cradled his head while his feet ended just above my wrist. He had a white scar that bisected the left half of his face, reminding me that he had been a living being with a meaningful life before these two humans had stomped into camp, captured him, and drowned him.

Yes, the drowning had been an accident, but he needn't have been captured in the first place. This whole thing could have been avoided if humans weren't such egotistical jerks who thought we were superior to all other creatures and had a right to capture them.

A flash of anger shot through me, and I looked the couple in the eyes, hoping they'd be able to see my rage. "You may not be able to see this pixy, Derek. But Lisa can see him just fine. Do you know what that means?"

Okay. Maybe I was overstepping here, but I decided I didn't care. I was supposed to help maintain relations between humans and those belonging to the supernatural community. This incident wasn't my fault, but I felt guilty that someone had lost their life and the humans didn't seem to care. It didn't matter that the victim fit in my hand.

"It doesn't mean anything," Lisa said, but she had wrapped her arms around her middle as she watched me cradling the pixy.

"Actually, it means that you have a little bit of something more than human in you, Lisa." At the last second, I decided not to label her as a witch. I had no idea how her husband would react. I didn't want to be responsible for her getting burned at the stake or something. "That's why you can see the pixy here," I nodded toward the body in my hand, "and why you can see my four-legged friend when no one else can."

"Your what?" Derek asked, looking around him.

Sensing my plan, Ramble moseyed over to Derek and took his cue to shoulder check the man in the thigh. Derek almost leapt out of his pajamas. He jumped in the opposite direction, knocking into Lisa who took a stumbling sidestep. She'd seen Ramble's approach though and managed to keep herself and her husband upright.

For his part, Ramble made contact, then moved slowly past the couple to stand at my side. I saw the sheriff look down at the ground as one of Ramble's giant, clawed paws left a sizable imprint in one sandy section of the campsite.

When the couple recovered, Lisa gave me an angry look. "We're good Christian people, and I'm just a regular, God-fearing woman."

"You might want to start fearing more than that. You worked together to kill this pixy. His..."

I mentally flailed around for the next word and Artemis helpfully supplied it before I looked too stupid and lost the couple's attention. "His clan will want revenge."

"What?" Derek said, still keeping an eye out for the giant invisible dog. "What do you mean, revenge? It was just an accident."

I shrugged. "A human court would call this involuntary manslaughter." I saw the sheriff open his mouth to protest and kept talking before he could ruin my momentum. "But we all know that no one believes in pixies. You won't go to court. No." I shook my head maybe a little melodramatically and added a sigh to it. "You won't be that lucky. What you two will face will be worse than anything a court would do to you."

"He's not a person," Lisa said, pointing at the body in my hand. "And besides, it's not like we're staying here. Those things can't follow us home."

The sheriff cleared his throat. "Didn't you two call the station because your vehicle wouldn't start, and you suspected sabotage?"

"Well, yeah, but..." Lisa stopped. She looked at Derek who still seemed a bit freaked out that there was a canine present that he couldn't see. When she turned her gaze back to me, she asked, "You think those...that the pixies put something in our truck's gas tank?"

Boy. She just really wasn't getting this. Like, at all.

"I think," I started slowly, feeling my way forward. "That until you decide to negotiate some sort of truce with this pixy's clan, you're going to start having a lot of random, unexpected problems in your life. Pixies aren't tied to one place," I added, "They can go anywhere you go—they just usually choose to be out in the wilderness by themselves."

Okay, I honestly had no idea if the pixies would actually follow this ridiculous couple back to their home, but Artemis had made it sound like they could.

The threat didn't seem to make a difference though. Lisa still looked determined to leave the scene of the crime with zero cares. Derek, on the other hand, stood stock still while darting his eyes around the area for any signs of Ramble. Or maybe he was afraid the pixies would come back.

"We're not going to negotiate with something that isn't human," Lisa said flatly.

In one last attempt to convince the couple they should negotiate with the pixies, I turned to the sheriff and in a conversational tone, lied through my teeth, "You know, I heard an up-and-coming news anchor accidentally stepped on a pixy while doing a story. She couldn't see him like you could," I said off-handedly to Lisa, "so she didn't know what she'd done or even that she could negotiate a truce with the dead pixy's clan. That poor woman had the worst luck from that day on. Malfunctions with TV cameras, bad hair day after bad hair day, terrible acne that couldn't be covered by make-up, a cheating spouse..." I shook my head. "Totally ruined her entire life and career in, like, two weeks."

I turned back to the previously happy couple. "But I'm sure you two will be fine." I forced a smile and walked away, still holding the poor pixy in one hand.

Do you think threats to their looks and careers are going to change their minds, Vânători? You'd be better off threatening their lives.

That's not really the way people think anymore, Artemis. I silently explained. *Most people don't fear imminent death. It's something that's far off in the future and isn't something that they think about happening to them. Most people go through life thinking they're invincible and underestimate their chances of getting hit by a bus when they step off a sidewalk. However, what this couple care about, or at least, what Lisa cares about, is getting more followers on social media.*

I...do not understand. Followers?

I mentally shrugged. *Just trust me on this.*

The sheriff stayed with Derek and Lisa while I walked away. I caught a snippet of him saying something about how "she's the expert." I could only assume he meant me.

Huh. Me. An expert on something. It wasn't exactly true, but I could get used to it.

Ramble and I had made it all the way to the edge of the parking area when Lisa caught up to us.

"Wait." She gently touched my arm, the one not holding the pixy, and said, "I'm sorry. We... *I* didn't understand before."

I turned and searched her face. She seemed contrite, but I honestly didn't believe her. You don't go from not caring about having accidentally killed someone to suddenly having a conscience and feeling bad. I mean, maybe if the pixy had little kids and they showed up screaming for their dad, perhaps I might have believed she'd changed her tune on whether pixies should have the same right to life as humans... but even then, I would have been skeptical of Lisa's sudden change of heart.

The thing was, I didn't need to believe she'd changed how she viewed the pixy. My job, as I understood it, was to keep the peace between humans and the supernatural community. That meant, in this instance, I needed to keep these two idiots from being bad lucked to death by the local pixy clan.

After a quick mental conference with Artemis, I managed to maintain a neutral expression as I told Lisa, "We can try to negotiate with the pixy clan, but we'll have to wait until dusk. I don't think they'll come out before then, but just in case, you might want to catch a ride back to town and spend the day there."

I gave her my number, but before I turned to leave, she asked, "What are you going to do with him?" If her tone hadn't held a note of what sounded like sincere regret, I might have wondered if she wanted to keep the pixy's body as proof of his existence or maybe to try to take a picture of him for her social media channels.

It was actually a good question since I had no idea what I was supposed to do with the pixy's body. Should I bury him?

Give him a Viking funeral? Leave his body in the woods for his family to find?

Since the pixies will not come out until dusk, I recommend watch over his body and bring him back with us as part of the negotiation.

My gut twisted. *We're gonna bargain with his body? That's just...wrong.*

It is the only bargaining chip that these humans have, Vânători.

Suppressing a sigh, I relayed Artemis's plan to Lisa as well as to Sheriff Allen and Derek who had joined us at the edge of the parking lot.

"We'll see you back here at dusk," I briskly said and started walking toward the car again. The sheriff followed me as Lisa and Derek retreated to their tent.

"I told her they might consider catching a ride into town with you. That way they aren't stuck out here all day."

"Do you think the other pixies will come back?" He asked while shooting glances at my outstretched hand.

I was a little impressed that the sheriff was taking this all in stride. Then again, he'd recently learned his deputy had been part-witch who turned into a ravening beast and murdered some of the townspeople. I guess pixies were a little easier to swallow...no pun intended.

"I don't think they will, but better safe than sorry." I popped the trunk open and rummaged around looking for something to keep the pixy's body in. Guessing my intentions, the sheriff disappeared over to his car and came back carrying a roll of Duct tape and a small tissue box like the kind you find in hotel rooms.

"Will this work? I can't tell if it's the right size or not."

"That's perfect." I maneuvered the pixy through the small opening as gently as I could, which was tricky since pixies apparently weren't immune to rigor mortis. I then had the sheriff rip off a short bit of the tape to cover up the hole.

When that was done, I looked back out at the water and surrounding woods. "Do you know what time dusk is?"

"Around this time of year? Between around seven and seven-thirty."

"What do you say we meet back here at about six forty-five? That will give us a little buffer time."

"Sounds good. You gonna bring your silent partner then, too?"

Oh yeah...

"I'm sorry I didn't tell you about him before. His name is Ramble."

The sheriff grunted. "Do I want to ask what he is?"

"Um...maybe not. Just know that he's got our backs. And you can buy into his affections with any kind of food."

Ramble snorted beside me.

"Okay, okay." I turned back to the sheriff. "Greasy, bacon cheeseburgers are his favorite."

Ramble let out a deep rumble of pleasure, and I could see the sheriff fighting the urge to step back from the sound coming from what seemed like an empty space beside me.

He took a second to recover, then said, "Okay, See you at six forty-five. Oh," he paused before walking away, "make sure to start keeping track of your hours on the job and include mileage and travel time. I expect an invoice in my inbox for this tomorrow morning." He handed me his card so I'd have his email address.

"Um, yeah. Will do."

That's me. Always professional.

"Oh," I suddenly remembered the dead deer in the shed back at the cabin. "Would you mind giving that butcher guy a call about the deer?"

"Will do," he said, clearly copying me before starting off toward the couple still standing at their tent, watching us.

"Time for babysitting," I heard him mumble before he got out of earshot.

I couldn't help the smile that tugged at the corners of my mouth as I let Ramble in the car and got in after him. I kind of liked the sheriff which was a bit of a surprise since I'd found him a little too lax in reigning in his murder-beast deputy. Then again, it wouldn't do to let my guard down too much around him. He was still in law enforcement, and, though he'd said he'd ignore the fact that another state was looking for me, that could change at any time. I'd have to stay on his good side.

Of course, it helped that doing that meant accepting the money from this consulting gig. But it would still be smart to be careful around him.

Smart girl, Vânători. Now you're learning.

I rolled my eyes at the condescending necklace, started the car, and aimed us back toward town. I needed coffee in a bad way and the closest place I knew meant I might get some pie as well. Of course, I'd have to spend a little more money than I wanted to, but I could take the opportunity to ask some of the local folks in the supernatural community about the pixies.

Wait, did that mean I could charge the Sheriff's Department for my time there? And the coffee and pie?

Maybe this morning was looking up after all. I caught sight of the tissue box and my mood fell as I remembered the life inside that had been extinguished by human stupidity.

Was negotiating for Lisa and Derek really the right thing to do? It was tempting to just let the pixies mete out their own justice. After all, they were the wronged party here.

So far, it seemed that my interactions between the human and supernatural communities had resulted in humans getting what they wanted while those in the supernatural community got the short end of the stick.

It made me rethink my stance on Hyssop's garden. Maybe I should be fighting harder for him to continue living there. After all, when you thought about it in human terms, he'd been ousted from his home, assaulted by the new owner, and now was sort of like a refugee who was forced to look for a new home. Okay, yes, he'd sabotaged the new owner's plants, but I couldn't blame him for trying to fight back.

Abruptly, I asked the necklace, "Do you really think that Hyssop will be okay if we move the dirt from his garden to somewhere else?"

No. Not really, Vânători. *But it's the thought that counts—isn't that one of your sayings?*

"What do you mean, 'no?' We told him it would work! Why didn't you tell me the truth before we got his hopes up and made plans with him to find a new place?"

I told you before. Gnomes—and fairies and pixies for that matter—are small players in the grand scheme of things. They can't help you in your fight against Morvalden, but I applaud your efforts to gain their trust. Perhaps it could come in useful down the road.

How had I gotten stuck with such a cold, cynical, calculating being?

Chapter Eleven

I pulled into the Flying Pie restaurant's semi-full parking lot and found a spot near the back. Before we went in, I tried calling Rosalyn. I wanted to ask her what she knew about pixies. When she didn't answer, I hung up before leaving a voicemail. Maybe I'd learn something from Delores or Mitchell while at the restaurant that might give me a different set of questions to ask the witch.

I sighed and asked Ramble, "Ready for second-breakfast?"

He licked his lips in obvious agreement.

Inside, Halloween decorations had been swapped out for turkeys, pilgrims, and cornucopias. Thanksgiving would sneak up on us fast.

A young woman led us to a table set for two with coffee cups and little saucers in the main room. I tried not to be disappointed that it hadn't been Delores or Mitchell greeting us at the door. Hopefully they were around today. As the resident trolls, maybe they'd have some insight into the Power that Artemis was freaking out about.

If you think the trolls will be willing to help a Vânători, think again.

They helped me before. You just weren't juiced up on vampire blood to be awake enough to see it, I told her silently as I draped my jacket on the back of the chair then perused the menu. Maybe I'd try the triple-berry pie. I showed a picture of it to Ramble, and he wrinkled his nose in distaste before pointing out a picture of hot-fudge pie beside it.

"Are you sure you're allowed to have chocolate?" I whispered with a grin. He bared his teeth at me in a mock threat. Or, I hoped it was a mock threat. "Okay, okay. Fudge pie it is."

As I spoke, I caught sight of Delores exiting the kitchen with a pot of coffee. Her eyes found mine and she barely hesitated in her beeline for another customer's table. After refilling the other customer's coffee, she made her way over to me. I quickly flipped the coffee cup on the table upright and sat up straighter she filled it.

"Ah, the sweet nectar of the gods," I wistfully murmured.

I am a god, and I can tell you that is not nectar.

"Vânători. To what do I owe the pleasure of a visit from you and your friend?" Her eyes flicked around the area where Ramble sat but they never really landed on him. At least that was still normal. I had been getting nervous that everyone could see my not-so-secret sidekick.

Or maybe I was Ramble's sidekick. It was hard to tell sometimes.

"I'm dying for some of your coffee and a piece of hot-fudge pie."

"Just one?" She said with a raised eyebrow.

"Maybe I should get two this time," I said with an unforced smile. "I didn't even get to try the last pie you gave me. *Someone* ate it before we got back to the motel."

Ramble snorted and lay down, clearly settling in to wait for our slices of pie while I doctored my coffee with the sugar and creamer already on the table. I'd drink it black at the cabin since it meant saving money, but why be a barbarian if you had access to the finer things in life for free?

"Are you still staying there? I'd heard you were taking the witch's old place out toward the mountain."

I quickly swallowed the swig of coffee I'd been savoring. "Wow, word travels fast around here, huh?"

Delores flapped her free hand. "Small towns breed fast gossip. That and Rosalyn mentioned it when she was here this morning. How long you been up there so far?"

I set the coffee down to give her my full attention. "I just moved in yesterday, so last night was my first. Actually," I glanced around to make sure we didn't have anyone's attention—

—and suddenly locked eyes with the Hyssop's neighbor-lady who didn't have an aura.

Rather than jump right into asking about the pixies or the antler-man, I decided to focus on her identity first.

"There's a woman three tables away having breakfast by herself. She has on khaki pants and an orange blouse with a white cardigan over it. Do you know who she is?"

Delores switched sides of the table under the guise of brushing some crumbs off the tablecloth, giving her a perfect view of the woman.

"Oh, Hester? She's been a regular for the last ten years or so."

The lawyer had referred to her as Karen, but maybe that had been more for being a nosy neighbor.

"Huh. Have you noticed anything odd about her? Like, that she doesn't have an aura? She can also see my friend here." I added and nodded toward Ramble, hoping she'd get my meaning.

"Really?" Her note of surprise validated my suspicions of the woman, and I was impressed when Delores didn't glance at Hester again. "You might ask Rosalyn about her. She seems to have a finger on the pulse of most things in town."

I nodded to Delores in thanks, and she retreated to the kitchen. Sipping my coffee, I thought about how surprised Delores had been about my information on Hester. The question was, did it surprise her more that Hester didn't have an aura or that the woman could see Ramble? I was tempted to ask Delores more about Hester, but I'd gotten the feeling that the restaurant owner had said all she would on that topic.

I didn't think it would hurt to ask about my other problem though. When Delores returned with a slice of hot-fudge pie on a plate and another in a to-go container, I took the opportunity to try and get more information.

"Have you heard anything strange about the cabin I'm staying at? I mean, other than Cassandra's murder?"

Delores hesitated so I elaborated, hoping it might convince her to share any info she might have.

"I, uh, found a dead deer on my porch this morning. Any idea who would leave such a thing there?"

"You found a deer on your porch *this morning*? And it was your first night?" She shook her head. "That didn't take long."

"Wait, what? What didn't take long?"

Delores looked around and must have decided it was too crowded. "Why don't we go to the kitchen where your friend won't have to wait to have his pie?" Before I could protest, she'd picked up both the to-go box and my slice of pie and jerked her head for me to follow her.

I don't like this, Vânători. *It could be a trap.*

I ignored Artemis and grabbed my coffee cup, then at the last second remembered to pull my jacket from the back of the chair before following Delores as she expertly wove her way between the tables to the kitchen door. I would probably pay for ignoring Artemis later, but I didn't feel like arguing with her right now. To be honest, I was still annoyed that she had so little respect for what she deemed the lower beings in the supernatural community.

In the kitchen, Mitchell, Delores's husband, stood over an industrial-size stove, expertly flipping pancakes and keeping an eye on a pan of sausages and bacon so they wouldn't burn. It smelled heavenly, and I suddenly wished I could afford more than just a slice of pie and coffee. Ramble looked like he was having the same thoughts, and I kind of felt bad that I couldn't provide better for him. Not without using the fake credit card anyways.

The moment we entered the kitchen, Mitchell looked up from the stove and glared at me. Even with the glare, you wouldn't have guessed he could morph into a huge, four-hundred-pound troll just by removing the little Flying Pie pin from his shirt. I'd seen it happen though and was under no impression that I would live if Mitchell decided to stomp me into the ground.

"What does *she* want?" Mitchell asked, pointing his spatula at me.

"*She's* here on business, and there's no reason to make a fool of yourself again," Delores chastised as she led us over to a small wooden table with two chairs in the corner.

I had to bite back a laugh at Mitchell's expression then quickly sat across from Delores in front of the pie she'd placed on the table.

"We'll have to be quick because I'm short-staffed and am covering two sections." She opened the to-go box and set it on the floor for Ramble. The hellhound immediately started wolfing down the pie. Delores handed me a roll of silverware from her apron then gestured at the pie in front me.

Apparently, I was also expected to wolf down pie like Ramble while we talked. I mean, it wasn't the biggest challenge I'd had all week.

"So, you were saying you know who left the deer on my porch?" I asked, then got to work on the pie while taking sips of coffee in between bites.

Mitchell froze. "He's already made contact?"

"Who has?" I said around a mouthful of delicious pie. Ramble had made a really, really good choice with the hot-fudge pie. It went perfectly with the coffee, too.

"Pamola. Who else?" Mitchell said with an arched eyebrow.

"Who's Pamola?" I asked Delores since it was clear that Mitchell wasn't going to elaborate.

The Power, Vânători, like I've been trying to tell you. But no, don't listen to me. Go right ahead and listen to two trolls who have no reason to give you the truth.

As much as I wanted to continue ignoring Artemis, I couldn't keep letting her malign Mitchell and Delores. It didn't matter that they couldn't hear her. I could, and that's what mattered. *They directly benefited when I kept Rosalyn from being overthrown as the coven leader. So, yes, Artemis, they have plenty of reason to tell me the truth.*

Delores's tone was serious when she answered my question, "Pamola is a great spirit or Power who lives in Mount Katahdin—"

Told you, Artemis interjected.

"—he sometimes wanders the land surrounding the mountain, and your cabin is right on the outskirts of those lands. The local tribe of Indigenous People have many stories about him. They mostly describe him as having the head of a moose, the body of a man, and the wings and claws of an eagle. Since he's a Power, he can take on the shape of whatever he wants. His existence is tied with the mountain, so he's at least as old as it is.

Well shit. I guess that antler headed guy that had attacked the sheriff really had been one of these Powers.

"I think I ran into him yesterday evening. Actually, he attacked the sheriff and started to attack me, too, but he ran off when the sheriff fired his gun at him."

"Wait," Mitchell said, completely leaving the stove now and walking around to stand over us at the table. "He attacked you? And you lived?"

"I mean, he *sort of* attacked us," I tried to explain. "He came out of the woods, tackled the sheriff, and when I reached them, he turned as if he was going to leap at me but stopped when the sheriff fired his gun."

"But then he left a dead deer on your porch?" Delores prompted.

I nodded, then paused. "I mean, I think it's the same guy. Ramble thought it sure smelled like the same guy."

"What did the deer look like?" Mitchell stopped and decided to rephrase his question before I could tell him it looked like a dead freakin' deer on my front porch. "I mean, what did the body look like when you found it?"

"It looked like something had taken a bite from its neck, then threw it on the porch." I had a flash of sitting on the porch with the dead deer's head in my lap. I suddenly wasn't so sure I wanted to finish the last few bites of pie. I caught Ramble looking at my plate, so I scraped the last bit into his to-go container. It quickly disappeared into the hellhound's stomach.

"The stove, dear," Delores reminded her husband just as I started to smell burning bacon. Mitchell hustled back over and started flipping food while quietly cursing under his breath.

With her husband distracted, Delores turned her attention back to me. "It sounds like the deer was left as an offering."

I couldn't tell if she was asking me or telling me, so I went with, "Um, I guess so. But what does that even mean?"

"It means that if it was Pamola who left it there, then he has met you and likes you enough to leave you a gift. That's a good thing." She paused then carefully asked, "What did you do with the deer?"

"I dragged it to the shed, and a butcher is going to go out and take care of it."

"Hmm. I'm not sure if that's wise or not. The deer was a gift for *you*, not for anyone else."

"Well, if ol' Pamola would like to butcher the deer for me and leave me just the parts I can eat, that would be great."

Delores stared at me for a moment as if I was an idiot. "It's not wise to mock a Power, Vânători. You're lucky he's decided he likes you. To be honest, we weren't sure which way he would lean."

Whoa. I'm sorry? What's that now?

"What?" Was all I could bite out. They'd known Pamola, some big special Power, not only existed, but that he would eventually learn that I was living on the outskirts of his woods, and no one had decided to tell me about it?

"Does Rosalyn know about Pamola?"

"Of course. All of us in the 'supernatural community' do." She actually put air quotes around the words. Apparently, my phrase was spreading in town, and, though it was obviously being used to mock me, I noted that it was also catching on.

"And no one thought to maybe warn me about this guy?"

It was Mitchell who answered me this time. "Meeting Pamola has been used for years as a sort of litmus test to see if someone is a good fit with the town." He held up two burned sausage patties that he hadn't been able to salvage and said to the empty air to the left of Ramble, "Do you want these?"

Ramble huffed and somehow Mitchell understood that as a yes before throwing the sausages to the hellhound who snatched them both out of the air and ate them in less than two bites.

"Does everyone who passes this little test get a dead deer thrown on their porch?" I asked.

"Not that I know of," Delores said. "Usually, if he doesn't mind someone new in town, he just leaves them alone."

"What about the people he *doesn't* like?"

Delores shrugged. "It's been a long time since he didn't like someone. We're pretty particular about who we let live here, though."

Clearly, they hadn't tested Deputy Smith or the witch, Gabriella, against Pamola. Or maybe they had, and this Power just didn't care if people in the community were scheming murderers.

"I see." I tried to take all this in stride. After all, I was an outsider in this town, but it still rankled that Rosalyn and Donavon had obviously collaborated to get me in the cabin near Pamola. I'd thought they'd just been scheming to keep me in town, but now it was obvious they'd wanted to test me with Pamola.

I'm not sure that I had the right to be upset since I'd been in town less than a month, but I felt a little betrayed. Anger flickered to life inside me, and in that moment, all I wanted to do was flip the table and storm out of that kitchen, get in the car Donavon had loaned me, and drive away from this stupid town.

Yes, Vânători. We should go. Leave these pesky trolls and gnomes and werewolves behind. Get the vampire and your hellhound and let us disappear into Between.

I had to admit, in that moment, it was oh-so tempting.

Ramble watched me carefully, clearly sensing that I was not a happy camper.

Under the super-transparent guise of taking another sip of coffee, I somehow managed to take my boiling anger down to a simmer. Right now was not the time to explode. I'd made promises to Hyssop, the sheriff, and that stupid glamping couple. I meant to fulfill those promises. And get paid by the sheriff, damnit.

Then maybe it would be time to reassess our presence in this town.

When I felt more in control of my voice, I asked, "And now that Pamola has given me this deer, I, what, passed his inspection? Or do I need to expect more tests? Is this guy gonna show up in the middle of the night?"

The couple stared at me before Delores finally broke the awkward silence. "One never knows what a Power will do, but it doesn't seem likely that you'll be bothered by Pamola again. He gifted you the deer, which means he likes you. Or," She cocked her head in consideration, "at the very least, that he's permitting you to stay."

"Huh," I grunted. I wasn't sure I could continue to be civil, so I dug out some money and left it on the table for the coffee and our pies. After throwing back the last swig of coffee, I set the cup down and stood up abruptly. "I appreciate your time and the information."

I ignored the beginnings of a protest from Delores and caught Mitchell's firm headshake to his wife. He clearly wanted her to let me leave.

Ramble and I left the way we came in. I almost took a second to speak with Hester and figure out what her deal was, but I was too pissed to be polite at the moment and, if I'd learned anything, it was that it was always best to start from a polite standpoint with creatures I didn't understand than to go in on the offense.

Okay, I know, I know. I didn't always abide by that piece of wisdom. What could I say? I let my actions be guided by my emotions sometimes.

So sue me.

Chapter Twelve

I was quiet during the drive to the local grocery store and was happy to blow off some steam on the way back to the cabin by shouting at the people in front of us driving so slowly. I would have stopped at the lawyer's house to plead Hyssop's case, but I didn't think he'd be home since it was the middle of a weekday.

Besides, with the mood I was in, I would have just shoved him against a wall and screamed in his face.

I don't think you'd be able to do that right now, Vânători. We are too weak. Perhaps with a little vampire blood...

I ignored the rest of what she said and focused on the road. When I finally pulled into the driveway what felt like an eternity later, I saw Hyssop sitting on the stairs waiting for us.

As soon as we pulled in, he leapt off the stairs and came hurrying over to us.

"It's about damn time you got back! I've been waiting here all morning! Do you know who runs this area?"

Shit. Even the gnome knew about Pamola? Of course he did.

"Yup. It's the great and powerful Pamola. Spirit of the mountain or whatever."

"Shhh!" The gnome said, finger to his lips. "What is wrong with you?" He whispered. "Do you want to get whisked away and forced to live in his mountain? That's what he does, you know. And I don't think you want that."

Well, that was new information. Good to know.

I sighed. "What do you want, Hyssop?"

He suddenly looked like a kicked puppy. "You said to let you know when I found a new place to call home. Did you forget about me already?"

"No, I didn't forget." I grabbed the grocery bag from the back of the car. I had really been hoping for a little nap when we got home, but it didn't look like that was going to happen. "Let's go inside, and you can tell me about the site for your garden."

And maybe more of what you know about Pamola, I added silently.

Do you really think he *will have more information to add?* The vitriol Artemis held for what she considered "lower" supernatural creatures was kind of astounding.

I'm not sure if you've noticed, but you're a deity trapped in a necklace and must depend upon a recovering alcoholic to have any kind of connection with this world. So maybe you can just take a step back from the high-and-mighty attitude, I told her.

A spike of anger from Artemis lit up the back of my mind, but I ignored it and ushered Hyssop inside.

"Pretty sparse living," the gnome commented as we walked through the foyer and he peeked in the living room on the way to the kitchen.

"Yup. I like to keep it simple." I gestured to one of the dining table chairs, and he climbed onto it to watch me readying a pot of coffee. "Want some?" I asked him. I might not have any furniture, but I could still be a polite host.

"No, no," he waved away the offer as Ramble entered the kitchen and lay down near the doorway to listen to the conversation. "I don't drink that stuff. It's all flower nectar and slug juice for me."

I momentarily paused scooping coffee grounds into the machine, but after a second of internal debate, I decided that I didn't want to know. When that was done, I grabbed a packet of cookies courtesy of Rosalyn's gift basket and plopped it on the table before sitting down across from the gnome.

Pie, cookies, and lots of coffee. The lunch of champions.

"So? Where are your new digs gonna be at?" I asked him. He gave me a strange look, and I realized I needed to stop using slang. Like Artemis, it seemed many of the supernatural creatures didn't stay super current on human sayings. And who could blame them?

"Your new garden," I quickly amended. "You said you found a spot for it?" I shoved a cookie in my mouth while I waited for his response and tossed another to Ramble who easily snatched it from the air.

Hyssop's features brightened. "Yes. It's nowhere near as big as my old garden, but it would be my very own, and I don't think any humans are going to come along and *unmake* it," he growled.

"Good," I said rudely around chewing. "Where is it?"

"I'll have to show you. We don't put street names and labels on places the way humans do."

"Okay." I wasn't sure what else to ask him about the site he'd chosen and was afraid that I was setting him up for major disappointment, and worse, death, by leading him to try a new garden site. "We'll go right after I have some coffee." I waved to the coffee maker.

Hyssop's nose wrinkled in disgust. "Why do you smell like

a dead pixy, Vânători?" He pulled back a little from the table and looked horrified "Have you been hunting pixies?"

"What? No, of course not!" I quickly explained the situation with the couple at the camp, then asked, "Do you know anything about negotiating with pixies?" It wasn't the main question I'd intended to ask the gnome, but I figured I could use all the help I could get to prepare for the evening's upcoming negotiations.

I couldn't blame him for being relieved that I wasn't going around murdering pixies.

"Of course I know how to negotiate with pixies!" He practically chortled. Apparently finding a new garden had put him in high spirits. I had to push back that feeling of guilt again. I really hoped this plan for him worked.

"So, what do you think the idiot campers should offer the pixies?"

I wasn't sure I could forgive someone if they'd killed a member of my family. If there had been another driver who was responsible for my parent's fatal car accident, I don't think I would have been able to forgive them and certainly not as part of some weird negotiation.

"Pixies are easy," Hyssop said, scooting toward the table again as he warmed to the conversation. "You just need bright, shiny things. You're lucky it wasn't fairies. No negotiating with that lot." He shook his head. "I once had to let them destroy a beautiful patch of lupine because a little fairy boy decided to eat the flowers. It wasn't *my* fault the fairies didn't teach him lupines are poisonous. But nooo! I had to get rid of the plant or risk the fairies burning my garden and salting the dirt."

Jeeze. I opened my mouth to comment, but a huge BOOM from outside had me leaping to my feet.

Ramble jumped to all fours and we stared at each other for a moment, listening to the sound of small things hitting the side of the house. We waited until the sounds died before the three of us crept to the living room to peek outside.

My mouth dropped open at the sight.

The little shed where we'd stored the deer had been totally decimated. It looked like someone had just thrown a grenade inside and shut the door. Pieces of splintered wood were littered across the yard and must have been what we'd heard hitting the side of the house.

What the hell?

"Ohhh. You've pissed off the mountain spirit," Hyssop whispered, backing slowly away from the window.

Ramble recovered more quickly than I did and started for the front door. I wasn't so sure it was a good idea to go out there, but I guess if Pamola could blow up the shed and throw a huge deer onto the porch, then he could probably kick down a door. That meant I wouldn't really be any safer inside than outside.

I followed Ramble out and around the side of the house. Hyssop decided it was safer to stay on the porch and watch us from there.

We could see the damage better once we stepped outside. Not only was the wood from the shed all over the yard, but all the tools inside it had been tossed around, too. We were lucky the damage wasn't worse. Actually, I couldn't believe the windows of the house and car had been spared. As it was, I saw a trowel had hit the car, breaking one of the little lights under the headlight. I didn't need that light, right? Maybe Donavon wouldn't even notice.

We must go, Vânători. The sense of urgency in Artemis's voice was palpable. I almost agreed with her...but I just couldn't bring myself to run away from this weird threat.

Only then did I realize what I didn't see in the yard: no deer. I scanned the area again, looking for any signs of blood or gross entrails but couldn't see any. I stomped back inside.

Yes. Good choice, Vânători. Pack lightly. We must leave at once.

"I'm not leaving," I said out loud, not caring if Hyssop heard me. I returned to the kitchen with Hyssop on my heels and took a swig of coffee before retrieving my phone from where I'd left it on the kitchen counter. I punched in the number from the sheriff's card.

"Sheriff Allen." Was the swift response when he answered after the first ring.

"Sheriff, it's Vianne." He knew my real name, might as well use it. "Did your friend come and pick up the deer from the house?"

"What? Oh, yeah. He said he did. He also said it was the biggest dear he's seen in two seasons."

"Great," I grunted. "Hold on a second."

I hit the mute button and turned to Hyssop. "If Pamola left a deer on my front porch and someone came and took the deer away, do you think that would piss him off?"

"Apparently," the gnome said.

Super.

I unmuted the phone. "For the negotiations this evening, those newlyweds need to get something to barter with," I told the sheriff. "Pixies like bright, colorful things, so they need to look for something like that."

"So, what the heck are they supposed to get? Confetti?"

"I dunno. Maybe suggest they go to a big box store and look around to see if they can find anything brightly colored that pixies would like. I gotta go. See you at dusk."

I ended the call before he could ask me more questions that I didn't have an answer to.

"What do I need to do in order to get off Pamola's shit-list?" I asked Hyssop.

Hyssop shrugged, then stopped and looked thoughtful. "Maybe give him an offering?"

"Like what?"

"I dunno. Maybe something you hold dear? Pamola is legendary for taking women and men inside his mountain and keeping them there for a year. Would you be willing to do that?"

It says a lot that I seriously considered it. I mean, if I was trapped inside a mountain and couldn't get out, didn't that mean that vampires couldn't get in? It was tempting.

"What does he do with the people he takes to his mountain?"

"The First People say he married the females and forced the men to marry his daughters."

I could only assume that by First People, Hyssop meant the Indigenous People in the area. Great. So, either suffer this mountain deity's wrath or have sex with him. Not great choices.

You do have a third option, Artemis said dryly.

For the first time, I actually considered her suggestion to run away. It wouldn't be so bad, would it? I mean, who would blame me?

I looked at Hyssop, who only moments ago had expressed such high hopes for doing something none of his other people had ever tried before. I couldn't just abandon him in the middle of that. He needed my help. And so did the dumb glampers if they were going to negotiate with the pixies.

I sighed and accepted the idea that I might very well end up trapped in a mountain with an amorous mountain spirit.

Maybe I could just move back to the motel? After all, Pamola hadn't bothered me before I'd moved to the cabin. I couldn't think of anything I could use in bargaining with a mountain spirit, so I decided that distracting myself and getting away from the cabin was the next best idea.

"Let's go check out your new place," I said and grabbed the car keys. I hoped we didn't run into Donavon on the way there. I really didn't need him yelling at me for busting a light on Samuel's old car.

Of course, I would yell right back at him since I was pretty sure he must know about Pamola, too. He'd known I was right in the Power's path out in this cabin but hadn't said anything.

Yeah. Donavon, Rosalyn, and I needed to have a little chat soon.

* * *

Hyssop's new place was not quite what I'd expected.

We stood behind a small building that housed the local library. A brass placard welcomed guests to the library garden and thanked Mr. and Mrs. Sweeney (whoever they were) for granting the small piece of land to the library in 1959. Looking around, I wondered if that was also the same year anyone had bothered to upkeep the space.

Though I knew not much would be growing right now, I didn't think that explained the sad state of the garden. There was evidence of overgrowth and weeds everywhere I looked. Some type of ivy, now dormant, had left its mark up the side of the library's brick exterior. I hoped it wasn't poison ivy. A small bench that was supposed to be an inviting space for library patrons to sit and read looked like it now stood as a spider kingdom. It was honestly hard to tell it was a bench since it was partially covered by some kind of overgrown bush. What had once been a quaint cobblestone walkway now looked more like broken teeth going every which way.

I didn't think many people would be patronizing this garden in its current state, but I worried what would happen if Hyssop took it over.

"Well, it definitely needs your help," I told the gnome, "but isn't it a little public for you? I mean, aren't you afraid that someone will notice you if you make it beautiful and people start using it again?"

As I spoke, Ramble shoved his nose into the bush near the bench and startled a mouse into a mad dash for safety. Not that the hellhound bothered to chase it. He just watched it in a disinterested way before continuing his inspection of the garden.

"It is a risk, Vânători, and that's why no one else has claimed this spot. But," he held up a finger, "I hear that one of the book-people inside is a witch. She might be willing to help me if I get in a tight spot." He shrugged. "I've a sister, Posy, who shares land with a witch. They've a bargain that Posy can do what she likes with the rest of the land as long as she grows and tends to all the witch's herbs. Gnomes grow the most powerful and potent herbs, you know. My sister is a smart one." He gave me a proud smile.

I couldn't disagree. Having a witch on site would be useful if Hyssop was ever spotted by a human again. Really, all the witch would have to do is gaslight the human into thinking it was just a trick of their eyes. And if Hyssop appeared in a different spot in the garden the next day, then the witch could just say she moved him.

Now we just had to talk to the witch. Well, I guess *I* had to talk to the witch.

Checking the time against the library's posted hours, I realized I only had about an hour to convince the witch to let Hyssop stay.

Actually...

Can you tell if the witch is even inside? I asked Artemis. No reason to bother going in if the witch-librarian wasn't around.

She is inside, Vânători, Artemis confirmed, but something in her voice—a note of mischievous glee—made me hesitate. She clearly knew something I didn't and wasn't willing to share.

Fine. I could handle the witch on my own.

Leaving Ramble and Hyssop to continue exploring the garden, I walked around front and went inside. The building was kind of cozy. I could almost imagine myself coming here to pick up books or maybe grabbing a magazine and curling up in one of the faux leather chairs I spotted in a reading nook...

You're not staying here forever, Vânători.

I withheld a sigh and headed toward the empty circulation desk. Artemis was right. I didn't need to get attached to the small town's library. I'd just be moving on to another town down the road. Hell, I might have to skip town sooner than expected depending on how things went with Pamola.

There was some shuffling in a backroom behind the front desk before the witch-librarian emerged with a rolling cart of books. Suddenly, I knew exactly why Artemis had been so smugly gleeful earlier.

The witch behind the desk had a black cast on her arm and was trying to maneuver a stack of books from the rolling cart to the front counter. Sensing my presence, she looked up and couldn't keep the grimace off her face.

Right back atcha, Willomena.

I was not a fan of this witch and she certainly had made it clear while I was investigating the murders that she was no fan of mine, either. It didn't help that I was also still pissed at her coven leader, Rosalyn, for knowingly putting me in Pamola's path by having me stay in the cabin.

Just keep it professional, I told myself.

"Hi Willomena. How's the arm?"

That was professional, right?

"It's fine." She glared at me for a second as if I was the one responsible for the break when, in reality it was the giant murder-beast-dog that had attacked her. "To what do I owe the pleasure of the great Vânători's visit? You're not a resident, so it's not like you're here to check out books."

I would have been more upset at being denied library access, but honestly, if it meant I had to deal with Willomena every time I visited the library, it was worth it to miss out on borrowing books.

"Actually, I'm here on business." I maintained a neutral smile. "I have a client from the supernatural community who wishes to move into the garden out back. He's a gnome by the name of Hyssop who needs a new place to call home. He could update the garden a bit and then would maintain it year-round."

The witch continued moving books from the cart to the counter, but I could tell that I had her attention. "A gnome? Why would a gnome want to move out there? I thought they picked a garden at adolescence and moved in for life? Unless this gnome is a teenager picking his first garden?"

"They do usually pick a garden for life," I confirmed, slightly surprised at her knowledge on gnomes, "but Hyssop lost his first garden when the house it's attached to changed hands and the owner decided to remove his garden."

She stopped working and glared at me. "I see. So, you're just gonna take the human's side and make the gnome move, is that it?"

I tried not to flinch. Her accusation reflected my own guilty thoughts a little too well. "What would you suggest I do?" I asked a little defensively.

"You could stand up to the human for starters."

"Sure. I'll just go tell him he has to rip out the new backyard he just installed, then force him to change it back into a garden and let Hyssop live there in peaceful harmony. Yeah, right. Come on, Willomena."

"Then scare the homeowner off."

"And then what would happen with the next people who

moved in?" I shook my head. "It's not that simple. We're going to try and rehome Hyssop by finding a new garden." I wasn't sure if the witch knew how gnome magic worked, so I left out the part of moving some of Hyssop's old garden dirt to the library's garden.

"So why are you telling me?" She asked. "Sounds like you've already made up your mind to do it. You don't need *my* permission. Especially since you're clearly just going to do whatever you want in this town."

I didn't take the bait. Honestly, I had too many other things to do today than to waste time arguing with Willomena. "I'm *asking* because it would be good for Hyssop to have an ally here in the library in case someone spots him out there." Before coming inside, I'd asked Hyssop what kind of arrangement he would be open to when it came to negotiating with the witch. It seemed like the right time to bring up his offer. "He says that he'll grow an herb garden out back just for you if you're willing to occasionally help him if gets spotted by humans."

This made the witch pause, so I laid it on a little thicker.

"Gnomes are well-known for being able to grow the most potent herbs. You could have access to those kinds of ingredients without having to lift a finger to grow them, all for the price of promising to assist Hyssop should he run into problems with any humans who might notice him."

She stared at me for a moment. "What sort of help? I won't use magic to make humans forget—"

I waved away her concern. "You could just tell them you're sure they're seeing things. Or maybe that what they saw was just an animal or something. I don't think you'd ever have to use magic." *If you used your brain*, I mentally added.

She watched me for another moment before saying, "I'll think about it." Then she returned to moving the books with her one good arm. If she had been anyone else, I would have helped her, but I'd rather chew glass than kiss up to Willomena.

"It's kind of a time sensitive issue," I said, not willing to back down. "I'd actually like to move him in today if possible."

"Why the rush?" She picked up a scanner gun and began the process of scanning each book into the system.

Rather than explain how Hyssop's magic worked, I asked, "Would you want to keep couch surfing at other people's houses or get a place of your own?

It wasn't the best argument, but I couldn't think of anything better without giving away gnome secrets.

She paused in her task and used the scanner gun to punctuate her sentence by pointing it at me. "Fine. But only in return for the herb garden. And I get to use the space every full moon for witch work."

"I'll have to ask him about that last part. Hold on."

Before I could turn to go outside, she said, "Just bring him inside. I might as well get to know him."

I couldn't argue with that.

When I returned to the garden and explained Willomena's demand, the gnome hesitated.

"Will her witch work hurt my flowers and plants?"

"I have no idea, Hyssop." I tried not to get annoyed at being the go-between. "She said to come inside so you could negotiate directly. Let's go in. You can meet her and see if an agreement with her is the right choice. And," I added as a good idea hit me, "we'll get the agreement in writing. That way, if she ever goes back on her word, you'll have something to back up what you two agreed on."

"Human laws don't apply to the likes of me, Vânători."

"True. But that's why you have me." I smiled. "If we have something in writing, then the other people in the supernatural community can hold her accountable if she tries anything funny in the future."

He returned my smile before we headed inside.

* * *

HYSSOP AND I MANAGED TO NAIL OUT A PRETTY GOOD agreement with Willomena. We even worked in a clause for him to have access to library materials as long as they were always returned without damage. She reassured him that her magic wouldn't harm his plants, and then I wandered off to peruse the new arrivals section of books while they discussed the intersection between magic and gardening.

This could be beneficial information to learn, Artemis chastised.

"Are we planning on becoming magical gardeners?"

You know what I mean, Vânâtori. Any information on magic could be beneficial.

"I thought you knew everything about magic already?"

No one knows everything *about magic. It is a dynamic thing that is always ever-changing.*

I decided that it was better to just pretend to listen to the magic discussion than continue to argue with Artemis. I wandered back over and caught some of their conversation.

"I'll need to burn out some of the weeds before the growing season starts," Hyssop was saying. "When would be a good time that there won't be a lot of humans around?"

"We're closed on Mondays. Probably doing it then in the middle of the day would be best. Otherwise people might notice the flames at night...actually, we have a witch in our coven who can do that for you without creating much smoke." Willomena's eyes slid over to me, "You've met her, Vânâtori. She helped you lay Cassandra to rest."

Willomena's tone shifted a little as she mentioned the

murdered coven member. Clearly, she missed her friend and still mourned her. It made me dislike Willomena a little less.

Then I realized who she was talking about. "Alexis? The young red-headed witch?"

Willomena nodded.

"But I thought she was missing? Did she finally turn up?"

The witch looked surprised, "Missing? Not that I know of."

I shared the conversation I'd had with Rosalyn about Alexis's disappearance, then watched as Willomena pulled out her phone and tried to call her coven leader. No answer.

"Maybe she's busy with the store," Willomena said, though the doubt in her voice suggested otherwise.

I shook my head. "We drove past there a few minutes ago, and it looked closed." It was true. Though I hadn't intended on stopping even if it had been open, Rosalyn's store was on the way to the library, and I'd driven by only to find the place looking empty and the closed sign in the window.

The witch's face scrunched in concern. She still had the phone pressed to her ear and left a quick message for Rosalyn to call her when she had a chance. When she hung up, the look of worry stayed on her face. Somehow, I felt responsible for putting it there.

"Do you want me to swing by her house? It's not far from my next stop."

After a moment's thought, Willomena shook her head. "This is coven business, Vânâtori. We'll handle it."

Because that went so well last time, I thought but didn't say. Instead, I shrugged, said, "Okay," and turned to Hyssop. "If we want to get *your things* today and bring them back over here, then we need to get a move on. I have to be somewhere at six." I hoped the gnome understood that I was talking about the dirt from his old garden.

Thankfully, Hyssop got it. I took Willomena's phone

number in case Hyssop needed to contact her while he was with me, and we left for Hyssop's old place. I was glad I'd thought to grab the box of garbage bags before we'd left the cabin. Might as well start keeping them in the trunk. You never knew what kind of messes you might need contractor-strength garbage bags for.

I parked in front of Hyssop's old place rather than down the street since I didn't see the lawyer's car out front. Maybe we could just get in and out with the dirt without being noticed.

As we exited the car and walked toward the garden gate, I realized too late that I should have brought the shovel from the cabin. Looked like I was going to get my hands dirty today. At least it was just dirt and not deer blood this time. I'd take my wins where I could get them.

I felt super conspicuous as we crossed the lawn, and I quickly lifted the latch on the gate to let us into the backyard. If we just kept pretending that we belonged there, surely no one would know we weren't supposed to be there, right?

The feeling of being watched crept over me as we walked toward the pile of dirt at the back end of the yard. I looked up to find the creepy lady next door watching us again. What was her name? Hester?

I smiled and waved at Hester where she looked down at us from the same upstairs window as before. Did she just watch this backyard all the time? Weird.

She didn't wave back, choosing instead to completely ignore me. Whatever. I wasn't there to make friends. We were here to get the dirt and get out.

When I reached the dirt pile, I realized our mistake.

"Shit, Hyssop. It's frozen solid." I kicked at the side of the dirt pile to emphasize the problem.

"Of course it's frozen solid. Don't you know anything about dirt?

Apparently not. "How are we going to move it if it's frozen?"

"Didn't you bring the shovel from your place?" He asked.

He knew damn well I hadn't brought the shovel. He'd been with me when we left the cabin, and I hadn't loaded the shovel into the trunk. Though to be fair, I had to admit I had picked up the shovel and leaned it against the side of the porch so I wouldn't accidentally drive over it if I came back to the cabin in the dark. It was possible he thought I'd brought it with us.

I must have let some of my dark thoughts show in my expression because Hyssop suddenly lost his attitude. "There's a shovel in the desecrating-human's tool shed over there." The gnome pointed near the house where a perfect little red shed sat next to the backdoor.

I dropped the box of garbage bags, did an about-face, and made a beeline for the shed. Of course, just my luck, it had a padlock on it. Shit.

Luckily, I'd learned a thing or two from my time spent in jail. I could pick a lock with the right tools. That, combined with my experience of getting cuffed by the deputy and not being able to get away before he almost murdered me had taught me to always keep some kind of lock picking tool on my person at all times.

I pulled two bobby pins from an inner pocket of my jacket. A quick glance told me that peeping-Hester was still watching. I'd have to trust that she wouldn't call the cops on us.

I hope you enjoy the show, lady, I thought and set to work picking the lock.

Vânători, I worry that there is more to the woman than we know.

"Obviously," I said under my breath. "I mean, she doesn't have an aura, she can see Ramble, and she's just all around super-creepy." I was focusing too much on the padlock to really give much more of a response than that, but I could feel Artemis's annoyance edged with a wariness of Hester.

After another few moments of messing with the padlock, it finally popped open.

"Eureka," I quietly said. For some reason I felt like I needed to whisper while under Hester's watchful eye.

Hanging neatly inside the shed were an array of gardening tools. I honestly wasn't sure why the homeowner needed so many tools when he hardly even had a garden anymore. Each tool was perfectly clean, too.

I grinned. This guy was going to be really upset when he came home and found a dirty shovel locked up in his shed and most of his dirt pile gone. I could just imagine the phone call to the police to report stolen dirt. I couldn't help but smirk as I grabbed the shovel and headed back to where Hyssop was waiting for me at the dirt pile. He'd taken the opportunity to pull out a garbage bag and had it open and ready for dirt.

The moment I set to work with the shovel, I knew this was going to be a long afternoon. The metal blade barely made a dent in the frozen mound. I spent another half-an-hour chipping away at the dirt while Hyssop worked on the mound with a trowel he'd swiped from the shed. All that work earned us only about five pounds of dirt.

I paused, out of breath. This was ridiculous. At this rate, we'd be here well into the night which we couldn't do because I had plans for negotiating with the pixy clan, and I was sure the homeowner would be home from his law office before then.

"We need to work smarter, not harder," I murmured then looked around.

Ramble lay on the pristine wooden deck, soaking in the

sun. Clearly, he felt his paws were too delicate for this kind of work.

"Hey Ramble!" I pitched my voice so it wouldn't carry too far. I'd gotten over the whispering thing at this point. It was hard to stay cautious even under Hester's watchful eye when you were hacking away at frozen dirt.

The hellhound opened one eye and looked at me in question.

"Wanna light this thing up?" I pointed to the dirt.

"No!" Hyssop cried, running in front of the pile as if to protect it from Ramble who was more than ten feet away. "You can't let the hellhound breathe fire on it! He'll kill all the good stuff in it!"

I blew out an exasperated sigh. "Fine." We set back to work on the mound and this time the shoveling seemed to go a little faster. Maybe it was because we'd finally broken through the crust of frozen dirt on the top. Or maybe it was because the sun had finally hit an angle where it was warming up the dirt. Either way, the stuff underneath was much easier to shovel.

We filled a bag halfway full, and I switched to filling a new bag after realizing I wouldn't be able to haul anything heavier than that. The second bag went much faster, and we were starting a third bag when I heard the distinct sound of a car door slamming out front.

A quick glance at my phone told me we were out of time. It was after four now. I thought we'd have more time before the lawyer called it quits for the day. Weren't lawyers supposed to work crazy long hours or something?

"I think the owner's home, Hyssop. We gotta go." I said and dropped the shovel where it was. So much for putting it away with dirt on it. Ah well.

I twisted the third garbage bag closed and shoved it toward Hyssop since it was the lightest of the three bags.

"Ramble," I whispered and waved him to come with us. He ignored me and walked right up to the glass back door. A second later, I realized he was acting as a lookout.

That left me to haul the other two garbage bags of dirt.

Have you ever tried to haul bags of dirt before? It's not the same as lifting a sealed bag of dirt from a lawn store. With those, you could lift them up on a shoulder or carry them two-handed at chest height. With these, I had to grab them by the top of the bag and just drag them across the ground. I didn't want to drag them through the jagged white rocks since I figured doing so would easily rip a hole in the plastic, so instead I dragged them down the winding little wooden pathway. At one point where the path narrowed, I had to put one bag in front of me and the other behind me, which meant lifting the front bag, walking two or three steps while dragging the one behind, then dropping the front bag before starting again.

It was slow going.

A quiet whuff from Ramble sent me scrambling off the end of the pathway and onto the lawn just as the backdoor opened and the lawyer stepped out.

There was a moment frozen in time in which he spotted us, and his brain just didn't seem to compute what he was looking at.

"Hey!" He finally shouted in surprise. He wore black dress pants and a light blue, long sleeve button-up shirt under what I could only guess was a really expensive wool jacket.

Hyssop had reached the garden gate, but I'd closed it behind us earlier. With the latch at the top of the tall gate, Ramble and Hyssop had to wait for me to open it.

Shit! I should have left the gate open!

You must start thinking ahead, Vânători. A mistake like this with the vampires might be the difference between living and dying.

"Thanks a lot, Artemis," I puffed as I dragged the bags

across the grass behind me in a sort of fast shuffle-walk. "Super helpful right now."

The man disappeared back inside. I wondered if he'd retreated to call the cops or run through the house and stop us out front. I didn't have time to think about it. I was almost to the gate!

"Stop! Thieves!" The lawyer re-emerged from the house and ran at us. In front of me, Hyssop let go of his bag and put his hands in the air.

Uh oh.

I stopped my bag-draggin' shuffle and turned to face the lawyer...who was pointing a gun at me.

Shit, both Artemis and I said mentally in unison.

Chapter Thirteen

I immediately put my hands in the air. At least we hadn't made it to the front yard where everyone could watch the show. Nope. Instead, we were just providing entertainment for Hester.

"You again!" The lawyer glared at the gnome. "Why can't you just leave me alone?!"

"I would love to, puffball-brains, but as told you before, I need my garden to live!" Hyssop's voice started out low but gained in pitch as he finished. "You ripped it out, and now I have to find a new place to live!"

"You never lived here! This house was vacant when I bought it, and you showed up a few weeks ago and started ruining *my* backyard."

"Ruining *your* backyard, huh?" Hyssop squinted at the lawyer and took a step forward. "I'll show you—"

"Stay where you are and keep your hands in the air where I can see them." The lawyer sounded brave, but I could see that the tip of the gun was shaking a little. It didn't mean he wouldn't shoot me. In fact, if he was nervous and hadn't used a gun before, it seemed more likely that he would shoot me by accident.

"Whoa. Hold on. We're not here to hurt anyone," I quickly reassured him. "We're just here to get some dirt from his old garden so he can use it to start the new garden at a different place." I hooked a thumb toward Hyssop as I spoke but kept my hands in the air at shoulder height.

"It was never his garden!" The man said in exasperation. "I bought the house from the son of the previous owner when she died. It's *my* house. It's *my* garden. Now stop harassing me, or I'll have to call the police."

Actually, I didn't think calling the police would be such a bad idea. In this town, the only law was the sheriff. And with me consulting for the sheriff, he'd probably listen to what we had to say and might even side with Hyssop.

Perhaps I should have enlightened the sheriff about my afternoon plans of stealing dirt. Then again, maybe that wouldn't have been such a good idea. If the sheriff thought it was a bad plan, I wouldn't be able to ask for forgiveness like I could if he was called to the scene now.

"Go ahead and call them. I'm a consultant with the local law enforcement," I said, thinking quickly. "I thought we'd try to do this the easy way and leave the law out of this—"

"You can't leave the law out of things," he interrupted. "The law is *everything*."

I suppressed a groan. Lawyers.

After shoveling all afternoon then dragging the bags, my arms were starting to get tired and shaky from being held in the air for so long. I started to lower them, but the lawyer jerked the nose of the gun at me.

"Keep your hands up, thief!"

The combination of hunger and exhaustion overruled my sense of self-preservation.

"Do you really want to shoot us with a witness watching?" Without any sudden movements, I tilted my head toward Hester where she still watched us from the upstairs window next door.

"Imagine the headline: Lawyer shoots young, unarmed woman for removing dirt from his yard."

"You mean stealing dirt," he corrected.

"That's not what we talked about yesterday," I suddenly said as I struck on an idea.

"What?"

"Remember, I visited your house yesterday?" I asked and the lawyer looked confused for a moment.

"Yes, but you never asked about taking dirt..."

"Sure we did. Or at least," I leaned forward a little and lowered my voice, "That's what my friend from yesterday will tell people if you shoot me." I had no way to get my story straight with Donavon to have him back up my lie, but it didn't matter. The lawyer didn't know that. "And your neighbor up there will also tell the sheriff that we came here yesterday," I added.

The lawyer stared at me with his mouth open for a minute, clearly not sure what to do next.

I sighed. What the hell. Let's see if the truth had any effect on this guy.

"Look, here's the real deal. That guy over there?" I pointed to Hyssop. "He's a gnome."

The lawyer shot a look at Hyssop then back to me though he kept his gun trained on me the whole time. Of course, he didn't know that Ramble was presently standing a few feet from him, listening and staring at the gun in his hand. I couldn't tell if the hellhound was calculating whether he could leap and knock the gun away before the lawyer could shoot me, or if he was thinking about breathing fire at the lawyer. Hopefully he'd give me a second to fix this situation before he acted.

"Yeah, a real gnome." I nodded. "They exist. And the thing is, he actually lived here first. In fact, he's been living in this spot for over one-hundred years. But you came in and tore up his garden, ripped out his plants, and then covered up most of the yard with stones and stuff. And while *I* think it looks great, it doesn't provide enough plants for Hyssop to live off of." I paused watching the lawyer's face for any indication that he believed me.

This guy must have been a damn good lawyer because he sure did have a great poker face.

"Gnomes aren't real. You're just some crazy lady with a dwarf or a little person or whatever you want to be called who's trying to steal..." he trailed off.

"Steal what? Go ahead. Say it. Steal dirt? Isn't that a little crazy? Do you want to look in the bags to verify that's all we took? Go ahead. We'll step back and you can have a look-see."

The lawyer stared at me for a second, then jerked the gun over to the side, away from the garden gate. "Slowly," he cautioned.

With my hands still in the air, I moved slowly away from the garbage bags. Hyssop, after a moment's hesitation, did the same and came to stand beside me.

Keeping the gun pointed in our direction, the lawyer leaned down and used his other hand to twist one of my garbage bags open. He continually glanced from the bag back to us to ensure we weren't trying anything funny.

"What the hell?" he asked when he finally got the bag open and looked inside.

"See? I told you. It's just dirt. It doesn't mean anything to you," I explained, "but it means everything to Hyssop. It's his life. Literally. He needs some of the dirt from his old garden to be able to go on living in a new garden."

This earned me a dark look from the gnome. "Those aren't your secrets to give, Vânători."

"If you want the dirt, Hyssop, you've gotta tell this guy why you need it. Maybe he'll let you take it if he understands."

Hyssop stared at the lawyer, lips tightly sealed in a thin line.

"Hyssop," I urged, "just tell him."

After giving me a death glare, the gnome finally relented and turned his attention back to the lawyer. "What she said. I've lived on this land for well over one-hundred years. I kept my garden before the humans built the first house here. From then on, any humans who planted something in my garden found that their crops or flowers thrived."

The lawyer lowered his weapon to point at the ground. "Then how come the vegetables I planted did so badly if you were tending the garden here?"

Hyssop actually looked embarrassed and shuffled his feet a little while looking at the ground. He lowered his hands and put them behind his back.

"They woulda done okay, but I was mad... and I... I poisoned them." The gnome's voice dropped to a whisper at the end. And, were those tears in his eyes?

"I would never have done it if you'd have left me even one plant from my old garden. But you didn't! You ripped out every single calendula, dug up all the beautiful bearded irises that took me *years* to cultivate, and then you tried to get rid of me by throwing me in the trash on top of my plants!"

I flinched as the gnome's voice broke and large, crocodile tears slipped down his face.

The lawyer stared at the gnome, then looked at me. "I didn't know. I didn't know he was real. I thought he was just a stupid statue."

I slowly lowered my hands. "Look, he can't really live here anymore with the backyard like this, but if you'll just let us take this dirt to his new home, he won't bother you again."

The man looked from me to Hyssop, then nodded and moved away from the garbage bags. "Alright."

"Thank you." I didn't give him any time to change his mind. I nodded to Hyssop to grab his bag of dirt, unlatched the gate, and pushed it open before getting a grip on my bags again. Hyssop went first, then I started through, but the lawyer stopped me with a question.

"If gnomes exist, what else is out there?"

I thought maybe it was a rhetorical question but when I looked at him, he seemed to want an actual answer.

I took a breath before deciding to say, "A lot of other beings that we think are just fairy tales. It's really better not to think about it." I considered where he lived and decided to give him a little warning. "But if you're going to continue living in this town, it's likely you'll come across people who aren't quite human. You might not even realize it. Or maybe something at the back of your mind might tip you off."

The lawyer looked up at the window next door where Hester still watched, then back to me with a question in his eyes.

"I don't know what she is," I said quietly, "but it would probably be smart not to start any neighborhood spats with her. Or anyone else for that matter."

"Wait," he said in sudden realization, "were those animal attacks in town really that or something else?"

Do I tell the lawyer that the deputy he probably had met in a professional capacity at some point was actually a half-witch, hell-bent on murdering anything not human? That might be a little much for one day.

"Something else," I finally said and started dragging the bags through the open gate after Hyssop.

"Are you really working with the Sheriff's Department?" He asked as he followed me through the gate. At least he'd put his gun away.

"Actually, yes," I huffed. "I'm a consultant. For another case." Was it me or were these bags getting heavier?

The lawyer followed me all the way across his lawn, peppering me with questions about things that go bump in the night. When we reached the car, I finally dropped one of the bags and held up a hand.

"Look, I'll answer one more question if you help me lift these into the trunk."

He considered the dirty, mud-smeared bags and his own pristine clothes. He'd clearly just come from the office and hadn't had the chance to change before he'd spotted us. Or maybe he didn't bother changing out of his fancy clothes at the end of his workday because he didn't consider them fancy.

After a moment of indecision, he took off his jacket, carefully turned it inside out and folded it before laying it on the top of the car. Together, we managed to lift the bags into the trunk which dropped the back of the car down. When we finished, the sleeves and the front of his crisp blue shirt were streaked with mud.

He looked at the stains distastefully and retrieved his jacket from the roof of the car, careful to hold it away from his muddy shirt.

"Okay. One last question," I said, feeling like a genie granting wishes.

Wait, did genies exist?

Yes, but they are very rare. It is unlikely you will encounter them on this continent.

Good to know.

"What are *you*?" He asked bluntly.

I opened my mouth to say that I was human but that wasn't true, was it? I wasn't even sure that I could say I was *part* human because that wasn't really accurate either. As far as I knew, a human wouldn't be experiencing the kind of craving for vampire blood that I was having right at that moment. Apparently skipping lunch was a bad idea and, similar to my addiction for alcohol, it made me long for a hit of something.

I really didn't need an existential crisis right now, so I simply said, "I'm the person who keeps the peace between humans and nonhumans."

You are more than that, Vânători.

Maybe, I responded mentally, *but he only needs the Cliff Notes version.*

I ignored her sudden confusion as the lawyer asked, "So, you're like an advocate for those who don't fall into the human category?"

It was a better descriptor than anything else I'd heard. Trust a lawyer to come up with it.

"Something like that. Oh, and I also see things that other people can't. Like my four-legged friend there beside you."

Ramble gave a small growl. It was hardly scary, but it made the lawyer go very still.

"Don't worry. He won't bite. Not now that you put the gun away anyways." I shut the trunk then opened the back-door for Ramble. The lawyer watched in terrified awe as the seat cushions in the back compressed under Ramble's weight when he jumped in the car.

Hyssop got in the passenger seat and I walked around to the driver's side. "Thanks for your help. And for not shooting us." I paused. "I'm Vianne, by the way."

"What? Oh." The lawyer recovered more quickly than I thought he would. "I'm Preston Powers."

Nice alliteration. I wondered if that was his real name or if he'd taken it on to sound more impressive in court.

"Nice to meet you. Thanks for the dirt." I got in the car and we left the lawyer standing in yard as he watched us drive away.

"That was pretty close," Hyssop said a little too brightly for my taste. I couldn't tell if he was still just hopped up on adrenaline or if he'd actually enjoyed the close encounter.

I grunted in agreement, not really trusting myself with real conversation right now. My caffeine had definitely worn off because I was tired. And hungry. And angry at the idiot lawyer for pulling a gun on us. Yeah, it was a dangerous trifecta of emotions for someone with an addiction.

We drove to the library in silence. It took longer to unload the dirt than it had to load it since we didn't have Preston's help. When we'd finally dragged the bags down the path and behind the library, it was pushing five o'clock.

I said a hasty goodbye to Hyssop, telling him to let me know if the new garden worked for him, and then Ramble and I took off. I needed a shower in a bad way if I was going to meet up with the glampers and the sheriff for a negotiation with the pixies.

On the drive back to the cabin, I realized I still hadn't heard from Rosalyn. Was she avoiding me now that I knew she'd sent me to the cabin to be tested by Pamola? Judging by the pieces of splintered woodshed that still littered the yard when we pulled into the driveway, I didn't think I was passing the test.

I tried calling her again on the way to the cabin, but the call went straight to her voicemail. I didn't bother leaving a message because I wasn't sure how to broach the subject of her putting me directly in Pamola's path. I mean, what would I say? Thanks for letting me stay in a cabin on the outskirts of a mountain god's territory and oh, by the way, he seems to have noticed me?

Maybe I could swing by her place tomorrow and just talk to her in person.

Happily, there were no new surprises when we got back to the cabin. I hurried inside and jumped in the shower. Ramble, who hadn't done much to help with dragging or loading the bags of dirt, was still as clean as when we'd left the cabin earlier.

Whatever.

After showering, I braided my hair, threw on a clean shirt, brushed off as much dirt as I could from my pants, and made a mental note that when I got paid by the sheriff for helping with the pixy negotiations, that I'd need to buy a few more clothes. Especially now that I had an actual washer and dryer on site. It was fine to wear jeans a few times without washing them, but it would be nice to have some clean options.

"Do we need anything for the negotiations, Artemis?"

You will need something to show that you would like to initiate negotiations. A white flag typically signals this.

Huh. I didn't exactly carry white flags around with me. I started going through kitchen cupboards and found a white and blue striped kitchen towel. "Will this do?"

I suppose…but you must attach it to a pole.

There wasn't anything inside that resembled a pole, so I stepped outside and walked the yard, scanning the debris field. After a few minutes of searching, I found a long enough piece of wood that would make for a slap-dash flagpole.

I suppose that will do, Artemis said.

I gritted my teeth against her snobbery and tied the towel to the end of the pole while sitting at the kitchen table. I debated whether or not I should take my gun to this meet. It didn't seem like a great idea since the sheriff would be there, but we would be returning to the cabin in the dark, and I didn't want to chance another encounter with Pamola without some kind of weapon. In the end, I decided to take my small throwing knife. I couldn't sink that thing into the broad side of a barn, but at least it was something. And hey, it had worked against the beast, right?

As an afterthought, I grabbed a box of crackers from the

kitchen cupboard before we left, and together, Ramble and I finished the box long before we got back to the campsite.

The couple's truck must have been towed to a mechanic shop because it was gone when we pulled in next to the sheriff's car. Their tent had been taken down and packed away as well.

I grabbed my make-shift flag from the passenger seat and the tissue box coffin from the glove compartment where I'd kept it all day. It seemed odd that I'd been riding around with the pixy's body all day and had only thought of it a few times. I wasn't sure if it was because I was becoming numb to random death or if it was because I was as biased as Lisa was about nonhuman creatures.

I hoped it wasn't the latter, but what did it say about my life that the better option here was to just be numb to the idea of others dying around me?

"Alright, let's see how this goes," I told Ramble before we got out to meet the sheriff and the two idiot glampers.

"Vianne," the sheriff said with a nod as we approached.

"Hey Sheriff."

"How long do you think we'll have to wait?" Lisa asked.

I didn't hear any impatience in her voice, just curiosity, so I decided to answer her.

"I'm not sure." I knelt and set the coffin down on the ground, then used both hands to drive the flagpole into the ground. "It's possible they might not come at all. We just have to wait and see."

The sun slowly began to sink behind the mountains, creating one of the most beautiful sunsets I'd ever seen. It started out orange, then grew into a deep crimson before fading to pink.

Of course, the crimson just reminded me of blood. I could almost taste the metallic, salty copper on my tongue...

I worry that your cravings are not normal, Vânători.

No shit they aren't normal, I told her, trying to reign in the deep need for just a little blood.

Neither of us mentioned that it didn't matter since I'd have to give in to that need eventually if I wanted to maintain Artemis's power within me. It was the only way I'd survive the vampires and keep Morvalden out of my dreams.

Derek and Lisa sat on one of the flat rocks close to the water, leaving the sheriff and me standing near the flagpole.

"I got a call about you today," the sheriff said quietly so the out-of-towners wouldn't hear.

Shit. What now?

"Oh?"

"New guy in town, a lawyer, called to verify that you were acting as a consultant for the Sheriff's Department."

"Wow, he sure didn't waste any time." I shook my head but kept my eyes on the tree line watching for any movement that might be pixies. I'd left the coffin tissue box on the ground so the pixies would be able to see it. I hoped they understood that we were trying to return the body to them.

When the sheriff didn't say anything else, my curiosity got the better of me. I glanced over and couldn't help but ask, "What did you tell him?"

He shrugged one shoulder. "The truth. That you're consulting on an unusual case."

I sighed. "Preston—the lawyer—he knows about the things that go bump in the night now. I'm not sure he entirely believes in them, but..." It was my turn to shrug this time.

The sheriff gave me a sideways look. "Did you really steal dirt from his garden?"

"Technically, it's Hyssop's dirt," I said, then had to explain the whole mess to him.

The sheriff's amused grin was certainly not the way I expected him to react to the news that gnomes existed in his town.

He shook his head. "Sounds like you've had quite the day."

"That's not even the crazy part. Wait 'til you hear about the shed at the cabin exploding."

The sheriff turned to me with a serious question on his face but a flitting movement near the wood line distracted me.

"Look!" I quietly said and nodded to the tree line before remembering that he probably couldn't see the pixies approaching. "I think we have company," I whispered, afraid any loud noises or quick movements would scare them off.

"Here they come!" Lisa exclaimed, leaping up from the rock and rushing over to us. "They're coming!"

I turned and gave her a dark look. "Yes. We know." I probably should have cut her more slack. After all, it wasn't every day that you got to see pixies in their brightly colored clothes flitting around. They moved so swiftly that they were basically just blurry balls of color flying around. It was enough to make anyone feel a little lift of excitement.

Though the sheriff kept trying to see the pixies, he stayed rooted to the spot, not panicking that he couldn't see a group of supernatural beings heading our way. I was impressed since I was pretty sure I'd respond more like Derek, frantically looking around me for attacking pixies.

There must have been at least twenty or more pixies. When they reached the campsite, they swirled around our little group in a vortex that got smaller and smaller until, just before they would have touched us (and I think one of them did rake Derek with a sword because he cried out and clamped a hand to his cheek), they flew straight up into the air, then down like a group of choreographed starlings all following some unseen signal.

They finally landed in various spots around the tissue-box coffin. Now that they'd stopped moving, I could make out their almost cherubic facial features which were set in matching scowls at our little group.

"Uh, guys?"

I looked back to find that one of the pixies had landed on Derek's shoulder and was poking her sword into his neck. Unlike the rest of her colorfully garbed brethren, this pixie wore a black shirt with matching pants.

A quick glance at the other pixies showed me that they also all had small but sharp weapons.

It looked like this was going to be an interesting negotiation.

Super.

Chapter Fourteen

✥

O ne of the pixies, dressed in a bright red shirt and
yellow skirt, stepped forward from where she
stood near the tissue box coffin. She wore a bright
orange flower like a hat and held herself with poise as she
addressed me. I suddenly realized the flower was a crown, not
a hat, and this must be their leader.

Not just a leader, Vânători. She is their Queen.

"Vânători. These people captured and murdered our kinsman, Raindrop." Her voice sounded exactly like a human
woman's and wasn't high and tinny as I expected. "We seek
justice for his death."

Her speech felt very formal, and I struggled with how to
respond while still maintaining that same formal tone.

I inclined my head to show deference since Artemis said
she was a queen. "You are right to seek justice, though these
people did not realize their error when they captured your
kinsman. His death was an accident—not purposeful—and
they wish to make amends if they may, Queen..." I let my
voice trail off so that she could fill in her name for me.

She gave the truly tiniest of smiles as she responded, "I am Queen Brightstorm of the Cinders pixy clan."

"I'm sorry we must meet under these circumstances." I gestured to the box on the ground. "We wish to return Raindrop's body to his clan, and the humans would like to make an offering to the Cinder clan."

The idea of replacing the pixy with some random human goods sounded hollow to my ears. It seemed wrong, but their ways were not mine so who was I to judge?

Queen Brightstorm's eyes flashed as she looked down at the box. With a quick movement, she directed a handful of her followers to whisk the box away. When Raindrop's body was gone, she looked back to me, then beyond me to Lisa and Derek.

"What have they brought as an offering, Vânători?" Though she addressed me, she continued to stare daggers at the couple behind me.

I looked back at Lisa, waiting for her answer. She was intently watching the Queen while the sheriff and Derek didn't give any indication that they'd heard the queen's question. Maybe they weren't hearing any of this other than my side of the conversation. Ramble sat a few feet away from the sheriff, watching the exchange with interest.

"Lisa," I said, breaking the woman out of her intense stare. "What did you bring to offer to the pixies?"

"Oh!" She opened her designer purse and pulled out a plastic bag full of something that clinked together. As she moved, all the pixies took up fighting stances as if they expected she might be drawing a weapon. Derek made a surprised sound as the pixy on his shoulder poked him harder with her sword. Lisa, totally oblivious to her and her husband's danger, knelt to place the plastic bag on the ground. She opened it wide so that the pixies could see the brightly colored jewelry and bottles inside.

"You bought them nail polish?" I asked incredulously.

"And jewelry!" She said defensively, "If you had a brighter idea, it would have been great to hear it instead of 'find something brightly colored.' Well," she pointed at the vibrant variety of nail polish on the ground, "these are bright and," she added, realizing that the queen was closely watching our exchange, "they can use it to add more color to their ensemble."

Do you know those moments when you just want to facepalm so hard, but you can't because people are watching? This was one of those moments.

The queen stared at me, waiting for my reaction. Or maybe my explanation of the gift.

You are the negotiator, Vânători. The queen cannot talk directly to the humans. She must go through you, and the humans must do the same to convey their gift.

Awesome.

"Queen Brightstorm, the humans make you an offering of jewels and paints," I said, trying not to feel like I was one of the damn pilgrims negotiating a terrible deal with Indigenous People whilst screwing them over. This was a really bad trade no matter how you looked at it.

The queen's lip curled in distaste. "What would pixies need with human baubles and paints?"

Good question. Telling her that she could paint her nails or wear one of the rings like a belt was ridiculously demeaning. As in, "Oh, we killed one of your people? Here are some pretty things to make it go away."

Nope. I couldn't do it.

"This is only one part of what the humans offer, Queen Brightstorm." Very slowly so as not to cause alarm, I stepped a little to the side so that I could see both the queen and Lisa at the same time.

Lisa wore a confused expression. Clearly, she'd expected

that she and her husband would be able to fob off any responsibility for the death of another being. I just couldn't let that happen. If I was going to do this job of acting as the go-between, then humans needed to be held accountable for their actions just as those from the supernatural community would be had this been a human death.

But I was also flying by the seat of my pants here.

Are there any offerings that are customary for something like this, Artemis? I silently asked.

They could offer their first-born child.

That's not an option. How about a suggestion that's actually helpful?

She sighed and quickly explained another offer.

Actually, that might work, I said after a moment of thought.

"Well, Vânători?" The queen said. Her hands had gone to her hips which only served to remind me of the sword dangling in the sheath at her side.

"Queen Brightstorm, the humans also agree to owe a favor to the Cinders clan." As I spoke, I glanced at Lisa to gauge her reaction. When she opened her mouth to protest, I raised an eyebrow and added, mostly to Lisa, "It is a small price for the life that was lost here."

The Queen looked thoughtful as she gazed down at the bottles of fingernail polish and then back up at Lisa and Derek. After a moment of consideration, she proclaimed, "We accept these gifts and the favor from the humans and will consider their debt paid." She paused, then looked from me to Lisa. "It is not every day that one meets a human who can see our kind. We should not waste such a gift. We call on you to fulfill your favor now."

Shit. I should have added certain limitations to the favor. I realized too late that they could easily ask for Lisa's first-born child or something equally unacceptable which would cause the humans to renege on the agreement.

"The Cinders clan asks that the humans take my daughter, Summerstorm, and treat her as their own. Train her in the ways of the humans and help her find a life partner since they caused the death of her chosen life partner, Raindrop."

Before Lisa could protest, the pixy on Derek's shoulder let out an indignant cry and flew to stand in front of the queen. Seeing them standing near each other, the family resemblance was obvious. Both had dark brown hair, green eyes, and the same full lips under a rounded nose. The contrast of Summerstorm's black outfit, which I now realized must be mourning garb, against the queen's vibrant shirt and pants only served to highlight their physical similarities.

"How dare you, mother!" Summerstorm hissed. "I will *not* go with these bumbling humans after they murdered Raindrop!"

I mean, I couldn't blame her. I wouldn't want to be pawned off on the very people who'd murdered my fiancé. How messed up would that be?

The queen looked at Lisa, ignoring her daughter's protest. "Do you agree to this arrangement or should my clan follow you all the rest of your days, turning all that you love to cinders and ash in accordance with our clan's namesake?"

"We agree," Lisa quickly said. I wondered what Derek would think of this arrangement when Lisa explained it to him later. From their blank looks, I didn't think Derek nor the sheriff were getting a word of any of this.

The queen clapped her hands together with surprisingly loud results and said, "The agreement is settled."

As Summerstorm fumed at her mother, the other pixies swooped in to carry off the jewelry and nail polish piece by piece until only a bright red bottle of polish was left. The queen, followed by her daughter who was clearly still railing at this agreement, flew down to the remaining bottle and held her shirt up to it in comparison. The nail polish was on the neon spectrum and was a much gaudier red than her shirt.

"How could you do this, mother?" Tears coursed down Summerstorm's face.

"Oh hush. You didn't even *like* Raindrop. You were always mewling about how ridiculous he was and how you wanted to marry the pixy of your choice. Well, now is your chance. Go with my blessing and find new blood for our clan."

Summerstorm stared at her mother in horror for a moment before flying off. The queen turned to Lisa. "Return here for my daughter when you are ready to leave the human town and return to your home. She will be ready for you. She just needs time to accept her new circumstances."

And I thought *I* had it hard discovering my family's secret vampire hunting past. I couldn't imagine being sent to live with those who had murdered someone I was promised to marry. Not that it sounded like Summerstorm was very attached to Raindrop...but still.

With the show over, Ramble lay down on the sandy campsite with a groan. I'd promised him dinner right after this and was looking forward to it myself.

The queen wore a look of pure curiosity while watching Ramble. "How did you come by a one-headed hellhound, Vânători?" She'd dropped all formality now that the official negotiations were done.

"I freed him and named him," I said, suppressing the desire to shrug. One does not shrug in front of royalty, right?

The queen's mouth dropped open for a millisecond before she caught herself. "You named a hellhound...and he didn't eviscerate you?"

"He's free to do as he wishes and so far, he's decided to stick with me. I don't really have an explanation for it other than to say we watch each other's backs."

If I was being honest, it was really Ramble who watched my back. Not the other way around.

"Your dog's a hellhound?" Lisa asked, also looking at Ramble. Hearing this, the sheriff followed the woman's gaze and, realizing that Ramble must only be a few feet from him, took a nonchalant step away.

Smooth.

"He is," I told Lisa, not liking the interested tone in her voice. So much for keeping that little nugget of information from the sheriff.

"Can I pet him?"

Oh my. That was a first. Without my having to answer, Ramble got up with a huff and stalked off toward the lake. I guess Lisa got her answer. As I watched Ramble, I caught a flash of the waning light off something in the distance across the lake.

"Is someone watching us from over there?" I asked and jerked my head toward where I'd seen the flash.

Queen Brightstorm flew straight up into the air, then came back down to flutter a few feet from my face. "It's only the woman who watches."

"I mean, yes...that's what I meant when I asked if someone was watching..."

"No, Vânători. She is the woman who is *always* watching."

Okay...then it clicked. Ten bucks I knew who the woman was: Hester.

"Sheriff, I've gotta go. I'll send you an invoice." *Once I figure out how to do that,* I mentally added. To the pixie queen, I dipped my head in respect and said, "Though the circumstances were unfortunate, it was a pleasure meeting the Queen of the Cinders clan."

"And you, Vânători. I hope our paths cross again under happier circumstances."

I didn't have anything else to say to Lisa or Derek. Her

being part-witch wasn't really my problem. It seemed her gift merely allowed her to see and hear things that others couldn't. It could be a useful gift, but once they went home where there were probably a lot less supernatural beings, I didn't think it would be a huge factor in her life.

Calling Ramble, I hustled to the car. When he was in, I told him, "I think Preston Powers's neighbor Hester is over there watching us. What do you say we pop over and say hi and find out why she's following us?"

Ramble blew out an annoyed sigh from where he sat in the passenger seat.

"I know. I'm sorry. But I promise we'll get dinner right after this. I'll even splurge on bacon burgers. Okay?"

He grunted and looked pointedly at the window. I rolled it down without complaint and tugged my winter hat on. It had been a pretty nice day, but as soon as the sun began to set, you could feel the cold begin to creep in. Not that having the window open made any difference since we didn't have heat in this damn car.

A quick search on my phone told me that Hester was at the little public area that Rosalyn and I had once parked at to have a private conversation. Had that really only been last week? It felt like a lifetime ago.

It was easy to navigate over to the public area, which was good because just as I pulled in, Hester, in her blue Subaru, was about to reach the exit. I quickly pulled across the entire lane, effectively blocking the woman from leaving unless she wanted to ram me. It was a calculated risk, but hey, this wasn't my car, and I'd already broken one of the lights on it. Might as well add T-bone damage.

Moving quickly, I got out and walked around to the driver's side of Hester's car. She looked surprised and a little scared at being confronted. Her hand moved to the neckline of her shirt and pulled out a silver cross necklace. She pointed the tiny cross at me in one hand without taking it off.

Wait...did she think I was a vampire?

"I'm not a damn vampire," I laughed, then motioned for her to roll down the window. When she didn't comply, I said, "I'm not here to hurt you. I just want to talk. You've been following me, and I want to know why. It would be a lot easier to talk if I don't have to shout through a closed window."

After a moment's hesitation and maybe the realization that her cross wasn't working on me, she dropped the crucifix and rolled down the window but waited for me to break the silence.

"You're Hester, right?" At her hesitant nod, I continued, "I'm Vianne Vânători." A little flicker of recognition crossed her face. Was this how famous people felt? I almost had to shake my head to refocus. One bad night of sleep and a day of crappy eating habits had really caught up to me.

"Why are you following me?" I demanded.

"So you *are* a Vânători. I'd heard stories, but I wasn't sure if they were true or not. There's not much data on the Vână-tori, you see."

I stared at her, trying to make her understand that *No, I did* not *see.* When that didn't make a dent in her sudden interest in my family history, I put on my I'm-tired-of-this-bullshit expression and tried again. "Why. Are. You. Follow-ing. Me?"

"Oh. I'm not following *you*, specifically. I'm here to observe those beings in this town that are not, strictly speak-ing, human. I'm a cryptozoologist, you see."

"A what?"

"A cryptozoologist. I study entities that others don't believe in. For example, the fairies you were talking to—"

"They were pixies, not fairies," I corrected, feeling annoyed—my stomach rumbled—and hungry.

"Oh goodness! That's good to know," she said and grabbed a small leatherbound book from the passenger seat to furiously scribble some notes inside.

I watched her for a second, then said, "You're not exactly human yourself. What are you that you can see those that others can't sense?"

She looked up from her notebook, snapping her eyes first from me then over to Ramble still in the car. She clearly wanted to ask questions about him or maybe take some more notes but decided that it might be smart to humor the angry lady asking questions.

"I'm *quite* human," she responded with a surprising amount of disappointment. It was obvious she wished she fit into the supernatural community rather than being lumped in with humans. "I take a special herb that allows me to see your four-legged friend there." She opened her mouth to ask what I assumed would be a question about Ramble, but I cut her off.

"And your aura? Why don't you have one?"

This caught her attention. "I don't have an aura?"

I shook my head and she looked thoughtful for a moment before saying, "Perhaps it's a side effect of the herb..." She tapped her chin as she mulled it over, making her shirt sleeve slide down to reveal a tattoo of what looked like a "W" with an eye in the empty space at the bottom of the letter.

A Witness, Artemis hissed with a venom she usually only reserved for vampires.

What do you mean? Is that a thing or are you just saying that she's a witness to our pixy negotiation tonight? I silently asked.

They are a society sworn to watch and observe nonhuman entities without interfering.

Well, that was new. *Is she an enemy then? I mean, is she dangerous?*

All Witnesses are a danger to the Vânători.

I gave the woman a closer inspection. She didn't seem much of a threat in her white cardigan, purple blouse, and beige khaki pants. Actually, she looked more like a manager at a clothing store that targeted middle-age shoppers.

While I thought Artemis was wrong about a lot of things, I thought it best if I treat this woman with some caution. I'd learned the hard way that not every dangerous creature looked terrifying. Some put on a pretty front to draw you in before they ripped your face off.

My mental conversation with Artemis left an uncomfortable silence in the air with Hester, so I asked, "Why were you watching Preston Power's house?"

"Boy, you're just full of questions, aren't you? And here I thought *I* was the researcher." Her smile suggested that she'd stopped being afraid of me. I considered whether I should remedy that or work a more friendly angle to get information from her. Before I could make up my mind, she answered my question.

"After hearing about the animal attacks, I happened to rent the house next door a little over a week ago. The attacks sounded like the work of a werewolf, and thought I'd look into it." She shrugged as if following the signs for a potential werewolf were no different than checking out a yard sale. "But then the attacks suddenly stopped so I shifted my focus to the drama unfolding next door. With the herbs, I could see the gnome, you see, and watched the poor little man lose his garden to the homeowner."

I didn't think Hyssop would appreciate being called a "little man" but decided to let it pass for now. However, if this lady wanted to have any kind of real interactions with those in the supernatural community, she was going to have to shift her approach to be less offensive.

And less creepy. I mean, no one wants to be watched like they're an animal in a zoo or have notes taken on them like a lab specimen.

"But you're a Vânători!" Hester suddenly blurted, as if realizing she was missing out on an opportunity. "You could answer *so* many of my questions!"

"I can?" I was a bit taken aback by her enthusiasm. She'd gone from being terrified of me to being excited that she could pick my brain.

"Oh yes! I'm sure you have oodles of information the cryptozoologist community would love to hear!"

She can have information over our dead body, Artemis growled.

Easy there, I cautioned, *I'm the one with the living body here, remember? You'll just keep trucking along in your incorporeal state in the necklace if I die.*

I stared at Hester for a second. It was getting dark quickly. Both Ramble and I needed to eat, and I needed to make an uncomfortable call with Louis to ask for his blood. I considered the idea of talking Hester into buying our dinner in exchange for information but thought better of it since Artemis was being so weird about the lady. That and just the thought of Louis's blood sent a little wave of need through me. I didn't think I'd be able to concentrate on a conversation with Hester right now.

I looked over at Ramble who, I swear, was grinning at my predicament. Jerk.

"I can't chat today," I told the woman and, honestly? Did not feel bad when her face fell. I was too hungry and too tired to care that much at this point. I was also feeling a little bit jaded by the supernatural community. I mean, who thinks it's a good idea to send their daughter to live with the people who just accidentally murdered their daughter's fiancé? Pixies, that's who.

I was not exactly in a particularly chatty mood.

Before I could head back to my car, Hester produced a business card and shoved it in my face. "Please, take my card and when it's a better time, maybe we can chat."

I had to admit, her ability to bounce back from disappointment was admirable. I took the card. "It was great to meet you," I said before getting back in the car.

See? I could be sociable.

In the car, I turned to Ramble. "Not a word, you." Then added, "Actually, you're probably the one she wants to talk about, so you should be thanking me that I didn't throw you to the wolves. Remember, she can see you. Which means you can communicate with her just as well as you can with me."

Burn that card before you're tempted to call the Witness, Vânători.

"Calm down," I told the necklace and dropped Hester's business card in the console's cup holder before turning the car around and heading away from the lake. Hester gave me a little wave goodbye like we were buds leaving a fun picnic.

"She really doesn't seem that bad," I said to Artemis and Ramble.

The hellhound rolled his eyes and stuck his head out the open window to enjoy the freezing-ass cold evening breeze.

Not that bad? Artemis's voice boomed in my head. *A Witness was the reason that Gawenna Vânători fell to Morvalden.*

Chapter Fifteen

✤

"What does that mean?" I asked Artemis out loud so Ramble would be able to hear the conversation. I'd relayed the necklace's side of the conversation as we drove to the little diner in town to pick up some burgers to go. They were way more expensive than I could really afford right now, but I'd promised Ramble.

It means, Artemis huffed, *that you should stay away from Witnesses.*

I rolled my eyes as I explained her answer to Ramble, then told her, "You can't say something like that about my ancestor then withhold information. It's manipulative and kind of a dick move. I won't be controlled by half-truths, so why don't you just tell me the story." When the necklace didn't respond, I plucked Hester's card from the console. "Okay, I bet Hester would be willing to tell me for a little trade of information..."

Do not threaten me, Vânători.

"Then don't leave me in the dark! Tell me what you mean. If you don't, I'll have to assume that Hester and the Witnesses or whatever aren't the threat you say they are."

There was another moment of silence, but this time it was filled with indecision.

Finally, Artemis caved. *Witnesses, as I said, are a society made up of humans that are supposed to watch nonhumans without interfering. Those they watch include the Vânători. But one Witness, Bernard Cooper, broke the rules. He started a relationship with Gawenna Vânători—the last full-blooded Vânători to possess the necklace and my power.*

I pulled into the diner's parking lot and killed the engine, relaying Artemis's words to Ramble. As much as I wanted to tell Artemis that she didn't need to remind me who Gawenna was, I stayed silent, even ignoring her little jab about not being a full-blooded Vânători for fear that she would get pissy and clam up again.

I warned Gawenna that having any kind of relationship was dangerous, Artemis continued. *It was a weakness that any creature could use as leverage against us, but she didn't listen. She was...besotted with the mortal. Eventually, as I predicted, Morvalden learned of Gawenna's relationship with the Witness and spirited him away to use as bait. I tried to convince her that Bernard would not wish her to put her life at risk to rescue him, but she would not hear it.*

Here Artemis paused and gave a weary sigh before explaining, *The Vânători are like a blade with two sides. On one side of the edge is a noble power that maintains a balance between mortal humans and those who are other. But should a Vânători fall over that sharpened edge, they experience their other, darker side. A side that is filled with unchecked needs and desires.*

This explanation had a familiar ring to it. When I'd been on the run from the vampires with the hunter, Jax, he'd taken us to get help from a powerful witch named Myra, AKA: The Lady of the Woods. She'd said something very similar, only with less cloak and dagger.

"The Vânători women have a dark side that involves being

drawn to gambling, sex, and alcohol," I said, paraphrasing Myra's words.

Yes. Gawenna's weakness was the man, Bernard. And Morvalden put that knowledge to good use. He promised to release Bernard in a trade for Gawenna. Only, when Gawenna arrived, she found that Bernard was no longer human. He had been turned into a vampire.

"That's awful..." I said but trailed off in thought. "Wait, wouldn't that actually make him stronger and a better ally?"

It felt as if Artemis pinned me mentally with a flash of anger. *No, Vânători. It made him Morvalden's puppet. You see, Gawenna was not killed by Morvalden. She died by Bernard's hand.*

"Oh," I hadn't seen that twist coming. I couldn't imagine being murdered by the one I loved. I mean, I'd almost been drained by Louis, but he was just an ally, not my lover.

With that thought, my brain helpfully supplied an image of what it might be like to be Louis's lover. I had to shut down that train of thought or be swamped by both blood lust and another kind lust.

I needed to eat.

"Anything else I should know about the Witnesses?"

They are wily, and their curiosity is insatiable. Information is a form of currency for them, and they will go to great lengths to gain information that they deem important.

Hmm. I wondered if that meant Hester was actually here to watch me and not here to investigate the murders as she'd said. And if she was here to watch me, did that make her dangerous? She didn't strike me as the dangerous type, but that didn't mean I shouldn't be on my toes around her.

I asked some more questions but that seemed to be all I was going to get from Artemis, so I did a quick burger run while Ramble waited in the car. It wasn't a terribly long drive back to the cabin, but before we'd left the diner parking lot, I unwrapped one of the burgers for Ramble so he could eat while I drove. I took a few bites of my own burger, but it was kind of a hassle trying to juggle that and drive, so I finally gave up.

Full dark had fallen when we pulled into the driveway. Yet again, I hadn't thought to turn on any outdoor lights so there was a bit of fumbling around on my part to get up the stairs and in the house. Ramble had no trouble and easily picked his way through the dark. I'd have followed his glowing red eyes, but he mostly had his back to me, so I couldn't really see them.

On the porch, my shins slammed into something near the door that gave a little with the impact.

"Damn it!"

Ramble snorted, clearly of a mind that my human eyes were pretty puny. "Thanks for the warning." Feeling around in the dark, I realized the thing I'd run into was a cooler.

Okay, I thought and hoped that it wasn't parts of another dead body that Pamola had decided to leave on ice for me this time.

After unlocking the house and dropping the food on the kitchen table, I gave Ramble a stern warning and added a waggle of my finger. "Don't eat my burger. You have two more in the bag. The partially unwrapped one is mine."

This earned me a harrumph, but I ignored him and headed back to the front porch.

Do you think you should perhaps arm yourself, Vânători?

"It's just a cooler," I murmured. "I don't think anyone's gonna jump out and steal me from the front porch. Otherwise, they'd have done it while I was feeling my way around in the dark." I also still had the small throwing knife tucked in my boot.

With the light on, I could see that it was a medium sized, red cooler with a white lid. A note had been taped to the lid. I pulled it off and read it aloud. "Hey Vianne, sorry I missed you. Bart said to just leave this with you, and you could get the cooler back to me along with the fee for butchering the deer. I kept some of the parts most people don't want but the rest should be good eating. Throw it in a stew if you don't know what to do with it. Your friendly neighborhood butcher, Ray."

Below that, Ray had written $45.

So Sheriff Allen's friend had already butchered the buck and dropped the meat off with me. That was quick. I guess that meant I'd save some money by not having to buy meat anytime soon. I opened the cooler and found it half full of several packages of plastic wrapped venison. One of the packages on top looked suspiciously like a heart.

I wrinkled my nose. Was I supposed to eat that?

Raw deer heart is good for you, Vânători. It will help give you the heart of a warrior.

"Uh...I think I'll just stick with cardio for that, thanks."

You'll drink vampire blood, but you turn your nose up at fresh venison? I do not understand you, Vânători.

"Right back atcha," I said as I hauled the cooler through the door. I flipped off the porch light and was just about to close the door when I heard a branch snap in the woods off to the left. I froze.

Quietly, like someone else might be able to hear her, Artemis whispered, *Shut the door, Vânători, and go get your gun.*

Behind me, Ramble let out a growl that made the hair on the back of my neck stand to attention.

GO! The necklace yelled at the same moment I slammed the door closed.

But the closed door didn't make any difference. Someone dashed onto the porch and shoved the door open with such force that I was thrown backwards. The door flew with me, landing on top of me and knocking the air from my lungs. Struggling to breath, I watched as Ramble took up a protective stance over me against what could only be Pamola.

A man with dark brown hair and antlers growing from the sides of his head towered over Ramble. Though his chest was bare, fur started at his navel and grew thick below his waist. Thank god because he was buck naked. Around his thighs, the fur blurred to something between feathers and fur, then the rest of his legs were covered in feathers and ended in bird's feet complete with razor sharp talons.

Ramble growled up at the being that Artemis called a Power.

This only served to piss off Pamola, and he suddenly unfurled giant wings that couldn't fully open because their span was wider than the foyer. They smacked the walls as he let out a rumbling basso noise.

Get up, Vânători! Run! He will crush us!

I fought to breathe while Ramble dodged a well-aimed swipe of Pamola's clawed foot. When I was finally able to take a shuddering breath, I worked my way out from under the door just as Pamola's great wing connected with Ramble and slammed him into a wall.

"No!" I screamed as the antlered birdman stomped over to where Ramble lay dazed. Pamola raised his clawed foot to deliver a fatal blow to Ramble's head, and I quickly pictured Ramble beside me.

POP!

Ramble disappeared just as Pamola's foot crashed down and left deep gouges in the hardwood floor. With another POP, Ramble reappeared on the floor next to me. He was still moving slowly, but at least he'd avoided Pamola's killing blow.

I scrambled to my feet just as Pamola managed to turn around in the tight space. He let out another basso roar when he saw Ramble beside me. I quickly stepped in front of the hellhound to shield him from the Power.

What are you doing? Run, Vânători! You cannot beat him!

The Power stepped closer and roared again. A wave of magic accompanied the sound this time and crashed over me. It filled my mind with that sound, and without Artemis's help in blocking it, I'm sure it would have done much more than just send me crashing to my knees.

"Argh!" I clapped my hands over my ears as if that would stop the magical assault. "What is your problem?!" I yelled into the sudden void of silence when the noise died away.

Remembering that Hyssop thought maybe the deer was a gift from the Power and that he was pissed that I'd given it away, I flipped the cooler lid open and pulled out the first piece of deer meat that I put my hands on. It was the heart. Working quickly, I yanked the throwing knife from my boot and used it to cut open the plastic surrounding the heart.

"I took your gift," I said, holding up the slippery heart. There was no time to be squeamish. This guy could clearly wipe me from the earth if he wanted.

"Look, it's right here! I just needed someone to butcher it for me so I could eat it. So just...chill out!"

Telling a being that terrified other members of the supernatural community to chill out probably wasn't the best plan, but come on! He was freaking out about nothing!

He bellowed again, but this time no wave of magic accompanied the noise, and it was quieter, like he wasn't sure if he should still be angry or not. He took one step forward, which was a little too close for comfort.

Look!" I tossed the heart at Pamola's feet. He stopped moving and stared down at the heart. With some difficulty, he maneuvered into a kneeling position and picked up the heart.

Holding it to his face, he sniffed it, then looked at me with a question in his eyes.

"Yeah, see? I didn't give away your gift." I explained, then more quietly said, "There's more of it inside, see?" I pointed at the open cooler.

Pamola peered inside then after a long moment, he snuffed and looked at me.

Now what? I thought. *How do you host a giant, antlered man with wings and bird talons?* Do I just invite him to a cup of tea or something?

I carefully put the knife on the floor and held out my hand, palm up, to indicate that I wasn't a threat. (Like he would even see me as one.)

"Thank you for the gift," I said, mentally flailing around to figure out what to say next. *A little help would go a long way right now!* I mentally told the necklace.

Now you want my help? You didn't listen when I said to run away, why start taking my advice now?

And she wondered why I wasn't a big fan of hers. Gee. I wonder why.

It looked like I was on my own here.

Before I could open my mouth to speak, we were both distracted by the sound of a car on the gravel driveway outside. The vehicle shut off, then someone got out and slammed their car door shut.

Shit! Why were people just showing up at my house all the time?

I wasn't sure what would be worse, warning the person and possibly startling Pamola or having a human, maybe even the sheriff, happen upon our little awkward gathering here.

Figuring that the arrival and subsequent freak-out from whoever had just pulled up once they saw the antlered and winged man would end up startling Pamola anyways, I decided to try and warn the newcomer.

"I don't know who's out there," I said, causing Pamola to swivel his head back toward me, "but this is maybe not the best time. Can you...maybe come back tomorrow?"

The footsteps came to halt.

"Vânători?" Louis's voice was pitched at just the right volume to carry inside but not so loud that he was shouting. Embarrassingly, the sound of his voice stirred up memories of me latching onto his arm and taking in his cool, coppery-tasting blood. It sent a tingle down my spine that made me shiver in anticipation.

Pamola saw the reaction and for some reason, was really, really unhappy with it. He turned his head to the ceiling and let out a sharp, angry bugle that carried more power than before.

Artemis couldn't shield me as well from this assault, and the magic stole away my breath, hearing, and sight for a few short seconds. It was as if his magic overwhelmed my sensory input and my puny body just couldn't handle it. When I was able to function again, I had tears streaming from my eyes, making everything blurry.

I could hear Ramble growling and what sounded like fighting. Someone slammed into a wall—Louis, I thought—and slid to the floor. As my eyes grew clearer, I realized it was a calculated move that allowed him to dodge Pamola's strong hands. Ramble was harrying the Power's feet, barely dodging those razor-sharp claws.

"Stop!" My shout was barely loud enough for *me* to hear. Why was my throat so damn dry? I swallowed and stood before trying again. "Stop! Stop fighting!"

This earned me a quick glance from Ramble, but he was too busy avoiding Pamola to actually stop. Louis also spared me a quick look, but it didn't look like he'd be able to stop either. We'd have to stop Pamola in order to keep things from escalating further.

What can I do? I thought. I mean, I had the throwing knife, but that wasn't gonna do me much good. There was the gun in the bedroom. Pamola had run from it once before, but my allies could die before I could get it and get back to the foyer.

Artemis sighed. *You are going to be killed, Vânători. Your friends are giving you the opportunity to run. You should use it.*

"I'm not leaving them," I said, more than a little scared at the idea of dying here, in this cabin, in the middle of the Maine woods. But Ramble had always had my back. I wasn't about to run away when the chips were down just because I was scared. "So, tell me what to do to stop them from fighting."

Fine. But it will take all the rest of my power. You will have *to drink from the vampire in order to recharge.*

"Tell me what to do. Quick!" As I spoke, Pamola had maneuvered Ramble and Louis into the corner. The only thing keeping them alive this long was Louis's vampire speed and their ability to move more quickly than the Power in such a close environment.

Let me take over, and I will end this fight.

I wavered. Artemis had wanted to take over my body before, but I was adamantly against it. Maybe it had something to do with being a recovering alcoholic and needing that sense of control, but I got a really bad feeling about giving her full control of my body.

Quickly, Vânători! We don't have much time!

She was right. Louis was bleeding from a gash on his side and Ramble was limping and leaving bloody footprints on the floor.

"Promise me you won't hurt Louise or Ramble, and that you won't kill Pamola."

Silly girl. I couldn't kill the Power if I tried. His magic and existence are tied to the very mountains here.

Promise me! I mentally shouted at her.

Fine. I agree to your terms.

I nodded, then closed my eyes and opened myself up to

her. I imagined holding onto a thick cord of control and then just letting the cord slip from my hands.

Suddenly, I was a backseat driver in my own body. I could still see everything that was happening, but I had zero control of what I was doing.

It was terrifying. I wanted to change my mind and take my body back. But it was too late for that. Artemis was in control now.

She turned our neck, making it pop while she flexed our fingers. Then, she focused our attention on the antlered Power trying to kill my friends. Now that I viewed the world through Artemis's filter, I could see that Pamola was almost blurred by bright green and brown magic surrounding him.

In a booming voice, Artemis easily gained his attention.

"Great Power," Artemis said through me, her voice ringing with an authority and magic I didn't know I possessed. "There is no need for bloodshed. We are allies. Not enemies."

Pamola's head jerked toward us. Taking advantage of the distraction, Louis moved to attack the Power.

"Stop!" Artemis said with that same ringing authority and, amazingly, Louis halted mid strike to whip his attention to us. "Did you not hear me, vampire? This Power is not our enemy. We must stop fighting."

A flicker of confusion crossed Louis's face before it locked back down into his normal, neutral expression. I hoped he understood that it wasn't really me talking. I didn't want to lose his trust just because Artemis was anti-vampire.

There was an awkward moment of silence broken only by Ramble's heavy breathing. I could only assume that Louis didn't need to breathe. Finally, Artemis broke through the quiet with a slightly lower volume that still held that note of magic.

"We are grateful for your gift, great Power." She inclined

our head as she spoke. "We wish to coexist with you peacefully in this region and have no reason to fight you. We are here as allies to protect those nonhumans in the area."

Pamola blew out a puff of air while he thought this over. If it had been Ramble doing that, I would have translated it as annoyance. Finally, he let out a small bugle devoid of magic. It felt like he was agreeing to a truce.

Except then he took one step forward, swept Ramble up in his big arms and ran out the open doorway before we could stop him.

Ramble! I shouted after him, unable to actually voice my cry since Artemis was still in charge. *Go after him!* I shouted at the necklace.

"There is little point in chasing after such a Power, Vânători. He has clearly decided to accept the hellhound in retribution for the insult you paid him. We must accept his decision or risk being crushed by his considerable power.

I didn't insult him! I screamed at her. *And fuck accepting him taking Ramble! That's not your decision to make. Give me back control of my body!*

But instead of running after Pamola, she said, "You are too careless with your life and have let our powers wane to the point where we are weak and unable to defend ourselves. I am relieving you of control, Vânători, until I am satisfied that you are able to make better decisions.

And just like that, I realized I'd possibly made the worst decision in my life by allowing her to take control of my body.

Shit.

Chapter Sixteen

I tried several times to take back control of my body. When that didn't work, I tried to call Ramble and help him disappear and reappear like I'd done before. Still nothing. I might have lost my shit for a little bit after that. I railed at Artemis, screaming at her to give me back my body and tried to claw my way back into control, but no matter what I did, she didn't respond. It was like pounding my fists on a brick wall.

As I screamed at Artemis, she turned to Louis and told him quite matter-of-factly, "Vampire. We require your blood." Then asked in that same calm tone, "Will you bargain with us?"

Louis stared at us.

I tried to calm myself down by focusing on the vampire. It didn't look like he'd taken massive damage from Pamola, but his lip was split and bleeding, and his clothing was completely disheveled. The gash I'd seen earlier in his side seemed to have stopped bleeding. He wore the neutral expression that I was beginning to hate, so I couldn't tell what he was thinking. Did he realize Artemis had taken over my body? Did he even care? When he opened his mouth to speak, I made my racing mind quiet down so I could hear his response.

"You are not the Vânători."

"No," Artemis said. I felt her purse our lips. "I am not. I am the power within her necklace and will remain in control until I feel she is ready to fight on her own." She paused. "Will you treat with me, vampire?"

I was almost impressed that she managed to keep the disgust from her voice when she said the word vampire. Then again, if she wanted him to bargain with her, she needed to play nice.

I swear, Artemis, if you don't give me back control RIGHT NOW, when I do regain control, I will throw you to the bottom of the ocean and let you rot. Is that what you want?

Idle threats will not get you what you want, she silently replied. *Without me, you are powerless against the vampires. You would not last one day alone.*

As much as I wanted to argue that I'd lasted just fine without her, I knew I'd be lying. I might be able to outrun the vampires without her, but without her shielding me from Morvalden, he would be able to reach into my dreams and pull me through to him.

Artemis turned her attention outward again, back to Louis who was watching us carefully. I suddenly realized he hadn't moved so much as an inch from where he'd stood when Artemis had told him to stop. Interesting. Was he...was he afraid of Artemis? Was she really that powerful?

"Well, vampire?"

Her words seemed to shake Louis out of his almost statue-like stillness.

"I will treat with you, Artemis," he made a very slight yet formal bow, then looked up in the middle of his bow and directly in our eyes, "but only on one condition."

Artemis cocked her head to the side and held out a hand

in a "come here" gesture. "Speak, then, vampire. I would hear your conditions."

"I will agree to provide blood," he said while watching Artemis carefully, "but only to the Vânători. I will not give my blood to you."

Apparently, that was not the right answer. Rage poured through our body like nothing I'd ever felt. I had no idea Artemis was capable of such anger, and it freaked me out that it had happened in an instant. Like the flip of a switch. I began to wonder if Artemis was altogether sane. Being locked in a necklace for hundreds of years would probably make anyone mentally unstable but this was on a whole new level.

Even scarier, Artemis grabbed hold of that rage and stuffed it deep down into herself, but not before Louis saw it. Did he realize the depth of insanity he was dealing with here?

"That is not acceptable, vampire," Artemis bit out.

"Those are my terms," he said with exactly zero emotion. Though I expected him to shrug and play nonchalant, Louis did no such thing. He simply waited motionless for her response.

Her rage leapt back up like a sudden wave crashing over us.

"I could *slay* you where you stand, *vampire*." Her words dripped with disdain and held just a taste of the power she'd wielded against Pamola.

Louis tipped his head to the side in a quick, noncommittal shrug. "You could, but then you'd be out a vampire. And we both know that the Vânători needs my blood—that *you* need my blood—to stay clear of Morvalden's reach." He stopped and assessed Artemis before adding, "You used a lot of energy here today. I think you know that there isn't another vampire close enough for you to retain your power over the Vânători. You played your hand too soon, and now the Vânători knows your true face. She will gain the upper hand against you with or without my help. At least by making a deal with me, you'll continue to exist and have some power."

As he spoke, Artemis's anger rose and fell. As much as she loathed Louis for what he was, I also sensed an odd kind of respect for his strategic gambit. In one last ditch effort, she quietly said, "I could simply take your blood. Then what?"

Now Louis truly did smile, though it must have been painful with that split lip. "I think you know more about me than you tell the Vânători. You know that you would not be able to capture such a one as me. Not in your fading state at any rate."

With her last effort thwarted, Artemis shifted her plan. More slowly this time, she spooled her anger back into herself like a skein of yarn, then directed her attention inward, back to me.

You must understand, Vânători, that what I did today was necessary. You are not yet ready to wield such power.

And then the real issue here hit me: She wasn't justifying taking over my body, she was defending her rationale for holding back her full powers from me. What I'd experienced so far while wearing the necklace had just been a taste of what we were capable of. I thought of how she'd used only the power of her voice to make Pamola listen and how she'd stopped Louis in his tracks.

My own anger threatened to rise up and swamp me, but I'd already found that yelling and screaming at the necklace would get me nowhere. I needed to regain control of my body so I could go after Ramble before something bad happened to him. So, instead of having a temper tantrum like a toddler, I took a page out of Artemis's book and bottled up that rage with the promise that I would release it at a later time.

Totally healthy, right?

With a clearer mind, I quickly assessed the situation.

Louis was right. If Artemis didn't get vampire blood soon, her powers would fade and, I could only assume, I would once again be in control of my body. That meant Louis was truly doing me a favor by refusing to provide his blood to her. I was going to owe him. Big time.

Great.

But it was my only option.

Give me back my body, I finally said to Artemis, *and I will forgive you for holding back the full Vânători powers.*

Without a parting word, Artemis dropped all control. I could suddenly move my body again. My knees buckled in sheer elation, and I couldn't help the tears that sprang to my eyes as I reveled in my freedom. How could I have ever been so stupid as to let her take control?

For her part, Artemis faded into the back of my mind. She clearly knew that I was not interested in speaking with her just now. Or even having her around. In fact...

I yanked the necklace off and threw it to the floor. It was such a temptation to destroy it. Artemis would never again be able to control me like she had. But if I destroyed it, I wouldn't survive Morvalden.

And I wouldn't be able to rescue Ramble.

I quickly wiped the tears from my eyes and forced myself to pick up the necklace and shoved it in my pocket.

"Vânători?"

I paused, remembering that Louis was there. When I looked up, I wondered how I could ever have forgotten the vampire. When my eyes met his, I felt an almost gravitational pull toward him. His whole demeanor went from on the edge of doing murder, to becoming a walking sexual invitation. I didn't know how he did that, but I honestly didn't care right now.

I fought my body's instincts to jump his bones and instead closed my eyes so I could concentrate. "Wait," I held up a hand, "I have to try and call Ramble back. Maybe now that I have control again..." I trailed off, picturing Ramble in the foyer with all my might.

Nothing happened. I kept trying but it didn't seem to matter.

"Why isn't it working!" I yelled and slapped the floor in frustration. "What is the point of this stupid bond between us if it doesn't work when it counts!"

Louis came closer. I guess he was convinced by my very human theatrics that I was truly me and not Artemis playing mind games with him.

"It is likely Pamola's magic is too strong, and that is why you cannot get through to Ramble."

Shit. He was probably right. I liked that he called Ramble by name rather than just hellhound as Artemis would. When I looked up again, he was standing over me, offering his hand.

Without hesitation, I took it and he helped me to stand. I had trouble looking away from his eyes though.

"Are you hypnotizing me?" I murmured while realizing that I was still holding his hand. His skin was cool where it touched mine and his grip had just the right amount of strength, though he could easily have crushed my hand if he so desired.

What would it be like to have that hand caress my skin? I wondered with an embarrassing shiver I couldn't suppress.

"No," he answered, his voice was silky rather than emotionless this time, and when he spoke, he moved forward, pressing his body to mine.

It was overwhelming having him so close to me. The scent of vanilla overpowered everything else. I wanted to taste those lips that were dark with his blood.

We stood motionless for a moment. Then his hand gently touched the curve of my hip, sending a wave of need through me. Reflexively, I rocked my hips forward against him. I could feel that he wanted me just as badly. His caress became more of a controlling grip on my hip that pulled me against his hardness while simultaneously moving us so my back was pressed against the wall.

I couldn't seem to look away from him. Was he hypnotizing me, or was it the blood on his lips that held me captive?

Slowly, as if afraid he might spook me, he lowered his head and slowly placed a kiss on my neck. I gasped and pulled him harder against me. When he lifted his head and pressed his lips to mine, I responded with a ferocious need that astounded me.

I wanted this. I wanted him.

I felt his hands traveling from my waist to my butt and then he hiked me into the air and pressed me against the wall. My legs automatically went around his hips as he thrust against me.

I had a moment of annoyance that my jeans were in the way, and then I tasted a coppery-salty decadence on my tongue. Louis's blood. I lost a few seconds of time after that. All I could think of was his blood and how I wanted it. I wanted more than he could give me from his lips though.

"Vânători." Louis's voice broke through my lusty brain-fog. It sounded ragged and on edge. Like he was under enormous strain.

I opened my eyes and found that somehow between my last lucid thought and now, we had migrated to the bed. Louis lay on top of me, and my legs were still wrapped around his waist. We were still fully clothed, and part of me wondered how I could remedy that while a smaller part of me screamed that we were wasting time and needed to go after Ramble.

I spotted a drop of blood on Louis's lips and tried to move to pull his mouth back down to mine but found I couldn't move my arms. Louis had my wrists pressed firmly against the bed.

I was...not against this situation.

"Vânători." Louis tried again. My eyes flicked from his lips to his eyes. I could see that he was fighting some internal drive. "Focus, Vânători. We cannot do this right now." As he spoke, I caught a flash of fang. Rather than make me afraid, the sight only made me more aroused. I tried to move against him, and he closed his eyes and gave a little gasp that fully bared his fangs.

What was wrong with me that this was so hot?

He lowered his head but instead of kissing me again, he dropped his forehead against my chest.

"I am not a saint that I can fight against this need to have you, Vânători." He murmured against me. I started to tell him not to fight it, but he continued, "We don't have time for this right now. Your friends are in danger and I do not believe that you would forgive me if I took advantage of you on this night and kept you from aiding them."

That finally got my brain working again. My breath hitched and I stammered my next words.

"W-we have to go after Ramble."

"Yes." He kept his head on my chest, then with a suddenness I wasn't expecting, his weight disappeared, and he was suddenly across the room. I felt...lost without his body against mine. It was that same feeling of loneliness I'd had while living in Indianapolis after being granted parole. Part of me longed for his touch, but another, saner part tried to get it together.

Now that I wasn't looking up into his eyes or fixating on his blood-stained lips, I could think clearly again. I sat up and found that Louis had turned his back to me and stood by the bedroom door.

"If you are to retrieve your companions, you must drink

from me. You will not be powerful enough to stand against Pamola if you don't."

He was right. With just that little taste of his blood, I felt a little better than I had a few minutes ago but I was still pretty weak. All that power Artemis had been throwing around had completely zapped my energy. It took a moment for his words to sink in.

"My companions? As in plural?"

Louis gave a curt nod. "Ramble, Rosalyn, and one of her witches."

I sucked in another breath, trying to get my head around the situation and get my mind out of the gutter it wanted to sink into at the thought of Louis's blood.

"He took Rosalyn?" Her radio silence suddenly made so much more sense. "And Alexis," I said as the realization hit me. That was why the gift basket had been dropped on the front porch. Pamola must have seen the young witch when she stopped by to leave the basket for me, and he'd decided to take her.

Louis kept his back to me but turned a little now so I could see his profile. It meant he didn't have to actually look at me. "Rosalyn contacted me when she thought one of her witches had been taken by the Power. She didn't want to get her coven involved for fear that they would all be taken into his mountain and have no chance of escape." He shook his head. "She said she was going to try to contact Pamola and didn't listen when I told her it was a bad idea. I didn't hear from her after that. Then tonight, one of her coven members called the motel to ask me to connect with you."

I sat up and scooted to the side of the bed, straightening my clothes and trying to pretend I hadn't almost just had sex with a vampire.

I had one guess as to which witch had called Louis: Willomena. I started to get annoyed that she hadn't just called me directly then remembered that, though I had her number, she didn't have mine.

"But why suddenly take Alexis and Rosalyn?" I asked. "I mean, Cassandra lived out here on the outskirts of his mountain, so it's not like Pamola didn't know about the witches."

Louis turned around at my movement. "Pamola has been dormant for many years now. I believe the presence of the magic in the necklace woke him." He paused, nostrils flaring, and glanced at me then at the bed before stating, "I need to leave this room."

With that, he strode out of the bedroom and down the short hall.

Alrighty then. I stood and followed him into the kitchen where we sat at the table across from each other. Totally nonsensual, right? I definitely wasn't having to fight the image of him taking me right on the kitchen table. No-sir-ee.

"Vânători." His tone held a note of warning.

Shit. Could he sense my arousal like Donavon could? Not cool.

I shoved those feelings down and tried to stay focused.

What were we talking about? Ah yes, that I'd somehow woken up a super-powerful being with antlers. That's right. A few minutes ago, I would have argued that the necklace was less powerful than the magic I'd seen Rosalyn wield, and that it seemed unlikely I had been the one to awaken the Power, but now I knew otherwise. Thinking of the witches, though, reminded me of something Deloris had told me.

"I thought those in the supernatural community used Pamola to test whether someone was a good fit for the town or not? That he protected nonhumans? How could that work if he's been dormant this whole time?"

Though I caught a glint of amusement at my use of the term, his tone was still serious as he shook his head and said, "Pamola has never tested nor protected anyone in this town.

Why do you think he didn't stir when the murders occurred? Pamola has just been used like a boogeyman in a children's fairytale to keep the 'supernatural community' in check." He smiled as he used my phrase, and I tried to ignore the little tug of desire that smile caused.

"So basically," I said slowly, "you're saying that my presence with the necklace woke him up."

Louis nodded and looked out at the damage in the foyer before adding, "And somehow, pissed him off."

"Hey, I had things under control before you showed up!"

This earned me a look. "I doubt that very much, Vânători." His lips tugged into another suggestion of a smile that made me catch my breath.

"So, what do we do? How do we rescue them all from Pamola?"

He began rolling up his sleeve. "You will have to drink from me to be strong enough to go after your friends."

I tugged my attention away from his bare arm and found myself staring in his eyes again.

"I'm not so sure it's a good idea for us to do that. What if I take too much again?" I asked, and while I did genuinely worry that I might kill him if I drained him too much, I was also concerned that it would be too easy to lose ourselves to desire again. "Last time—"

"Last time was a mistake." His eyes pierced me like a knife and his anger was so strong that I stopped in my tracks. "As was what happened a few moments ago." He quickly dropped his eyes. "I'm sorry, Vânători. It has been a long time since I fed directly from a human, and your Vânători blood is even more alluring and...intoxicating."

I guess I'd take that as a compliment.

"We can be smart about this, Vânători. You do not need me present to drink my blood."

I quirked an eyebrow at this and opened my mouth to ask

how that would be possible, but he stood with preternatural vampire speed and took a glass of water from where I'd left it by the sink. He poured the water into the sink, then returned to his chair, more slowly this time, and set the glass on the table between us.

"You will go and shower to get my smell off you while I leave you my blood in this." He tapped the glass.

At my look of confusion, he further explained. "Judging by his reaction to my arrival earlier, I don't think Pamola likes me very much." His lips gave a tiny hint of a sardonic smile then slipped back to neutral. "It would be best if you don't enter his domain with my smell on you."

Only then did I realize that Louis wouldn't be going with me to rescue Ramble. For some reason, I'd just assumed he'd help me negotiate Ramble and the witches' release. I felt a little abandoned but tried to tell myself that Louis was right. Pamola clearly didn't like him. It would be dumb of me to try and bring Louis along in a negotiation.

Damn.

Louis watched me, waiting for my reaction. I nodded my agreement with his plan but asked, "How do I get them out though? I mean, I can't go in there, guns blazing. Artemis was able to hold him on her own for a few seconds, but I'm not giving her control again, so that's out."

"For what it's worth, I do not think that she could hold the Power long enough for your friends to escape his mountain anyway."

"So, I'll have to negotiate with him." My spirits deflated.

Now it was Louis's turn to nod and ask, "Do you know what he would be willing to trade for?"

"No," I said slowly as an idea took formation in my mind, "but I think I know someone who might."

Chapter Seventeen

A cold shower helped jumpstart my brain and kept my mind off what I knew Louis was doing in the kitchen.

Nope! Not gonna think about him leaving a glass of his blood for me.

Instead, I worked out my next move. As if rescuing Ramble wasn't enough, I was going to have to free the two witches from Pamola as well. In all honesty, I was kind of pissed at Rosalyn for putting me in this situation in the first place. She'd clearly known about the existence of the Power and had maneuvered me right in his path. Was it really to test me as Delores had suggested? I wanted to believe that the coven leader wouldn't do something like that, but how well did I really know her?

As much as this train of thought pissed me off, it at least took my mind off Louis. I heard the front door shut and his car leave, so I turned off the shower and toweled off, shivering in the cold air. I hadn't bothered starting a fire in the woodstove—mostly because I would have failed without Ramble there to get it going.

I threw on some semi-clean clothes and made my way to the kitchen. I'd pulled the necklace from the jeans that apparently smelled like Louis and shoved it into the jeans I had on now. Thankfully, Artemis stayed silent when I touched the necklace. Good. I wasn't in the mood to talk to her just yet.

On the kitchen table was a glass of red liquid. Louis's blood.

Seeing it, I had that familiar, paradoxical sensation of craving the vampire's blood while simultaneously feeling completely revolted by the idea of wanting it. It felt like the universe was conspiring against me here and forcing me to give in to this new addiction. If I'd said this about alcohol to my substance abuse counselor, she would have said that it only *seemed* that the universe was conspiring against me.

I wondered what she'd have to say about this situation with the vampire blood and the whole magical necklace thing.

Staring at the glass, my palms began to sweat. A visceral part of me wanted that blood but I knew it wouldn't be the same as drinking directly from Louis. Without him there, drinking his blood somehow felt like a dirty act.

Where's a therapist when you really need one?

Maybe it was best not to think about it further. I stepped up to the table, grabbed the glass, squinched my eyes shut, and held my breath as I downed the blood.

I was good for about a milli-second until I realized that the blood was still a little warm. My eyes flew open, and I sucked in a breath, almost choking on the blood. Now I could taste the coppery notes and, on my inhale, got a big whiff of that underlying scent of vanilla that was pure Louis.

My saner side tried to reject this act, and my throat began to constrict. I stopped drinking and let the half-empty glass dangle by my side for a moment as I tried to get a hold of myself. I thought of all the times Ramble had saved my ass. Of how he always had my back even against bigger and scarier things than him. Hell, he'd just stood up to a Power to protect me.

Was I really going to let the idea of being grossed out by a little blood keep me from powering up and rescuing my faithful hellhound?

Hell no.

Steeling myself, I lifted the glass back to my lips and forced myself to drink all of Louis's blood down to the last drop. Once I'd finished, I put the glass in the sink and washed my mouth out with water.

Only then did I notice that I felt much better than I had for the last few days. Louis's blood was invigorating. If I'd had any injuries, they would have been healed just by his blood alone. When combined with wearing the necklace, which was still in my pocket, I would gain access to what felt like unlimited strength and power. Of course, now that I'd seen Artemis unleash her true power, I knew that what I'd felt before was just a tiny taste of what I could be capable of with the necklace.

The problem was, now I didn't trust Artemis.

As much as I wanted to leave the necklace here, I needed her power if I was going to get Ramble back from Pamola.

Remembering how I'd been swept up in power the last time I'd worn the necklace and then had Louis's blood, I took a deep breath and gritted my teeth against the onrush of power. When I felt ready, I fished the necklace out of my pocket.

The moment my fingers touched its surface, I could feel its power filling me.

Where before I'd felt refreshed and reinvigorated, now I was filled with a power so great that it threatened to completely swamp me. With that power, came a natural clarity of what each decision I made could lead to. My initial idea of who I needed to call returned to me, and I assessed it with this newfound clarity, turning the idea over in my mind like a rubix cube and examining all the possibilities.

I waited a few moments before putting the necklace on, thinking that if Artemis tried to take me over, then I could simply drop the necklace.

I cannot take over unless you give me control, Vânători, Artemis quietly said from what sounded like a distant corner of my mind. Though I could tell that her power had grown stronger with Louis's blood, her tone was that of defeat.

I didn't trust that tone one bit, but I didn't have much choice.

I put the necklace on and dropped it below the neckline of my t-shirt then said to the empty room, "Time to make a house call."

* * *

It was late when I hit the doorbell and stepped back from Hester's front door to watch the windows. Her car was parked out front, so I knew she was home. When none of the windows lit up, I stepped forward and hit the doorbell again.

We do not need help from the Witness, Vânători.

It was the first thing Artemis had said to me since we'd left the house. I started to ignore her but decided that playing stonewalling games wasn't the best option. If I was going to survive going into the mountain, I'd need Artemis's power and knowledge.

"We do need her help if I'm going to get Ramble back."

I felt more than heard Artemis's deep sigh and had a feeling she was going to suggest we not try to rescue my four-legged companion. Luckily, she was interrupted when Hester suddenly flipped the porch light on and opened her front door. She blinked at me in obvious surprise.

"Hello, Hester," I said. "Want to trade some Witness secrets for Vânători ones?"

Her mouth dropped open. I'm not sure if it was from me knowing she was a Witness or if it was because a Vânători had just showed up on her doorstep in the middle of the night. She floundered for what to say for a moment before stopping, composing herself, and taking a step back from the doorway.

"Please, come in." She gestured us inside. Once the door was closed, she led me to a well-maintained living room. Had I not been high on vampire blood and busy evaluating the situation, I would have been envious of her leather couch and matching chairs. Apparently, the life of a Witness was a lucrative one.

Clearly, I was in the wrong line of work.

Hester perched on one of the leather chairs. so I sat on the couch facing her. Several times, Hester opened her mouth to say something, thought better of it, then pressed her lips tightly together.

She finally decided to go with, "To what do I owe the pleasure?"

Nice, safe, neutral response.

"I thought I'd take you up on the information thing. You see, I need information about a nonhuman entity, and I thought you might be able to help. In return, I'll answer your questions. Does this sound acceptable?"

This is worse than what you did with the vampire, Vânători. Have you not sullied yourself enough for one night?

I'm sorry, I mentally responded with as much acid as I could. *Did you not just try to take over my body a few hours ago like I was some sort of meat-puppet you could traipse around in? News-flash: I am not like your old Vânători. I'm a 21st century woman, and*

I have the final word on who I sleep with. I didn't even sleep with him anyway! And YOU *no longer get a say in things until you can earn my trust back. So, take a seat and shut the fuck up unless you have something useful to say.*

Though I responded to Artemis only in my mind, it's possible that Hester sensed my anger since I'm pretty sure my face turned red. I know I was grinding my teeth to keep myself from screaming out loud at her. My outburst (inburst?) was met with blessed silence both in my mind and within the room. I looked at Hester and lifted one eyebrow.

Had she not heard my earlier question?

"I'm sorry," she explained cautiously. "You seemed... preoccupied?"

"I was. My apologies. I'm listening with my full attention now."

My speech pattern felt weirdly formal. Since when did I talk like this? Was this indirectly related to the powers of the necklace? Was it influencing the way I spoke? I didn't remember it doing that before...then again, the last few times I'd been high on vampire blood, I had been doing a lot more than sitting around talking to someone.

Hester nodded, still cautious. "I'm curious to learn how you knew I was a Witness. I was told you might not be aware of our society as of yet."

Translation: She thought I was young, stupid, and had no allies to provide me with information about those in the nonhuman community.

"I saw the tattoo on your wrist and put two and two together." I paused and decided to deliver my own barb. "As I'm sure you're well aware, there have been...partnerships forged between the Witnesses and the Vânători before."

Now it was her turn to lift a brow, though her expression spoke more of disdain than impatience. "There was a relationship between *one* Vânători and *one* unprofessional Witness. He is no longer a part of the society though."

I wanted to ask if that was because he was long dead, an undead vampire, or because he'd had a relationship with Gawenna Vânători. In the long run, it didn't really matter so I kept the question to myself.

When I didn't say anything, she pressed on. "I see you've lost your hellhound friend. Does the hound no longer serve you?"

Ooh. Tricky, tricky. The ability the necklace gave me to see several different paths at once suggested that how I answered her question could give away more information than I wanted, but that doing so could lead to the outcome I desired: getting information on Pamola and how to get Ramble back.

My lips tipped into a half-smile and I enjoyed how it caused Hester to involuntarily drop her mask of indifference. Was I a scary bitch right now? I wished I could look in a mirror.

Focus, Vânători, came the whispered admonition.

I didn't bother to respond to Artemis and instead gave Hester my full attention which she clearly was not excited about anymore. "Ramble never served me. He is a free agent and an ally. However, he *is* why I've come to you tonight. He has been taken by a Power named Pamola. I need information on Pamola. Specifically, what the Power would be willing to trade in order to release Ramble."

Hester's mouth dropped open. "You named a hellhound?" She squeaked out. Then as her brain caught up to the rest of my sentence, her eyes widened. "Pamola? As in *the* Pamola?"

I nodded, waiting for her to wrap her mind around what I'd said. She stopped talking, closed her eyes, and held a hand up as if she needed a minute to process. Was it really that big a deal to have Pamola coming after me?

When Hester opened her eyes again, she looked more in control. "First, you named a hellhound, and he didn't immediately rip you and everyone else in the vicinity apart?"

I shrugged. "I guess he liked me. Besides, aren't you Witnesses supposed to know all this stuff about me anyways? Weren't you really sent here to watch me, not check out the murders?"

She opened her mouth, then closed it before admitting, "I truly was sent here to investigate the murders. There was conjecture that the local werewolf Pack might be experiencing a hostile takeover from an outsider. Imagine my surprise when it turned out to be a coup among the witches. And then you, a Vânători who was supposed to be all but extinct, suddenly showed up."

I wasn't sure I wanted to know the answer to my next question. "Did you know what was going on with the witches before I arrived in town?"

I took her stony silence as a yes.

I stared at her in shock. "Why didn't you tell the witches? Or the werewolf pack? Or hell, me? You might have saved people from being murdered!"

"I am only here to Witness. Not to interfere."

"What the hell do you call this?" I asked and lifted a hand to indicate our little midnight chat.

The Witnesses do not interfere unless it benefits them with new information, Artemis murmured in my mind.

Wow. The more I learned about the supernatural world, the less I understood it.

I shook my head and tried to stay on track. I was here to get information in order to save Ramble. I wasn't here to judge the woman who sat before me.

"So, your little secret society wants information?" I asked. "Great. I've just given you information regarding a hellhound's ability to refrain from going on a murderous rampage when named and freed. In return, I need information on the Power who took him."

Hester shook her head slightly. "We don't know much about Pamola. Only what is generally already known to the locals. He protects his lands and, once upon a time, would choose a human to take back to his mountain to marry him or to marry his daughters. Legends suggest he might be open to a trade to free those he's taken, but it hasn't happened often."

I was curious about his daughters but forced myself to stay on track. "What kind of trades has he accepted in the past?"

"That we know of?" Hester shrugged. "Stories say he trades one person for another, but we've never been able to fact check that or anything else about him."

Crap. It was sounding more and more like I was going to have to go live with Pamola in exchange for Ramble's freedom.

Great.

"I've heard he lets people go after a year in his mountain. Do you know if that's true?" I asked and tried to keep the note of hope from my voice.

Vânători, you cannot possibly be considering trading yourself for the hellhound! You cannot lose a year of your life to captivity!

It would be a year of all but guaranteed safety from Morvalden, I grudgingly answered her. *And I would rather be imprisoned in a mountain than imprisoned in my own head by you again.*

Hester must have sensed that I was having an internal conversation again because she waited until I was fully focused on her again before saying, "The stories suggest that Pamola marries the women and releases them after one year. But they are cautioned never to marry again, or he comes and takes them back to his mountain and they are never seen again."

Artemis clearly wasn't happy about what I was thinking of doing. *Where do you think he gets his daughters from? He uses mortal women as his vessels, Vânätori. That's why he keeps them for a year. Is that what you want? To be a vessel for some Power's child?*

Getting knocked up by the powerful spirit of a mountain wasn't really high up on my list of things to do, but maybe I could figure out an alternate arrangement with Pamola? Not that he'd seemed that interested in actually communicating with me so far. I actually wasn't sure we even *could* communicate.

You can speak with him, but you'll need my help.

Oh, let me guess, I silently griped, *you'd need to take over my body again to do that?*

Her silence only confirmed my suspicion that her "help" would mean I'd have to give up control.

That's not happening again. Ever. I turned to Hester. "Is there anything else about Pamola that I should know before I negotiate with him?"

She shook her head and I abruptly stood to leave.

"Wait," Hester said standing as well. "I'd like to go with you."

I stared at her. "Unless you know how to communicate with him, then you'll only be in the way. I don't know how Pamola will respond to you. He could be offended by your very presence."

Hester looked confused. "Why wouldn't you be able to communicate with him? In stories from Indigenous People, Pamola could speak with them."

"He hasn't said anything that sounded remotely like a language to me." I thought about my encounters with the Power so far. I'd spoken to him when I'd shown him the deer meat to calm him down, and he'd seemed to understand, but he hadn't tried to communicate back. "Mostly it's just been animalistic grunts."

"Fascinating," Hester said, clearly ready to grab a pen and her notepad to document my experience. "Let me get my things and I'll come along."

I shook my head. "I don't know how dangerous this will be, and I don't have time to babysit you. Pamola is just as likely to decide that he wants to take you for his next wife."

Hester shook her head. "This is a once in a lifetime opportunity to study a Power. Only one other Witness has ever had the opportunity before, and he died to get a pitiful amount of information back to the order."

I might have looked at her like she was crazy. "You would be willing to die just to get information about Pamola for your secret society?"

She nodded. "This is what we're trained for. It is our very purpose in life: to live and to witness so that others can learn."

Oh my. The Witnesses were a crazy cult. Who were they even teaching this stuff to? It sure as hell wasn't the general public. Or to the Vânători.

"Fine. We leave in five minutes," I said and stepped outside to wait.

Are you sure you want to do this, Vânători?

You can't talk me out of it, Artemis, I mentally responded. *I'm going to get Ramble back. I owe him that. If it means facing Pamola, then I guess that's what I have to do.*

You're willing to stand against a being of Power but not Morvalden? Her tone suggested I was a complete idiot.

"I'm not planning on standing up against Pamola," I told her out loud this time. "I'm planning to try and negotiate with him. It's totally different than it is with Morvalden. I can't exactly negotiate with *him*."

Just then, Hester stepped outside, pulling her door shut and locking it before shifting one of those little sports bags that wasn't quite a backpack higher onto her shoulder. She'd changed into dark sweatpants and a black, zip-up hoodie that made me think she was about to go for a jog.

She saw me lift a brow at the bag and explained, "Just a few things for taking notes. And a flashlight. You know, that sort of thing."

Shit. I hadn't even thought about a flashlight. Mine still sat in my backpack at the cabin. I made a mental note to start carrying it in the car where it might do me more good. We got in my loaner car, and I started to head back toward the cabin, but Hester stopped me.

"I'm not sure where you're headed, Vânători, but the best place to start would be the lake. There are a few trails we can follow up the mountain and into the heart of Pamola's territory."

I thought about it. Though Ramble and Alexis had been taken from the cabin, I had no idea where exactly Pamola had taken him.

"You know where Pamola lives?" I asked.

"I have a general idea of where he might be, yes."

"Alright," I relented. "Tell me where to go."

Hester guided us to the same campsite where I'd met up with Lisa, Derek, and the sheriff only a few hours ago. The couple was most likely long gone along with their new Pixy housemate, and the area was empty on this chilly night.

As soon as we exited the car, Hester dug a flashlight from her bag and snapped it on. "This way," she said and began leading me toward the forest.

So much for just watching without interfering, I thought, but was glad we had someone who knew the way and had thought to bring a flashlight.

Artemis made a sound of agreement but stayed silent other than that.

It didn't take long for us to find the trailhead.

"Lore says that Pamola lives on the mountain and that there's an opening to his domain somewhere on this trail."

I looked at the trail sign. "This says it's a thirty-mile loop." Hester's expression didn't change. Did she not understand the problem here? "So we have to search along thirty miles of trail to find an opening no one else has ever been able to find?"

"Well, to be fair," she said, "others have found it which is why we know it exists. They just couldn't remember *where* they'd found it."

"Great. That doesn't exactly help us, does it?"

Hester bristled. "You're a Vânători. I thought maybe you'd be able to figure it out from here."

While I was trying to think of a way to respond that didn't involve smacking the woman with her own flashlight, a firefly lit up near the trailhead. When it floated closer to us, I realized it wasn't a firefly but a pixy.

And not just any pixy—it was Summerstorm.

"Why are you stomping around my clan's woods at night, Vânători?" She flew close enough that I could see her facial expression but stayed just out of reach. Her glow seemed to radiate from within and was the same yellow-green as a firefly. "And since when do Vânători consort with those who watch?"

It was interesting that she knew Hester was a Witness, even if she didn't name her as such. That meant she or her clan had had dealings with them before. For her part, Hester just stood watching the pixy, her mouth partially open in a sort of awe. I guess that meant her special herb allowed her to see the pixies just like she could see Ramble.

I filed that information away for later and ignored Summerstorm's questions to ask one of my own. "What are you doing out here? I thought pixies only came out at dusk and dawn?"

Summerstorm's eyeroll was so exaggerated that I could

practically hear it. "Come on, Vânători, you didn't buy into *that* old wives' tale, did you?" When I didn't respond, her glow became tinged in purple and she laughed. "Vanatori, every nonhuman creature has some tale they've let the humans believe in order to keep themselves safe. If humans think we can only come out of our homes at certain times, then the rest of the time they won't hunt us."

"Like the whole vampires and sunlight thing," I said out loud while internally, I tried not to be too snide to Artemis as I said, *Looks like you don't know quite everything there is to know about the supernatural community.*

"Exactly," Summerstorm said then glowed green again. "So? Your turn: what are you two doing out here in my clan's woods in the middle of the night?"

Since there was no reason to keep our goal a secret, I didn't see the harm in sharing information with Summerstorm. That and if I didn't tell her, she could bring her whole clan down on our heads. I'd seen the aftermath of their wrath. I preferred to avoid that, thank you very much.

"My companion, Ramble, was taken by the spirit of this mountain—

—Antler-head took your hellhound?" She interrupted then rolled her eyes again. "That nosy Power. He's like a crow —always interested in shiny new things."

"You're not, I dunno, afraid of him?" I asked. Everyone else I'd met in the supernatural community had seemed terrified of the Power.

"Meh. He's got firepower, but he knows he needs to get along with his neighbors or we'll make his life a living hell. He and the fairies had some beef a few years back. To piss him off, they helped humans create this trail that goes right by his front door."

"Wait, do you know where the door is?"

She fluttered a little closer, her wings moving so fast they reminded me of a hummingbird. "I do." Her lips turned up in a mischievous smile. "What's it worth to you, Vânători?"

I resisted the urge to groan. What was it with people around here? Everyone wanted some sort of trade. What happened to just doing something out of the goodness of your heart? I wasn't in the mood to negotiate. We needed to save Ramble.

"How about I go tell your mom that you didn't go home with Lisa and Derek?"

"Try again, Vânători. Those two never came back to the lake to fulfill their end of the bargain."

"What? Are you serious?" I shook my head, but really, was I that surprised?

"Yup. My mom is *pissed*. And you know who she blames?"

I sighed. "Let me guess: me?"

Summerstorm's smile turned into a grin. I decided to try a different tact.

"I can't imagine that your mom would want you helping us out then, huh? Might as well fly back to your clan and tell her where we are. This will be pretty dangerous anyways." I jerked my head at Hester to follow me, and we started up the dark trail with Hester lighting the way.

"Whoa, hey! Wait a second!" Summerstorm zipped past me and stopped in mid-air, hovering about two feet from my face. We stared at each other for a few seconds until she harrumphed. "You're no fun, you know that, Vânători?"

"So everybody says," I murmured mostly to myself, then louder, said, "I need to find that door, Summerstorm. I'm willing to do whatever it takes to get Ramble back."

Out of the corner of my eye, I noted Hester watching our discussion with almost fervent interest. I bet she wished she could whip out her notebook and write all these fascinating interspecies relations down. I tried not to roll my eyes for fear that Summerstorm would think it was directed at her.

"How about," the pixy said, "I'll show you where the door is if you agree to take me on to find a new life partner. You're a lot more interesting than those human idiots, anyways."

I hesitated. I already had one companion, and he'd been kidnapped by a damn mountain spirit.

Exactly, Vânători. Having friends or lovers, she practically spat, *would only compromise you. You must stay focused on learning to use my abilities so we can annihilate Morvalden once and for all.*

I'm not hesitating because of that. I'm hesitating because I don't want anyone else to get hurt because of me.

The thing was, if I didn't accept Summerstorm's offer, I might not get to Ramble before Pamola hurt him.

"Fine," I said. "I agree. Do we need to shake on it or something?"

The pixy broke into a huge smile and flew a few inches higher while the yellow of her glow intensified. "You won't regret this, Vânători. A pixy is worth a thousand times her weight in gold."

Before I could respond, she continued, "Follow me. I'll show you the door." And zipped away up the trail. Hester and I hurried to keep up, and the forest quickly swallowed us. I had to stay close to Hester with her flashlight or risk tripping over unseen branches and jutting rocks.

We tromped along in the dark for what felt like hours when we suddenly came upon a clearing where starlight revealed two tall, giant boulders leaned against each other, forming a little triangular opening between them. Behind the boulders was a sheer rock face. The trail we were using continued on past the clearing and appeared to start rising in elevation before it rounded a bend and fell out of sight.

Summerstorm stopped in the clearing. Hester shined her flashlight on the opening between the rocks.

"This is it!" The pixy proclaimed. She landed on the left

boulder and stood with her hands on her hips. I tried not to think of Tinkerbell.

It couldn't be that easy, could it? If that little triangle of space was the opening to Pamola's mountain, surely someone would have found it by now, right? I took a steadying breath and hoped Summerstorm and Hester didn't notice my hesitation. Before I could chicken out, I slipped past Hester and strode toward the hole.

With Hester standing behind me with her flashlight, the opening was cast in shadows. Hester stopped just short of the opening. I put a palm out touching one of the boulders and jerked my hand back in surprise when I found the boulder was warm. Weird for such a chilly night.

Then again, I told myself, *you're about to walk inside a mountain because it's home to a super old being who has antlers sticking out his head and eagle's feet. Oh, and wings. Can't forget those. So, what's a warm rock compared to that?*

Steady, Vânători.

I ignored Artemis and, with one hand in front of me, felt my way forward through the dark opening. After three steps, my fingertips hit hard rock. It was the cliff face behind the boulders. Huh.

It's a doorway, Vânători, Artemis neutrally said in mind. *You must use my powers to open it.*

Man, I *really* didn't want Artemis's help already, but short of shouting "Open sesame!" I had no idea how to proceed. The only other time I'd opened a "magic" doorway was when Ramble had helped me find a physical door that we were able to open to the Between. But it had been a literal door with a handle.

How the hell was I supposed to open a doorway where there was no door?

Artemis saved my sense of pride by offering me assistance

rather than waiting on me to ask. That was new. Clearly, she was trying to get back in my good graces.

Close your eyes, Vânători. I am going to flood you with the power to open the door. When I do, touch the rocks on either side and think of the word "open."

I followed her instructions, placing each hand on a rock, then braced myself and closed my eyes.

Artemis wasn't kidding when she'd said she was going to flood me with power.

The moment she opened the floodgates, I gasped. Her power burned through me. It literally felt like I was on fire!

Breathe, Vânători!

I sucked in some air, suddenly aware that I'd been holding my breath against the pain.

The pain will fade as you grow accustomed to the power. This is only a taste of what you could wield. You see now why I withheld this from you?

I nodded, tears streaming down my face as I tried to convince myself that my skin was *not* on fire. Maybe if I kept telling myself that, I'd believe it. Suddenly, the burning lessened a little and I could breathe again.

Better? Artemis asked.

Though she couldn't see me, I nodded and breathed a little sigh of relief.

"You okay, Vânători?" Summerstorm called. She must have heard my sudden gasp.

I took another shaky breath and hoped my voice at least sounded steady as I responded. "I'm good. Just...figuring things out. There's an entry point here but it's closed off. I'm going to have to open a doorway."

I wondered if I should tell them to stand back or cover their ears or something. I still didn't really understand how magic worked. Shouldn't opening a door in an otherwise normal rock wall be explosive or something?

They will be fine. Now focus, Vânători. You must open the door. You now have the power to do so. Concentrate and think the word "open" at the rock wall in front of you.

I squeezed my eyes shut, took a deep, steadying breath, and focused all my being on not just the word open but the very idea of opening. In my mind's eye, I pictured a vault, then imagined it starting to shake before its giant metal door popped open.

The ground began to shake.

That's too much, Vânători! Just think the word!

The giant boulders above me began to quake. My eyes popped open.

Uh oh.

Run! Artemis screamed in my head.

I didn't have to be told a second time.

I turned and dashed out from the space between the boulders mere seconds before one of them was shaken off balance. It fell toward us in slow-motion, giving us plenty of time to retreat to the center of the clearing. As it slipped forward, the other boulder shifted sideways. The thud as the first boulder hit the ground was deafening.

Eventually, when everything stopped moving, the left boulder was leaning against the right one that was now horizontal on the ground.

"So much for secrecy," the pixy remarked.

Hester was silent, her lips pressed tightly together in clear disapproval as she watched the boulder fall. I got the feeling that she felt that I'd desecrated some sacred Witness site or something. It was Summerstorm who suddenly pointed at the cliff wall behind the boulders.

"Look! You did it, Vânători"

She was right. A dark, cave-like maw had opened behind the boulders. Unfortunately, it was now partially covered up by the giant boulders.

Shit.

Once we were sure nothing was going to move again, a closer inspection revealed that there was just enough space that if we climbed on top of the fallen boulder, we could slip to the right of the leaning boulder and shimmy through the top of the cave opening.

I looked at my companions. As much as I didn't want to go into that cave alone, it would be my fault if we all got trapped in there. Or worse.

"There's no guarantee we'll be able to get out once we go in. These rocks could shift and trap us in there after we're through." I hesitated but forced myself to continue. "Maybe you two should stay here."

I looked at Hester who gave a little shrug and grin. "I'm along for the ride."

"You made an agreement with me, Vânători," Summerstorm said. "Now I go where you go. Besides," she added with real zeal, "this is an adventure! Why would we want to stay behind?"

Your companions are idiots.

I couldn't disagree with her, but I was also secretly grateful to not enter the mountain by myself.

With that, we climbed onto the fallen boulder, squeezed through the opening, and entered the dark cave that would hopefully lead us to a being of Power.

Chapter Eighteen

⚜

As we entered the cave, I wondered if this would be at all like going into Between. I didn't want to lose time inside this mountain and come out with a horde of Morvalden's vampires waiting for me back at the cabin. But the cave was nothing like Between. One major difference was that Hester's flashlight could actually pierce the dark, giving us flashes of the rocky walls on both sides. It was really more of a long, rocky corridor than a cave.

Summerstorm flitted a little ahead of us, but not too far. Though she'd been excited to go on this adventure, it was clear that she wasn't eager to separate from our little group to go wandering around by herself.

Eventually, the path began to slope down and curve. We went another two-hundred feet like this before I realized we were in a kind of spiral that was winding us down to the bottom of the mountain.

Good thing I wasn't claustrophobic about having all that mountain on top of us.

I felt like my inability to see past the space Hester's flashlight lit up only allowed me to focus more on the weird tingling feeling that still lingered on my skin from Artemis's magic. It was a sort of itchy feeling, but no amount of rubbing or scratching made it go away. The sensation reminded me a little of when I'd been swarmed by an army of bugs not long ago. At least I'd had Ramble by my side then.

We walked for what must have been another half-an-hour before anything new happened. I was beginning to wonder if Pamola had set up this dark, endless tunnel just to mess with us when Summerstorm spoke up.

"Is it just me, or is it starting to get a little brighter in here?"

She was right. But the light wasn't coming from the tunnel ahead. It was more of a glow coming from the very walls around us. The further we walked, the brighter it got. When it was light enough in the tunnel that we could all see, Hester switched off her flashlight and stowed it in her bag.

"Do you think he knows we're here?" I asked.

"After the noise you made when you dropped that boulder? How could he not?" Summerstorm helpfully said.

The tunnel widened and then…things got weird. Not that I expected any less when visiting a mountain spirit who liked to kidnap people and force them into marriage.

The floor became a mosaic of beautiful dark and light rocks, polished to shine like fine tiles. At the same spot where the floor tiles began, the walls of the cave took on a dark smoky glass-like surface. Further along, when the glow behind the walls became brighter, we could see shadows moving in the light. Were we being watched? I couldn't tell if the shadows were just a trick of the light or if they were people moving back there.

I was so distracted by the shadows that I plowed right into Hester when she came to a stop.

"Sorry," I whispered.

"Look, Vânători. There's something ahead. Perhaps you should take the lead now." She gestured ahead.

Though there was enough of a glow from the walls to see where we walked, it wasn't bright enough to make out many details of the dark shapes Hester indicated. They looked like trees, but what kind of tree could grow inside a cave? I hesitated, trying to decide if we should continue forward. It wasn't like we had much choice at this point. That, paired with the fact that none of the trees were moving, convinced me to keep trudging forward.

As we approached the tall shapes, light from the ceiling grew exponentially brighter and, rather than coming from behind the high cave ceiling as a glow, it came from one point directly over the shapes we now walked toward.

Summerstorm flitted closer to the light source then quickly zipped back to us. "I'm not sure what it is, but it doesn't have the same feel as sunlight."

The brighter light now revealed that the weird tall shapes were, indeed, trees. They grew right from the tiled cave floor. What the hell? We continued moving but now kept our heads on a swivel as we entered this strange forest.

At one point, I started to touch one of the trees just to see if it was real, but Summerstorm darted in front of me.

"Not a good idea, Vânători. When in the realm of a Power, it's best not to touch anything." She looked around the odd forest. "You should also avoid eating or drinking anything the Power gives you."

"I thought that was fairies," Hester said, pausing beside us.

The pixy shook her head vehemently. "Not wood fairies. They're about as useless as a stick in mud and about twice and boring. You're thinking of fae. Not fairies." She flew closer, a suddenly serious expression on her face. "And if you meet a fae, don't take *anything* from them. Ever. Just clear outta there. You can't outsmart a fae. No way, no how. Just run."

She is not wrong, Vânători.

"Okay, steer clear of the fae. Good to know. How about Pamola? Any ideas how we're supposed to find him and Ramble in this cave?"

Suddenly Summerstorm whirled around. In a flash, she'd unsheathed the sword at her hip and pointed it at the trees to our left. I followed the point of her sword to where a woman emerged from behind one of the weird trees.

As the woman drew closer, I realized that I recognized her. The flannel pajamas Lisa wore were a dead giveaway, though they'd definitely seen better days.

"What the hell?" I said, taking a step toward Lisa. "What are you doing here? Did Pamola take you, too?"

"Careful," Summerstorm quietly cautioned. "I don't think she's all there right now."

I started to ask what the pixy meant but when Lisa drew closer, I suddenly understood. Not only were Lisa's pajamas caked in mud, but her make-up was also smeared, and her hair was in complete disarray. I didn't know this woman very well, but it seemed like she was having much more than just a bad hair day. The glazed look in Lisa's eyes only confirmed Summerstorm's need for caution.

"I guess this explains why she didn't come get you before she left, Summerstorm."

Lisa came to a stop about three feet from where I stood and grinned at me, her eyes vacant of the joy that should have accompanied that expression. It seemed that she only had eyes for me as she completely ignored my two companions.

"Vânători!" She chirped, and I just about jumped out my skin. She waited, staring at me with that grin as if waiting for a reply.

Summerstorm darted a look at me as if to say, "Well?"

"Yep. That's me." I confirmed. "You don't look so good, Lisa."

Her grin didn't falter. "You must follow me, Vânători. The great mountain spirit wishes to meet you."

"We've met." I couldn't help my dry tone. "He took my friends." I tilted my head to the side a little at a faint flicker in Lisa's eyes. But it was gone too quick to identify it. "It seems that he's taken you, too."

Was Lisa being steered around by Pamola like a meat-puppet? Could he do that? Was he doing that to Ramble, Rosalyn, and Alexis right now? I suddenly wasn't so sure I wanted to negotiate with him. I already had one being in my life who wanted to take control of me. I certainly didn't need another.

She is a lesser witch, Vânători. It is likely only because of this that Pamola is able to control her so easily.

I guess that was reassuring...?

"Vânători, the great mountain spirit wishes to meet you." Lisa's facial expression remained fixed in that creepy state of joy as she repeated herself.

"I heard you." I looked at Hester and Summerstorm then shrugged. "I guess he knows we're here." I turned back to Lisa. "Lead the way, I guess."

Keeping that same smile in place, she turned and began walking through the trees in the direction she'd just come from. Only then did I notice that she was barefoot, and her feet were also caked in mud. At least it wasn't as cold in the mountain as it was outside.

This does not seem like a wise plan, Vânători.

Neither did walking into this guy's house after breaking his front door, but we're here, aren't we?

Without another word, we turned and followed Creepy Lisa through the odd forest under an impossibly tiny sun. At one point, we passed through a small clearing where a small group of people had gathered. There were two young women, one teen boy, and a man and woman I pegged to be in their mid-to-late sixties.

They all appeared to be Indigenous People and their clothing styles were all over the place. It was like they'd gone into a vintage thrift store, chosen pieces from different eras, then mashed them together into outfits. Interesting.

Lisa walked past the group like they weren't even there. They made space for her and kept a wary eye on us, especially Summerstorm.

"Easy, guys," I murmured to my companions as we slowly approached the group. I smiled at one of the young women, but she, along with the others in her group, just stared at us like we were both terrifying yet fascinating.

They didn't have that same, glazed look in their eyes like Lisa did, so I paused near the older couple.

"Hi. We're not here to hurt you. Have you seen..." I trailed to a stop, realizing I couldn't tell them I was looking for my hellhound companion or even a dog since it was unlikely any of them would be able to see Ramble.

The man said something short and clipped to the woman beside him in a language I'd never heard before. She said something back to him that, language barrier or not, sounded like a reprimand.

Hester quietly said, "I think...I think these might be some of the Indigenous People that Pamola was rumored to have taken to his cave to marry or for them to marry his daughters." Her voice brimmed with the excitement of a historian who'd just rediscovered a historic piece.

"Stop screwing around, you two," Summerstorm admonished, zipping back to Hester and me. "The puppet-lady isn't waiting for us."

Shit. She was right. Creepy Lisa had continued past the clearing and had disappeared into the woods. I hesitated.

Shouldn't I try to free these people as well as my companions? Maybe we could get them out if we escaped the mountain and came back this way? Or maybe I could negotiate their release, too?

I didn't have time to dawdle since it seemed that Lisa wasn't going to wait for us. We'd just have to hope we could help these people later.

I turned and quickly jogged after Summerstorm as she flew off in the direction we'd last seen Lisa heading. Hester was quick on my heels as we passed through a tight copse of trees and then were finally free of the creepy forest. As the trees receded, so did the bright yellow light from above. The cave grew dark again, and we could only just make out Lisa as she continued to lead the way.

In time, I began to hear the sounds of a waterfall. As it grew louder, the cave began to brighten again. The ground changed from those black and white tiles to random patches of grass here and there until eventually the grass overtook the tiles and we were walking in a lush, green field. The light here glowed a more bluish hue and emanated from the top of the giant waterfall ahead. The water seemed to come straight out of the cave wall, which wasn't that odd. What *was* odd was the verdant green plant life and beautiful flowers that graced the area around the waterfall.

Were the plants actually able to grow in that blue light from above, or were they simply kept alive by Pamola's magic? I'd thought he got his power from the mountain, but it looked more like he used his magic to maintain everything within the mountain instead.

We kept following Lisa, skirting the pool that the waterfall cascaded into and continuing on our way, deeper into the mountain.

Just as before, the light dimmed as we left the area with the waterfall. I only knew we were getting closer to something else because the light began to come back up, this time with a greenish hue. When we reached a small, familiar wood cabin, I could only shake my head.

"What?" Asked Summerstorm.

"It's an exact replica of the cabin I just moved into."

This was just too weird. Pamola had even recreated the blown up shed with all the debris spewed around the yard. The only thing different were the cars in the driveway. I wasn't completely sure I remembered correctly, but I thought one of them might be Rosalyn's car.

"Looks like someone *liiikes* you," Summerstorm said, flying a little closer. I gave her a look and she skittered back a few inches. "What? Pamola wouldn't be such a bad life part-ner, would he? I mean, I bet he could make you whatever kind of house you want to live in here." She waved her arms to indicate the mountain.

"I wouldn't call being held captive here for a year by a controlling guy who forces you into a marriage a very good relationship. It wouldn't be a house; it would be a cage."

"Tomato, tomahto," she shrugged a tiny shoulder. "To my people, this would be a great compliment."

"Then maybe *you* should marry him." I might have been a tad on the grumpy side at this point.

The outside porch light flicked on by itself. It, too, had an odd green glow to it.

"I guess he knows we're here," Hester commented.

And to think, I'd come *this* close to having a real home with my own washer and dryer. On the bright side, maybe Pamola could provide that here. And hey, no rent for a year! Unless you counted a forced marriage and probably the required conjugal visits from the Power. I tried not to picture sex with Pamola. It was just... disturbing.

I sighed. "Might as well go get this over with." I forced myself to start toward the cabin.

My little entourage followed me up the stairs and onto the porch. At least Pamola hadn't recreated the deer blood that still stained my real porch.

Lisa just stood there on the porch to the left of the door, giving me her creepy, vacant smile. Not knowing what else to do, I knocked.

Nothing happened. There were no noises from within either.

"Did we come all the way here and he's not home?" Summerstorm asked, her hands on her hips in a cocky attitude.

With still no response from Lisa, I shrugged and tried the doorknob. It was unlocked. With a quick glance at Summerstorm to let her know I was going in, I twisted the handle and shoved the door open.

I don't know what I was expecting, but it certainly wasn't the cozy house we walked into.

Though the outside might look like my cabin, the interior was a different story. It was more like a second home for the rich and famous. It was still a wood cabin, but it had a totally different layout inside than my place did. The front door opened onto a huge, open plan living area with a ginormous, medieval fireplace that I could literally have walked into without banging my head.

I might have blanched a little when I saw the hunting trophies mounted on the wall. On either side of the fireplace, were the heads of men at different states of decay. I was surprised I couldn't smell them. Maybe that was part of the illusion or magic or whatever.

I didn't think it was a good sign that Pamola was cool with displaying human heads on his walls. If I was going to be in charge of decorating for the next year, those would be the first thing to go.

Everything else in the room seemed normal. Brown

leather couch tastefully worn from use. Two wingback chairs near the fireplace with a bear skin rug between them—the rug suddenly moved, and I almost lost my shit until I realized what it was.

Ramble stood in front of us, his red glowing eyes looking at us like he wasn't sure we were real. Suddenly he darted toward me, and I couldn't help but go down to my knees to hug the guy. His spiky fur was rough under my hands, but I didn't care. He shoved his head against my neck. It was the only time I'd ever seen him actually seek out affection. Sure, he'd comforted *me* in the past, but it had never been the other way around.

"I'm so sorry, Ramble. I didn't mean to let him take you." I pulled back, taking his head in my hands to get a better look at him. "Are you okay?"

Of course he's okay. He's a hellhound. They're made of sterner stuff than most.

Ramble gave a snort to let me know he was a tough guy and was alright. I looked at him for another second, then stood so as not to embarrass him.

"Do you know where Rosalyn and Alexis are?" I asked.

Ramble gave me a shrug and snuff that suggested he wasn't sure. I turned to the only other person who might know.

"Hey, Earth to Lisa. Where are the rest of our friends?"

"The Power would like to meet you," Lisa said through that smile that just got creepier and creepier by the second.

"Well? We're here. Where is he?"

A knock sounded at the front door. For some reason, it sent a shiver down my spine.

I could have sworn we'd left it open behind us. Now it was closed.

"Someone is at the door, Vânători," Lisa helpfully said.

"Yup. Thanks for the newsflash."

It's possible that I get snarky when I'm nervous.

"Hey," Summerstorm said, zipping over to hover a few inches from my face. She jerked her head toward the door and grinned. "Someone's at the door."

I gave her a look that I hoped she rightly interpreted as me wanting to murder her. Then, there was nothing else to do but answer the door.

I tried not to shake as I strode over, grabbed the door-knob, and yanked the door open.

Chapter Nineteen

T here stood Pamola, glaring at me and my small entourage.

There was an insane moment where I considered just shoving past him and making a run for it, but there was no way I'd be able to outrun him even with help from Artemis. I also briefly wondered if I could get Ramble to pop out and save himself. Then again, if Ramble could have done that, I'm sure he would have blown this pop stand long ago.

Time to face the music.

Pamola looked from me to Ramble now standing defiantly beside me. When his eyes flicked back to mine, his brows drew down, and he let out a screeching bellow I'd only ever heard on nature shows. It was the sound of an angry moose. If you've never heard what that sounds like, look it up. Then imagine that sound right in your face.

It made me jump backwards a little, which knocked me into Hester. She steadied me as Pamola took a step forward toward where Ramble still stood.

The hellhound reluctantly backed up a few steps but kept his eyes on the approaching Power.

He's amassing power, Vânători! Artemis yelled in my mind.

What? What do I do?

I'm going to dump power into you, and you're going to think of a wall as he throws his power at us. Brace yourself!

The flood of power rushing into me was almost too much. I let out a gasp and luckily Hester was still steadying me, or I would have gone down to both knees.

Breathe, Vânători! Artemis screamed in my head. *And when I tell you to think of a wall, do it!*

I managed to suck in a gasping breath, looking very much like a fish trying to breathe air on dry land. My body was on fire and that feeling only seemed to be intensify in waves. I sucked in another breath, but when I let it out, it began to turn into a scream that I couldn't stop.

Not yet, Vânători. Wait for it. Wait.... Now!

I forced my brain to think of a wall, but the thought got twisted up with the feeling of being on fire. Instead of producing an invisible wall or a wall of stone, I manifested a twisting cyclone of fire between us and Pamola.

It apparently got the job done though because we didn't get pulverized or whatever by Pamola's power. He bellowed again behind the wall of fire.

I can't keep this up, Artemis. I mentally ground out. *You have to pull the power back, or I'll pass out.*

If you would just let me—

No. Not ever again. Just pull back on what you're dumping into me!

If I draw back on your power, then the wall stopping Pamola will disappear.

I can't keep it up forever, anyways. Let me step back a few paces, and then pull back on the power.

To Hester, through gritted teeth, I said, "We have to pull back a few paces. Give him some space."

She nodded and immediately started helping me back up

about ten steps. Summerstorm flitted near my shoulder, and Ramble stuck by my side.

The burning pain receded slightly until it was more like having a really bad sunburn. As the power drained from me, the fire-twister slowly dissipated until it was nothing but a puff of smoke.

The moment it was gone, Summerstorm flew into the space where it had been, brandishing her sword at the Power. "Oi! You've had your pissing contest with the Vânători, now, Pamola. It's time to quit playing games. And since when do you have the authority to snatch friends of Clan Cinder?"

My mouth dropped open. Not because of Summerstorm's ferocity (which was impressive) but because the great spirit of the mountain jerked back when he saw the pixy.

Pamola bellowed something at the pixy but she cut him off.

"Nope! Come on, Pamola. I know you speak English. Stop yanking the Vânători's chain and start telling us where her witchy friends are so we can get on with negotiations." As she spoke, she poked her sword at the Power to emphasize her points.

Pamola tried to bugle back at her but she cut him off again.

"Do you *really* want me to go get my mother? Because I can't imagine you'd want to talk to *her* after she learns that you've been messing with a friend of the Cinder Clan. If you thought the fairies did you wrong by building that trail near your front door, just wait 'til you see what a pissed off pixy clan could do."

There was a bit more grumbling, then Pamola suddenly morphed from his part-animal shape into a human form. He had long dark hair and wore blue jeans paired with a colorful but modern jacket that suggested he wasn't unfamiliar with the current world.

Also, he was hot. Like, straight up model-from-a-photo-shoot hot.

"Are you happy now, pixy?" Pamola's voice was just as nice to listen to as he was to look at. I suddenly understood why the women before me had agreed to stay with him for a year.

Yowza.

"Much better," Summerstorm agreed as she sheathed her sword then put her hands on her hips. "Now, where are the Vânători's witchy friends?"

Pamola sighed dramatically and snapped his fingers. Rosalyn and Alexis popped into existence on the living room couch. Both had their hands bound in front of them with some kind of glowing green magic. It must have kept them from being able to use their own magic. They both looked surprised to suddenly be in the room with us, but when Alexis spotted Pamola, her eyes lit up with a tint of red fury.

That was new. I'd never seen a witch's eyes turn a different color. I realized I really knew next to nothing about the young witch. Unfortunately, this wasn't the time for small talk.

Pamola continued glaring at Summerstorm. "Are you going to do all of the Vânători's negotiating, pixy?"

"Actually, I think I will." Summerstorm didn't need her sword when she had such a sharp smile. If one pixy was this formidable, what would a whole clan of them be like? I was starting to realize just what kind of hell we'd saved Lisa and Derek from.

The thought reminded me of the other woman in the room who was still wearing that vacant grin. I jerked a thumb in Lisa's direction. "Fix her, too, would you?"

Pamola quirked an eyebrow at me. "Are you sure?" There was a sly undertone to his question that I didn't like.

"Yes. No one should be a meat-puppet like that."

Pamola shrugged and just like that, Lisa was released from

his spell. She dropped to the floor like a sack of potatoes. Hester, who had been gripping my arm this whole time, mesmerized by the scene around us, moved to check on the woman. Her concern surprised me since Artemis had made it clear that the Witnesses didn't care about those they watched.

Sensing that my thoughts had turned to her, Artemis suddenly piped up. *We should leave, Vânători.*

I'm working on that, Artemis. It's not like I can just thank Pamola for a great time and walk out the front door.

I jerked when I realized that Pamola was studying me as I spoke to the necklace in my head. Could he hear our conversation?

As if in answer, he smiled. "Ah, yes. The great Vânători and her powerful ally."

At first I thought he meant Ramble, but then I realized he was talking about Artemis. I wasn't sure how to respond to that, so, rather than do the sensible thing and stay quiet, I responded, "Ah yes, the great and powerful Pamola." Then I couldn't help but ask, "What's up with pretending not to understand me at the cabin?" I looked around. "I mean, before. At my real cabin."

"I'm not in the habit of explaining myself to mortals, Vânători."

I shrugged. "Suit yourself. But it just seems kinda weird." Despite knowing that this guy had a ton of power at his fingertips, it was hard to be in a perpetual state of fear. Especially when the guy flinched at the threats of a tiny pixy. Not that Summerstorm wasn't scary. It was just that I wouldn't have thought the Power would be afraid of someone so small.

"It's not *weird*, Vânători. It was a test. I wanted to see how the *great Vânători* would react to a creature who didn't appear human."

"You thought I'd attack first and ask questions later, huh?"

His smile was somewhat smug as he jerked his head at Lisa. "Humans aren't exactly great at accepting something that's different from them."

Before I could respond, Summerstorm cleared her throat, drawing attention back to herself. When all eyes were back on her, she turned to Pamola. "Well, *great mountain spirit?*" She said, with an overabundance of sarcasm. "What's the deal here? Are we gonna negotiate, or are you gonna bicker with the Vânători all day?"

Pamola squinted at her, clearly trying to decide if he should be offended by her tone or not. Finally, he crossed his arms over his chest and put a little thunder in his voice as he said, "The witches and hellhound are mine, Vânători." Then he smiled. "That is, unless you wish to take their place and stay here for a year and a day with me."

I mean, now that I'd seen him as a human and saw what kind of digs I'd be staying in...

Vânători! Artemis admonished. *Do not even think about staying here with the Power!*

I sighed inwardly and started to respond but Summerstorm beat me to it.

"You haven't been paying attention, Pamola. The hellhound is not part of these negotiations. He is a friend of the Cinder Clan and, in accordance with the treaty you signed with the pixy clans of this forest, you are prohibited from abducting him."

The mountain spirit threw up his hands. "You pixies with all your legal nonsense—*I* am the Power here!" The cabin shook with the might in his voice. He closed his eyes for a second as if to calm down, and when he took a deep breath in, the shaking stopped.

"Fine," He said and opened his eyes to point at Ramble. Before I could step in front of my companion, Pamola added,

"You're free to go, hellhound." And poof! Ramble disappeared.

I raised an eyebrow at Pamola, and he cut me off before I even started to speak. "He's fine, Vânători. I dropped him on your front porch." He turned to Summerstorm. "Are you happy now, pixy? Does that suit your treaty?"

Summerstorm nodded

"Any other *friends of the pixy clan* here that I need to know about?"

"No."

"Wonderful. Can we get on with the negotiations then? Or is there some other ace-in-the-hole that you're going to whip out like Jessica Fletcher?"

My mouth dropped open. Was that a *Murder She Wrote* reference?

The Power glared at me. "What? You don't think I've just been sitting here in my mountain, twiddling my thumbs for all these years, do you?"

I shrugged. "I've heard a lot of different things about you, honestly. None of them seem to live up to the real you though."

He squinted at me for a second as if trying to decide if I were insulting him or not, then broke into a grin. "Is the great Vânători stalling?"

"No." Maybe. Hell, I didn't know what I could offer the guy. He didn't seem so bad...except for the part where he'd kidnapped my friends and forced people to live in his mountain with him. Honestly, it kind of just sounded like he was really lonely.

That didn't mean I wanted to live with him for a year though. Even if he was super-hot.

"Well, then? What will you offer in exchange for releasing the witches, Vânători?"

"Me," Summerstorm said.

I jerked my head at the pixy. "What? No. You don't have to do that Summerstorm. I've got this."

She gave me a look filled with amused pity. "You clearly don't, Vânători." She turned back to the Power. "Well? What d'ya say, big guy? Would you be willing to trade the witches for a year a day with the daughter of Queen Brightstorm?"

Pamola rubbed his chin in thought. "Perhaps. The two witches are quite a catch though. Especially the fiery one. She was quite fun to spar with." Alexis jerked against the magic holding her on the couch. It looked like she had a lot to say about that.

"Three witches." Summerstorm held up three fingers, then hooked her thumb at the still unconscious Lisa.

"And the people we passed on our way here," I added.

Pamola turned his full attention on me, and I suddenly wished I'd let Summerstorm continued handling the negotiation.

"They are not part of the bargain, Vânători. And they would not survive in your world. They are from a different time and only staying here in my mountain keeps them alive."

It kind of seemed like they should at least have a choice in the matter instead of him speaking for them. I opened my mouth to say as much, but Summerstorm zipped in front of me and gave me a look that made me shut up. Clearly, I was screwing up her negotiations.

"We can't save everyone, Vânători." She must have sensed that I wouldn't be able to just leave them there though because she added, "I agree with Pamola on this, one. It's not likely they would be able survive outside his mountain. Magic is funny like that. But if I stay here, I'll make sure they are well-taken care of and will negotiate that they have the choice to leave."

"I'm not sure you're worth all that, pixy."

"Ha!" Summerstorm whirled around and flew a little

higher to put herself at face level with the Power. "I'm worth *way* more than that, antler-head. Besides, this is just the beginning of our negotiations. I expect we can hammer out some new pacts between you and my clan that would make everyone happy."

"You don't have to do this, Summerstorm," I said again. I didn't want to be responsible for the pixy losing a year of her life to playing house with Pamola.

She looked back at me. "I know. I'm not doing it for you, Vânători. I'm doing it so my clan will gain an edge over the fairies and we'll be less likely to be bothered by humans again with this guy on our side."

Pamola eyeballed Summerstorm as she pointed at him. Was he... was he checking her out? I suddenly pictured a swarm of pixy-sized Pamolas with eagle wings and antlers on their heads. Oh my. That would be...interesting.

After a few beats of silence, Pamola jerked his head in a nod. "Done."

Summerstorm grinned and looked back at me. "My mother is going to be so pissed when you tell her where I am."

"When *I* tell her?"

The pixy flew closer so I could see her better. "Uh, yeah. I just saved your bacon, Vânători. The least you could do is tell my mother where I am." She glanced back at Pamola.

"Fine." Out of the corner of my eye, I saw Hester's eyes light up like a Christmas tree. Clearly, she was going to ask if she could be there when I spoke to the pixy queen. Not gonna happen, lady.

I looked back at Summerstorm and hesitated, not knowing how to thank her.

"Listen, I—"

"It's okay." She reassured with a grin. "Besides, who else

can say that a Vânători owes them?" With a wink, she flitted back to Pamola. "Time to send them home, big guy."

For a split second, I saw Pamola rethinking his life choice as he considered arguing with the pixy for telling him what to do. Then, looking only slightly defeated, he let the issue go and turned to us. In that moment, I knew that Summerstorm would be able to hold her own against the Power.

"On your way, Vânători."

—and suddenly we were all standing in front of my real cabin.

Chapter Twenty

"That guy has some major power," I murmured.

It was still dark out and, yet again, I'd forgotten to leave the porch light on. I heard a scuff of something against the porch boards and turned, ready for whatever would emerge from the dark only to see Ramble dash down the steps. He shoved his head against me, nearly knocking me down.

"I'm glad to see you, too, buddy."

Rosalyn and Alexis watched as I gave the invisible hellhound a brief hug. When I straightened, I noticed that there were two cars in the driveway—neither of which were mine. Pamola had zapped us all here along with Rosalyn's car and what I could only assume was the car Alexis had driven over to my cabin when the Power had snatched her. Of course, he hadn't bothered to send *my* car from where we'd left it parked near the lake.

Great.

"We should talk, Vianne." Rosalyn drew my attention back from my car-less predicament. Beside her, Alexis and Hester were helping the now conscious but dazed Lisa to stand.

I suddenly remembered that we did, indeed, need to talk. After all, Rosalyn had planned for Pamola to notice me by putting me out here in Cassandra's cabin. She just hadn't factored in that the Power would decide to take her and her witch hostage.

"For what it's worth," Rosalyn said, watching me mulling over how to respond, "you saved Alexis from losing a year of her life to the mountain spirit. He was quite taken with her. She has a powerful gift of fire. It's why my house burned down not long ago, actually."

Huh. I guess that explained the scorch marks on the porch stair's bottom tread. She must have tried to defend herself when Pamola snatched her from my place.

My place. It had been so amazing to finally have a place to call my own. Now it seemed like that had just been a fantasy. I shoved down the emotion that threatened to overwhelm me when I realized that I wouldn't be staying here much longer. How could I after all this? It was clear that the people I'd thought I could trust weren't as trustworthy as I'd hoped.

I wouldn't be leaving tonight though. I was too exhausted. Artemis had burned through most of the power I'd gotten from Louis's blood during our encounter with Pamola. As much as my pride urged me to get in a car and drive away from this town, I knew I was too tired to do so right now.

That and I'd made a promise to Summerstorm to tell her mother about her daughter's decision to stay with Pamola. And I honestly wanted to make sure that Hyssop's magic would return with his new garden. Plus, I didn't have a car to drive away in unless I stole one from the witches. Knowing my luck, they probably had some kind of magic LowJac that could track the car.

So, rather than saying something I might regret later, I

shook my head at the witch. "You lost a lot of my trust with this, Rosalyn."

"I understand, Vianne, but I did what I felt was necessary to ensure the safety of my coven."

"By trying to have me kidnapped by a mountain spirit?"

She shook her head. "By testing your loyalty to the nonhumans in our town." I rolled my eyes, but she continued. "Some of the Vânători have been notoriously vicious to people like us in the past while others, long ago, acted in good faith to keep the peace between us and the humans. We needed to know which type you were."

"Really? You couldn't tell that from me helping track down the people killing your witches? Or when I helped stop them from taking over your coven? That wasn't enough for you?"

"I am sorry, Vianne, but I had to be sure."

I didn't know what else to say. It was clear she'd probably do it all again if given a do-over. I think it wouldn't have hurt so much if I hadn't had glimpses of what my life could be like by staying here. It was the first time I'd felt that I fit in somewhere—not just since I'd found out about the whole *Vânători* thing, but since my parents had died.

It was clear, now, that I'd been mistaken. As much as I'd thought this town might be a place where I could make a life, I was clearly never going to be completely accepted by the supernatural community. And though I could pass for human, it was obvious that would always just be a ruse, too.

No, what sucked about Rosalyn's little test was that I knew it's results would never matter. They would never accept me here.

Yes, Vânători. I'm sorry, but now you know the truth of it. The Vânători are their own kind. They do not belong with others the way the rest of the nonhumans do.

"I think it's best if you just go, Rosalyn. Drop Hester and Lisa off on your way, would you?"

I thought the witch might say something else, but she decided against it. Instead, she gave me a nod and turned to help Alexis and Hester get Lisa into Rosalyn's car.

I sat on the scorched bottom stair. A second later, Hester approached me.

"What an intriguing night! I have so many notes to make! But..." she paused, "let's keep it between us that you knew I was watching the whole Pamola-thing."

"Sure." I honestly couldn't care less what story Hester cooked up to tell her bosses.

"And I'll need you to drop my bag off when you get a chance to retrieve your car."

I nodded. She seemed to take the hint that I didn't want to talk to anyone else. With a wave, she retreated to Alexis's car. A few minutes later, everyone left.

Ramble sat on the ground and leaned against my legs, flipping his head over backward in a move that I'd call silly if he were a normal dog.

"Just you and me again, buddy."

His doggy-grin suggested that that was a-okay with him. And... I had to agree. Who needed witches, werewolves, and vampires when you had an ass-kicking hellhound by your side?

After a few minutes, I got sick of feeling sorry for myself and stood to go inside and collapse on the bed. Of course, I'd totally forgotten that the outer door to the cabin was broken.

Shit.

Well, it wasn't going to fix itself and I really didn't want to go to sleep without something blocking the front door. With a sigh, I set about dragging the door out of the hallway and positioned it as best as I could against the opening.

"Good enough," I told Ramble. I kicked my shoes off and

ignored the marks in the floorboards from Pamola's talons. Good thing I hadn't put a deposit down on this place. Not that it would have mattered since my landlord was directly responsible for the damage to the cabin.

The place was freezing. For a moment, I stood there, trying to decide whether it was worth it to start a fire in the woodstove since it was likely that any heat would just escape through the front door before it reached the bedroom. I finally decided that it wasn't worth it. Besides, the sun would be coming up soon. It would heat things up eventually. I wasn't gonna freeze to death before then. Not with a hellhound beside me, anyways.

I shut the bedroom door behind us, pulled the curtains, and dropped into bed. Ramble climbed up beside me and curled up with his head facing me. I pulled the covers over both of us, careful not to cover his face.

"I'm glad to have you back, Ramble. I'm not sure I could keep doing this without you."

He looked at me for a moment, then let out a deep sigh of contentment to show me that he was happy to be back, too.

At some point during our nap, my hand found its way to the top of one of his giant paws and stayed there until we were rudely awakened by someone shouting outside.

"Vianne! Are you in there?"

"No," I mumbled into my pillow. Ramble grumbled beside me.

"Vianne?"

There was a loud thud as the outside door fell down in the hallway. Dammit. I worked hard to put that thing up.

"What the hell?" I could tell now that it was the sheriff. "Vianne?!" He called more loudly now the outer was open.

"Argggghhh," I complained and hoisted myself out of bed. "Are you coming?" I asked Ramble.

The hellhound curled up even more tightly and scrunched his eyes shut.

"Hey, I went into a cave and fought a being of Power for you, buddy."

He pretended to snore.

I mumbled something about getting no respect around here and yanked open the bedroom door. I wished I had started a fire now that I was walking around in the cold cabin in just my socks. *Maybe I should invest in some slippers or something,* I thought, then reminded myself that we didn't plan to stay here for much longer.

When I stepped around the corner, I found the sheriff pointing his gun at me. I quickly threw my hands in the air. "Whoa, there, Sheriff. It's just me."

"Jesus, give me a little warning next time, would you?" He said and breathed a sigh of relief before holstering his weapon.

"I mean, you are in *my* house. I thought *you* were supposed to give *me* the warning."

"I've been shouting your name for the past five minutes. Didn't you hear me?" At my shrug, he shook his head. "What the hell happened here?"

Only a few days ago, I might have made something up to keep the sheriff from suspecting what might be going bump in the night in his neck of the woods. Now? I didn't really feel it was my problem to keep things from him.

Careful, Vânători. Artemis cautioned. *You can't trust the humans any more than the nonhumans.*

It was the first time she'd piped up all morning and she sounded as drained as I felt.

I can't trust you, either. What's new?

My response shut her up.

"Remember the guy who attacked you the other day?"

The sheriff nodded.

"He paid me another little visit and tried to haul me off to live with him in his mountain."

The sheriff just looked at me.

"Look, if I'm gonna have to explain things, I'll make you deal. You start the fire in the woodstove, and I'll go make some coffee, then we'll meet in the kitchen for story time." Without waiting for his response, I walked into the kitchen. As I passed by the cooler full of deer meat still sitting in the foyer, I grabbed it and dragged it with me. It should still be good right? I mean, it had been cold enough in the cabin that it should be fine.

I started a pot of coffee then began putting deer meat in the freezer. I had no idea what the hell I was going do with it. Maybe I could sell it or something? As I worked, I heard the sheriff loading the woodstove. After a few minutes he joined me in the kitchen.

"Not gonna do much to heat the house with that front door open like that. You want the name of someone who can come fix it?"

"Sure. I'll pass the info to Rosalyn since she's the landlord."

We sat down and I gave the sheriff an abbreviated version of last night's events. I left Hester out of the picture since I wasn't sure where she stood in all of this or how she'd feel about law enforcement learning about her secret society. About halfway through, Ramble padded into the kitchen for water. The sheriff stared in open-mouthed awe as water from the bowl was lapped up by an invisible hellhound. Then he followed the sounds of Ramble's claws as the hellhound retreated to the living room to lay by the fire.

When he was sure Ramble was gone, the sheriff asked, "So, do you think this Pamola will leave you alone now that the pixy agreed to stay with him?"

I shrugged. "I hope so."

"What about the other people trapped in his mountain? Should we be concerned for them?"

I paused. I'd been thinking about them as well while rehashing what happened. "I don't think so... it sounded like they wouldn't survive outside the mountain anymore."

The sheriff nodded. "What about the pixy? You gonna inform her mother?"

I wrinkled my nose at the thought. It didn't sound like a very fun conversation to me. "I guess so."

"It sounds like you wrapped everything up pretty good with that one. Anything else I should know about in the supernatural community?"

I couldn't help but smile at his use of my term. "Actually..." I told him about Hyssop and his move to the garden behind the library. It seemed like it might be a good idea to have at least one other person besides me and Willomena who knew about the arrangement. I needed to let Donavon know as well. I made a mental note to give him a call.

"Gnomes?" The sheriff said. He closed his eyes for a second before nodding. "I guess I need to get used to being surprised about who we share the town with."

"If it makes you feel any better, that was a first for me as well."

We chatted for a little while longer and then the sheriff had me make him a handwritten invoice for my time on the pixy case. Since I didn't have any paper, I pulled the calendar off the fridge and wrote on the back of it.

"You need to figure out a way for me to be able to pay you by check so we can keep this on the up and up. For now, though," he pulled out his wallet and removed some bills. "This will have to do."

"Thanks." It was...weird to suddenly be paid for doing an actual job again. I had a weird moment where I wanted to hug him and cry and be shocked all at the same time. The sheriff, maybe sensing my emotional state, decided it was a good time to leave.

Next, I decided to track Donavon down. I was just calling him when he pulled into the driveway. Boy, apparently everybody wanted to have a visit with me.

Rather than have a repeat of the sheriff's freak out, I met him on the front porch.

"What the hell?" He said with a gesture to...everything. I looked around, surveying the broken door and the pieces of shed that littered the yard like confetti. At least the car with its broken light wasn't there for him to see.

"I had a visit from your friend, Pamola."

Donavon stopped. "Pamola? He came here?"

"Don't act so surprised." I put my hands on my hips and immediately thought of Summerstorm. "You and Rosalyn both knew that putting me out here would set me directly in his path."

"I mean...I..." He spluttered.

"Uh huh. That's what I thought." I stalked back inside and into the kitchen, thoroughly annoyed that Donavon really had known he'd put me in the path of Pamola. This clearly called for more coffee.

You cannot trust anyone but yourself, Vânători.

I can trust Ramble, I snapped back.

Donavon poked his head in the open doorway to the cabin then when he saw me in the kitchen, he let himself in and headed my way.

"It wasn't my idea." He said with a shrug. He wasn't pleading. I think he felt above anything like that. "Rosalyn thought it would be best to have him see you sooner rather than later." He looked back at the clear destruction of the door and the floor of the hallway. "He did all this?"

"It was mostly him, but Ramble and Louis tried to defend me. They might have left a few marks as well. The door was entirely him though," I pointed out, not wanting to get stuck with the bill for that.

"Louis?" He sniffed the air, then walked over to the sink. I hadn't had a chance to clean glass I'd drank the vampire's blood out of. Nostrils flaring, Donavon turned back to me and put crossed his arms over his chest, glaring at me.

Whatever. I'd faced a much more powerful being last night. I wasn't going to be afraid some big bad werewolf.

I sighed. "Yes, Louis was here and helped me." I brought my coffee to the table and then went over the same damn story that I'd told the sheriff. Well, mostly the same. "I didn't tell the sheriff about Hester so you might leave her out of it if this comes up between you two."

Of course, in both stories, I left out the part where Louis and I ended up in bed together. We hadn't done anything, but that was between the vampire and me.

Donavon sniffed out the omission anyways. Literally, sniffing the air. "So, you drank Louis's blood," he accused.

I shrugged. "It seems to be how this works, Donavon. I don't know what to tell you."

"Is there more to it than just the blood?"

I rocked back a little, not prepared for that line of questioning. The honest answer was I didn't know. I was definitely attracted to Louis whenever he vamped out, but I wasn't sure if that was because I wanted his blood or if it was more than that.

Donavan watched me as I considered his question, then got up and closed the distance between us. Before I could react, he leaned down and kissed me.

It was a full, delicious kiss that made me lean toward him. He put a hand on the back of my neck and held me to him. I had the stray thought that I probably tasted like coffee and then I was kind of swept away by the electricity of his kiss.

When he finally pulled back, we were both a little out of

breath. Donavon's eyes had that werewolf glow to them, and I was hot and bothered in ways I hadn't been with Louis. Where the vampire was cold to the touch, Donavon's skin was almost too warm.

"Looks like I might have a fighting chance," he said a little gruffly. And then, just like that, he left.

I was still sitting in stunned silence when his car pulled out of the driveway. Ramble padded in and gave me a curious look, one brow lifted in question.

"I have no idea," I told him. "But I think I may be in trouble."

About the Author

J.J. Russell lives on a small farm in Downeast Maine with her husband and two adventurous dogs. When she's not writing, you can find her growing veggies or out on a trail running (very slowly). Check out her author page at www.JJRussellWrites.com and sign up for the newsletter to hear when new books are released and get free short stories for characters in the Artemis Necklace Universe!

facebook.com/JJRussellWrites

twitter.com/JJRussellWrites

instagram.com/JJrussellwrites

Also by J.J. Russell